THE
TIGERS
OF
LENTS

THE
TIGERS
OF
LENTS

MARK POMEROY

UNIVERSITY OF IOWA PRESS | IOWA CITY

University of Iowa Press, Iowa City 52242
Copyright © 2024 by Mark Pomeroy
uipress.uiowa.edu

Printed in the United States of America
Text design and typesetting by April Leidig

Printed on acid-free paper

Library of Congress Cataloging-in-Publication Data
Names: Pomeroy, Mark, 1969– author.
Title: The Tigers of Lents / Mark Pomeroy.
Description: Iowa City: University of Iowa Press, [2024]
Identifiers: LCCN 2023025965 (print) | LCCN 2023025966 (ebook) |
ISBN 9781609389376 (paperback) | ISBN 9781609389383 (ebook)
Subjects: LCSH: Lents (Portland, Or.)—Fiction. |
LCGFT: Domestic fiction. | Novels.
Classification: LCC PS3616.O579 T54 2024 (print) |
LCC PS3616.O579 (ebook) | DDC 813/.6—dc23/eng/20230530
LC record available at https://lccn.loc.gov/2023025965
LC ebook record available at https://lccn.loc.gov/2023025966

Wendell Berry, excerpt from "Poetry and Marriage" from
Standing By Words: Essays, page 97. Copyright © 1983 by Wendell Berry.
Reprinted with the permission of The Permissions Company, LLC,
on behalf of Counterpoint Press, counterpointpress.com.

For Brooke and Nate

PART ONE
2010

1

THE NOISE OF SPEEDING VEHICLES cascades over the neighborhood in this far part of the city, cutting through the evening drizzle and breeze, filling her ears as she steps along the gravel road with two large trash bags on her back. Dark sweatshirt hood pulled up, sweatpants already mud-speckled, her muscled legs flex as she maneuvers around the potholes, eyeing the run-down apartments just visible around the curve, the dumpsters there. She stops and readjusts her grip, watching ahead for the landlord's white pickup, listening for voices, the usual drill, and hefts the bags again. Three weeks' worth of food scraps, night diapers, wadded TP. It's near dark, the air cool, tinged with freeway smell, and as she walks on she thinks of the Mexican kids who used to live in the apartments and how she'd play soccer with them right here on the gravel road, how they dug potholes for goalposts. The hours and hours out here playing, gravel embedded in kneecaps.

The houses along the road are small, mostly on the ratty side, some with chain-link fences around them, one place with a mossy Winnebago parked across the front lawn.

At the apartments' dim-lit back lot, Sara stops. No white pickup, no sign of anyone around outside. Both dumpsters with closed lids. Like always, there's the warm tightness in her belly.

When she reaches the dumpsters, she lowers the bags onto the cracked asphalt as quietly as she can. From here, she can see between the two apartment buildings, to the other parking lot out front, and there's the back end of a white pickup, but from this distance she can't be sure it's his. To hell with it anyway, though. Gently, she lifts the first dumpster's lid and raises it back, hoists one of the bags and sets it in there on top, but as she does, something shifts further down inside and a metallic clatter echoes. She freezes, waits a few seconds, hears no one coming, and picks up the second bag. It's then that the landlord comes jogging around the far corner of the building off to her right and yells, "Hey!" A tall, thickset man. From what she can tell in a quick glimpse, he's wearing a white T-shirt, suspenders holding up his jeans. "I told you—"

Sara runs. Hears him chasing, but doesn't look back. She turns east and picks up speed, her hood falling back from her head, and it all comes in snatches now. The murky spaces between houses, shadows of fir trees, a barking dog, and the freeway sound.

"I know where you live!" he shouts, still after her but losing ground, but she doubts that he knows. She keeps running the opposite direction from her house, though, and soon cuts across a divot-pocked yard onto 98th, turns an ankle slightly and hobbles a few yards before trying to run it off, teeth gnashing. The landlord is nowhere in sight, but she can hear him in her head.

On Foster Road she hangs a left, looping back toward home through the mist, and eventually slows to a walk. Pulls up her hood again. Ahead, the freeway looms, and beside her the traffic on Foster is rush-hour thick. Despite the sore ankle, she moves with a strong, athletic fluidity, a stocky balance, and though her forehead is sweat- and rain-sheened, she isn't out of breath. Marshall High School's star center midfielder, in midseason shape.

At the gravel road again, she makes another left and the tiny white house comes into view, her stomach tensing once more. One story, in need of a paint job (talk about scuzzy landlords), with the bare light bulb above the front porch. Overgrown shrubs. As she often does when she's stressed, she retreats into imagining some strange names, or now and then children's book titles, a habit from girlhood. The closer she gets to the house, the more she can feel the ankle.

Taterhead Hughes. Jade Saucedo-Skunkpants. Amelia Nasty.

Blocking out the pain, she pushes up the three front steps and hesitates for a few beats there on the concrete porch, her hand on the dented screen door, hearing the muffled TV noise mix with the freeway noise.

This is where she lives, right here. It's true.

2

SHE FINDS HER MOTHER in her chair with her swollen feet and ankles up, in her yellow robe and matching slippers, watching the local news, her wineglass has only melted ice cubes in it. Over in the kitchen, her younger sister Elaine is at the stove, some noodles are boiling, while at the hallway threshold her little brother, Adam, has his plastic blocks dumped out all over the brown carpet.

The stick-limbed boy looks up at her, spreads his arms out wide, and says, *"I love everything!"* He pauses, his brow knitted, arms still outstretched. "I love everything except stinky shoes and bad food." Apart from his pirate undies and green rubber boots, he's naked.

"What happened to you?" Melanie lifts her wineglass and notices it's empty.

"Nothing," Sara says, crossing in front of the TV.

"Hey? While you're up?"

Sara takes the glass and steps into the kitchen.

"Mama brought home hot dogs," Adam says.

"Mac and cheese, too." Elaine, still in one of her favorite school outfits—the long green skirt that helps hide her rump and thighs, the funky turquoise earrings from Goodwill—stirs the noodles, then drops four hot dogs into the other pot of boiling water. "You still going to that rally?"

"Kim's coming by in fifteen, gotta get cleaned up." Sara puts the bottle of zinfandel back into the fridge, slips a fresh ice cube in, and takes the glass back over to her mom, who's watching a story about a Portland man who yelled racial epithets on a city bus. For a minute she stands there watching, too, giving the ankle a breather, at one point muttering, "What a moron," but soon her eyes drift. On the wall behind the TV, her grandma's needlepoint of a dress-wearing brown bear in a rocker. To the left of that, her younger sister Rachel's watercolor of Haystack Rock down at Cannon Beach. Over by the front door, the tan curtains pulled over the window. Coffee table, two plastic TV trays. Her mom's chair, and then the old couch, where her dad always sat at the end with the frayed armrest, where he liked to set his beer after a long day of landscaping. Her dad gets out of prison in three weeks. What'll happen then she has no clue, the thought of it makes her chest feel tight. How will he be? Will they see him? What'll he expect? She forces herself to picture the Marshall auditorium, where the rally is tonight, to try to save the school from closing, but that only makes her chest feel tighter.

She can smell her mom's talcum powder and lavender lotion, her after-bath, after-work scent. From standing at her checkout station all day, the woman's ankles and feet look awful, which makes her tune in to her own ankle, the light pulsation there. Her mom, as usual in the evenings, appears wiped out. The glassy eyes, the corners of her full-lipped mouth turned downward some.

In the bathroom, she props her foot on the toilet's edge and peels down her white sock. The ankle looks swollen along the outside, but it's nothing compared to the sprain last spring. She gets out the old Ace bandage that smells of Icy Hot and wraps the ankle, then pops three ibuprofens, ties her sneaker again, and pauses to check her face. A face only decent-looking, no one would call her pretty, probably. At least no one ever had. The small gap between her two front teeth, thin brown hair pulled back like always, the slightly puffed eyes that make it seem like she's been crying or has some kind of allergy or something. Then there's her thick ass and the little pooch at her belly, even though she's in shape; she's always been on the chubby side. But hey, her skin's pretty good, she at least has that. Olive-toned, like her dad's. And she has the okay eyebrows, too, dark, smooth. She reapplies some eyeliner and considers her sweats, but hell, it's too late to worry about clothes, and the sweats smell fine; besides, does she ever wear anything much different to school? She watches herself chew a hangnail and spit it into the sink.

Before sitting down at the small table at the kitchen's edge, Sara goes over and pulls one of the TV trays up beside her mom's chair and takes the plate that Elaine hands her, sets the plate onto the tray, and asks their mom if she needs anything else. Elaine has already sprinkled some pepper onto the pile of mac and cheese and folded the piece of white bread around the mustard-coated hot dog. Without taking her eyes from the TV, Melanie starts eating, and at the table, Adam and Elaine have already set upon their food as well.

Spooning up the mac and cheese just as fast, Sara half listens to the national news start up, the lead story about a helicopter crash in Afghanistan, and thinks of the Salmon River up at her grandparents' place near the mountain. That silvery river smell, the mossy woods. That peace. She needs to get up there again soon, it's been too long.

"You going to the rally?" she asks Elaine, whose plate is already half-empty.

"Homework."

"Can I have more Pepsi?" Adam says.

Sara answers first. "Half glass, but that's all."

When the boy scoots off his chair, Elaine glances into the front room before meeting Sara's eyes. "Did you see Rachel today?"

"What."

"She had a black eye. I saw her in the hall after third period."

Sara stares at her. Adam's busy at the fridge, and the TV sounds go on filling the house. She looks over at their mom, who's eating absently. It's been two weeks now since their sister has slept at home.

"He did it, didn't he."

"I don't know. She wouldn't say."

Sara resumes chewing. Swallows too soon but doesn't choke. Her jaws flex as she keeps gazing at her sister. "She really stayin' with that fool?"

"I guess." Elaine's voice remains hushed, and when Adam returns to the table she focuses on the rest of her hot dog.

Soon a honk comes from out front, and Sara gives Elaine another look before wolfing down another bite of dinner. She takes her plate to the sink, then hustle-gimps to the bathroom and downs two more ibuprofens, and on the way out scratches the top of Adam's shaggy head and tells Elaine she'll do bedtime tomorrow, plus the dishes.

When she opens the door again onto the drizzly night, she glances back at their mom, who doesn't turn and ask where she's going. The woman's feet are still up, her robe pulled over her belly, the wineglass there on her tray with only the melted ice cubes in it.

3

"YOU WANT ANYTHING?" Kim says, looking over her shoulder, and Sara checks her wallet. Three bucks and change.

"Naw, I got it."

They're in line at the coffeehouse on 92nd and Foster where the antique store used to be, and after Kim orders her latte, Sara steps up to the counter and asks for a regular coffee, no room for cream.

Back in Kim's dented mini-pickup, her dad's old ride, they cruise down 92nd past shadowed Lents Park, past the tall dark firs and the playground, the band shell and the baseball field. On the stereo, some Amos Lee, one of Kim's picks. The silence between them is comfortable, as it almost always is, as it's been since middle school, and as they smoke their cigarettes and sip on their coffees they watch the neighborhood scenes flow by. Glimpses of the elevated freeway off to the right, the left turn to Marshall up ahead.

In the parking lot in front of the school, Kim backs into a space. The rally doesn't start for a few minutes yet. They sit there with the windows partway down, listening to the soft music and watching other vehicles stream into the lot. In the background, the freeway hums, Sara notices; it almost sounds like a jetliner, though some people say it's like a river or the ocean. Romantic bullshit.

She eyes the brick school, her school, the front doors where people are filing in, some carrying homemade protest signs, and she flicks her cigarette at the ashtray. Between her and Kim's seats, the cupholders full of crumpled Burgerville wrappers, Kim's pruners in their hard leather case.

Kim stares at the school, her alma mater, and as she does, Sara glances over at her best friend: the shower-wet short hair, the flannel shirt untucked, sleeves rolled up, the faded blue jeans hugging her long legs, her normal earthy look, the daughter of hippies. Kim always smells fresh and clean after her workday at the nursery, and the dim light catches the cords of muscle in her forearm as she takes another sip of her latte. All that pruning these past five months, the girl's getting some guns.

"Can't believe they're actually serious about closing it . . ." Kim takes a last drag and pushes her cig into the ashtray. "They're serious, aren't they."

"This rally's a joke."

After finishing the coffees and then downing a cold Coors each from the little blanket-hid cooler behind Kim's seat, they get out and head down the row of vehicles past a Chevy SUV with sandblasted splotches along the sides and a bumper sticker that reads CAUTION: DRIVER DOESN'T GIVE A SHIT ANYMORE.

"Who drives this thing?" Kim says.

"Superintendent."

IN THE PACKED, rowdy auditorium, they sit near the back and Sara looks around for her sister. It's tough to see the whole crowd with all the bobbing signs and banners, but she doesn't find Rachel anywhere. Spots a couple of Kurt's friends, but no Kurt and no Rachel. The audience quiets down, and Terence McDonald from her math class sits at the table on the stage off to the school board's right and adjusts the mic. Clears his throat. No other high school in the city is getting treated like this, he says. Then after a couple of minutes Mr. Mulligan, Kim's favorite English teacher, sits up there and says how the board is taking "the path of least resistance." It should be "ashamed of itself for kicking a community that's already, in many ways, on its knees." There's a moral issue here, he says, and the board "lacks imagination. There are other options for reducing costs, right here on the Marshall campus even . . ."

The board members all listen politely. The superintendent's face is mostly unreadable, though even from a distance it's clear enough to Sara that the woman feels superior to the crowd. Maybe it's just that she has her armor on, but she's a little too stoic, her chin raised a little too high at times. The board sitting up there like royalty, those concerned, understanding looks on most of their faces. Let the peasants vent. God bless them.

Sara sits there, thighs tensed, ankle throbbing, and watches her classmates and teachers, her community, beg.

IN THE FOYER AFTERWARD, people are all riled up, some saying there's still a chance, there was some strong testimony in there, and at one point she looks off down the long hallway and spies Kurt huddled with his buddies by some lockers. Tall, skinny Kurt Draker in his baggy, skater-dark duds, bangs in his eyes, the leader of his sorry-ass gang, four or five drugged-out fools. Without saying anything, she turns and starts down the hallway, and hears Kim break off a conversation.

She picks up speed, barely noticing her ankle now, zeroing in on Kurt, who's facing the other way, waiting on one of his friends who's digging something out of a locker. Farther up the hall, some kids are standing around talking. She still doesn't say anything, just picks up her pace even more and ignores Kim, who's jogging after her now, asking what she's doing, hang on dude. When she reaches the huddle, her fist is already cocked back. Kurt turns around saying, "What the—" and she tags him on the cheek. He staggers back a step, then takes a wild swing and slams her in the jaw, which knocks her off balance, but she manages another shot, this time to his Adam's apple, before Kim pulls her from behind and says, "Bennett's coming. Jesus." Anthony Ferris, Kurt's main homie, holds Kurt back and says, "What the hell?"

"You ever hit my sister again—"

"Better watch your back now, skank. You think I'm *playin'*?" Kurt's red-faced, his eyes flashing as he strains against smaller Anthony's grip. "What are you, her fuckin' mom?"

"That's right."

"Chick's *wack*," says Anthony. "Check her out."

Strands of her hair in her face, she locks her eyes on Anthony Ferris. "Coming from a guy with a goat's brain, poodle's face, and chipmunk's dick."

Kim's arms are stone-strong around her, and then Ms. Bennett's clacking heels are upon them, the walkie-talkie crackling. After Mr. Vincent, the paunchy VP, comes running up the hall, Bennett hears from everyone briefly, cuts off arguments, looks down at Sara again and says, "Come with me."

"Meet you out front," Kim says, while Sara glares at Kurt as Mr. Vincent leads him off in the other direction. The skaters disperse.

On the walk to Bennett's office, Sara's ankle feels fine. Her pulse still beats in her ears. Her movements suggest those of a bulldog's, how she often looks on the soccer field, she's been told. The spring-loaded energy. In Bennett's office, she refuses ice for her jaw.

"He hit my sister," she says in a low, even voice.

Bennett, sitting across the desk, looks at her as she's often looked at her for nearly four years now, that understanding mixed with impatience, a touch of pity maybe, too.

Sara retreats into herself. Feels the walls going up again. The familiar, encircling, comforting hardness.

Several seconds pass, the office quiet.

"You need to stay on track," Bennett says. "Sara, you need to graduate, then—"

"He hit my sister. Look at her eye if you ain't seen it already."

Staring at her, Bennett takes a slow, deep breath. The suspension will be for a day, she says. Sara can still play in the game on Friday.

"But if you go after him again, it'll be more. Count on it. And that's about the last thing you need."

4

KIM'S GREAT. At times like this especially. Knows when they need to just get into the mini-pickup and take one of their city drives.

It's raining full-on now, and gusty, and vehicles pass them left and right on the freeway toward downtown, Kim doesn't like to push the old truck.

"How's the jaw?" she says.

"Fine." Sara holds another can of beer to her face, looks out her window at the 43rd Avenue exit, and pictures the team bus taking that exit on Friday afternoon, less than forty-eight hours away, for the game against Grant. She rotates her swollen ankle some.

"Music?" Kim says.

When *Achtung Baby* starts up, another of Kim's favorites lately, Sara glimpses the lit-up downtown buildings ahead and feels the cold droplets blowing in through her cracked window. She takes another swig of beer, then lights two cigarettes. As they cross the Morrison Bridge into downtown, she peers down at dark Waterfront Park and thinks of her dad, how he would take them to the Rose Festival just about every year, to the carnival rides. Her, Elaine, and Rachel. Their mom usually working or wanting to rest at home.

Twenty-six days. The dumbass will be out in twenty-six days.

It's been six years since her dad helped his childhood friend Bruce break in to one of the new McMansions over on Mount Scott, the once-forested hill just south of Lents. She remembers when she was little how her dad would occasionally look up at those places and say how people up there probably thought they were above it all. She recalls, too, hearing snippets about the trial, how the break-in happened on a Saturday night, her dad and Bruce had been out drinking, Bruce had apparently been talking about the burglary for months, ever since he worked on a fence-building crew up on Mount Scott and got a good look around. They broke in through a back window while one of their other pals waited out front in the car. No alarm signs or window stickers anywhere on the property, and when they got in, there was no sound. Nothing. Just TVs and vases, electronic equipment galore. But it turned out to be a silent alarm, or the thing was malfunctioning. The police showed up, the friend outside got away, left the car. Her dad and Bruce? Red-handed. Two idiots in a partly trashed house.

She chews at another hangnail and drinks and smokes, looking out at the sleek buildings here in the other Portland, this other planet, less than twenty minutes from Marshall.

Soon Kim turns onto Broadway for the first loop, reaches over and skips ahead to "The Fly" and says it's probably one of her all-time favorite U2 songs, where The Edge cuts loose, a wildman, and Sara only nods, gazing out at all the people on their missions, people eating in tall-windowed restaurants. The fancy stores, peach-colored streetlamps. She gets another beer and the buzz thickens, her jaw and ankle start to numb, and now she's lost in the dazzle of streetcars, food carts, construction cranes, and all the traffic too, the cyclists and pedestrians. There's a gaunt man stepping along the sidewalk with a cat perched on his shoulder. On the third loop, they stop at a red light at Morrison and watch a group of street kids cross into Pioneer Square, six or seven kids right around their age, all wearing dark clothes, a few with tattered backpacks, one guy holding a wooden staff.

Kim's on her third beer, Sara her fourth, when they turn for one last trip up Broadway and spot a tricked-out white mini-pickup ahead with the words PUSSY WAGON in red bubble letters across the tailgate.

"Ready?" Kim reaches over and ejects the U2. Puts in her dad's Hilary Hahn and cranks the volume. They roll down their windows all the way. When they pull up alongside the PUSSY WAGON, the Bach starts up, that burst of fierce violin, and they look over at two Asian guys in their twenties, the driver with spiked hair and a stud in his ear, some Lil Wayne rattling the truck. The driver turns his head, his expression hard but also a little thrown off, lowers his volume, and then grimaces.

The light changes, and Kim lets out a laugh as she accelerates.

A few blocks farther, the WAGON roaring off into the night, weaving through traffic, Sara's grin fades and she kills her beer. "Swear to God, if he hits her again . . . Still have no clue why she's with him."

Kim glances at her as they chug down the freeway on-ramp, and then they're going over the tall, curving bridge, the downtown lights sheening the river.

"Time?" Kim says.

"Yep."

The sweetness of being with this girl, Sara thinks. This person in the world who understands her. Maybe the only person besides her sisters. This girl who's known her so long, knows where she comes from. She puts in Journey's *Greatest Hits*. Their driving home album, the one they always finish their nights with, every time. With their favorite song first. Their freeway-buzzed-and-stay-happy song. She cues "Don't Stop Believin'" and turns it way up, and when Steve Perry with his mountainous voice starts in, they start in with him, at the top of their lungs, two Lents girls letting it all out in the rain-soaked night.

"Just a small-town girl, livin' in a lonely world . . ."

As they turn onto I-205 and start heading south, though, she feels the buzz begin to die, like it usually does right about now. This stretch of freeway up ahead, where they had to raze five hundred homes to "clear the right of way," as her Gramps once told her. She listens to Journey and thinks again of her dad, who gave her most of his eighties rock CDs before he went away, and by the time they exit at Foster Road, more names start popping into her head.

Reekhamper Jonas. Hogsback Chunch.

They turn onto the gravel road and there's a large coyote. Standing next to a pothole, water dripping from the sides of its mouth. Orange eyes in the headlights, mottled raggedy fur. They watch it watch them, and Kim clicks off the music.

"Wild in the city," Kim says, and Sara fixes on its electric eyes. *Jesus.* The suddenness of seeing the thing, after just cruising on the freeway especially, being downtown. The coyote takes a few final slurps as if saying, *You'll just have to wait another minute,* then trots off across the street into old Ms. Hughes's flower-lined side yard.

In front of her house, she looks up at the porch with its naked bulb. The apartment complex lights just visible up around the bend. She leans over and hugs Kim, Kim kisses her cheek. That good smell of Kim's skin, that warmth. It's 1:15 a.m.

Inside, it's quiet apart from the fridge hum, the faint freeway hum behind that. The TV is finally off, the dishes washed. Her mom's bedroom door is closed, Adam's is cracked open. She goes in and retucks the kid's sheet and blanket so he won't fall out of bed, tucks his furry yellow Winnie-the-Pooh between the wall and bed, facing him, as he likes it, and then pauses at the doorway and watches his sleeping body in the night-light's blue glow. Rachel's bed across the room, empty.

She goes out and looks into the sparse fridge and takes a swig of OJ from the jug, leaving the last bit. She feels only slightly buzzed now, her ankle and jaw smarting again, but to hell with it. She tagged him pretty good. Wishes she'd broke his nose. Because no one hits somebody in her family. No one.

In her and Elaine's room, Elaine is sound asleep, the shadowed hulk of her in her bed, the labored breathing. Sara undresses and gets into her sleepshirt that says JUICY ET MOI across the front, the one Elaine got for her at Goodwill on one of her jewelry runs last month.

Before collapsing, she pads over to the dresser and writes out a note on one of the Post-its, then slips it into Elaine's backpack so she'll find it tomorrow at school.

You are a sexy beast and you rock. I love you. S

5

HER LIFE IS ABOUT TO CHANGE.

It's that October afternoon light that about breaks your heart, and as the bus pulls up alongside the field, she blocks out the soreness, the ankle taped well, the jaw all bruised, to hell with trying to hide it with makeup. When she gets off the bus with her duffel bag slung over her shoulder, she notices the nice houses across the street, some nice cars parked in front of them, and then the older Volvo directly in front of the bus, a bumper sticker that says DARWIN LOVES YOU.

There's already a decent-size crowd on Grant's sideline, plenty of parents and students, but as Sara steps onto the field and begins crossing to the Marshall bench, she blocks out everything but the grass field. She's all business now. Coiled swagger. The slanted sunlight accentuating the ripple of muscles in her legs, she moves with the electric authority of someone who has put in the hours. She feels her cleats—the cleats donated to her club team last spring—sink down into the mud a little too much; she should probably be wearing longer ones, but this is her only pair.

On the far sideline, she sits down on the grass and adjusts her socks, eyeing the Grant players warming up over by one goal. She knows some of them and they're all right, mostly, but there are no smiles today. A few others she knows from her club league, too, and they're not all right, not at all. Stuck-up rich girls: one of the worst things she can think of. They're big, strong girls, the Grant team. And fit. Currently first in the league. Girls whose high school isn't closing. Not in this neighborhood, no chance. She watches them running their precise shooting drill, the blasts on goal. So what if she has a chip on her shoulder? Whatever she can use, fair game. Will some of these girls have to travel out of their own neighborhood to a new school next year? Longer commute times, earlier wake-up times? Hell no.

The game starts and Grant scores in the eleventh minute. Lauren Chapman, from her club team, the league's leading scorer. The crowd yells, and Sara calls a quick huddle and tells the defenders to stay in front, lock down, she told them Lauren was fast.

In the twenty-eighth minute, Grant scores again. Lauren Chapman. Sara feels the familiar squeeze in her gut. She's been marked constantly so far, but she doesn't give up. Her team, once again, is clearly over-matched, but she will not give up. She fires a shot from twenty yards, left-footed, and it clangs the crossbar. More clouds have streamed in, occasional gusts bring the smell of rain, and in the fortieth minute Grant scores yet again, a ten-yard volley from a girl Sara doesn't know. They're fitter, tougher, better-coached. And still playing hard, like they should, no pity. At halftime it's 3–0.

In the second half, she tries to step it up. As the attacking center mid, she often switches the ball, sees openings, but her teammates usually can't keep possession. It's raining full-on now, mud city. Despite the score, the game's rhythm fills her, and she doesn't mind playing in the mud, it's always felt intense and sort of wild, almost taboo. It's like how she used to play a lot of times with the Mexican kids and come in all muddy and soaked. If her mom was home she'd say, "What on earth?" If her dad was home, he'd say something like, "Swamp Girl's here, watch out," then go back to sipping his Bud, watching one of his NBA games.

The rain, the crowd, the score: she ignores it all, she's lost in this sweet feeling, in the flow and the breathing, the working muscles, here in the moment. Right here, now, she's not a girl from Lents. She doesn't live on a gravel road. Her dad isn't in prison, her mom isn't a grocery store cashier. She *belongs* on this field and to hell with anyone who takes her lightly.

Sara feels the surge kick in, that angry rush, that second wind, and starts to take matters into her own hands. In the fifty-sixth minute, there's the burst of speed, the other gear she can hit, and she finds traction in the mud and beats two defenders, rockets a right-footed shot to the upper left corner. Some in the Grant crowd even cheer the goal, and she hears some guy with a loud deep voice say, *"Christ almighty."*

She doesn't see Angus Graham, the University of Portland women's coach, standing with his arms crossed in his black Adidas rain suit at the other end of the bleachers, one of his assistants standing nearby.

AS HE TAKES IN THE MATCH, rain sliding down his tanned bald head, Angus Graham temporarily forgets that Martin Crosley is next to him. Forgets, for a few moments, where he is—a rare experience in all his years of coaching.

Not afraid to mix it up, this one. Some grit.

Excellent vision as well. The speed, yes. In abundance. Something else, that.

The ferocity doesn't seem skin-deep. Martha mentioned that. A bit too much at times. Can be a difficult kid. Strong-willed, Martha put it, yeah?

She's a bit on the short side, but makes up for it in speed and strength. Likes to push forward, not shy on the attack, but she doesn't get back soon enough. A hint of laziness there.

But look at the girl. Like she owns the bloody field. Down two, not giving an inch.

AFTER THE GAME, as her teammates head over to the bus, she notices the UP coach and another, younger man with the same kind of rain suit approach Randy near the center circle. Randy Marinus, her pot-bellied coach in his dripping baseball cap and soaked nylon windbreaker, Randy who coaches the Marshall softball team, too. Her face and jersey mud-splattered, her hair plastered to her skull, she peels off the tape from around her socks and takes out her shin guards, looks up again and sees the three men coming toward her. Angus Graham moving with an athletic smoothness even though he's slightly overweight. Some of the Grant players pass behind the men, glancing at Angus Graham there with his hands in his pockets as he walks, in his new-looking Sambas that are getting all muddy. He showed up at one of her club games last summer, a game out at Delta Park on a ninety-degree day, and some of her teammates pointed him out.

The crowd still dispersing, she feels a gust cool her soaked jersey. Her cheeks flush. She can still feel the loss in her stomach, like always, as if she might throw up, but there's also a sudden warmth in there. Her soggy teammates are getting back on the bus now for the trip back out to their part of town. A busful of muddy, poor, drenched Lents girls who are now officially second from last in the league standings, no chance for the play-offs. *What in God's name would Angus Graham be doing talking with Randy?* They keep coming toward her and she glances over at the scoreboard.

HOME 4   GUEST 1

Randy introduces the men, and Sara only shakes their hands, doesn't speak.

"Tough result, that," Angus says, and gazes at her. Confident, kind, yet no-nonsense eyes, wrinkle-framed. He seems to her about forty-five and like he's spent a lifetime outside, the major crow's feet. He's five-eight at most, but something about him makes him seem taller. Martin Crosley, a thick-necked, fit guy of about thirty, stands a good six-two, which makes sense, since Randy just said he used to be a professional goalkeeper.

"Right," Angus says. "I'll be crisp so we can all go get dry." Another gust comes, driving more rain into them, but Angus doesn't flinch or squint. Just gauges her. "I'd like for you to come play for us next year, if you're interested."

Sara looks at his eyes for an instant. "At UP?" One of the best soccer programs in the country, she knows that much. She looks over at Randy and he's giving her a closed-mouth smile, his chin tucked into his neck.

"That's right." The thick accent. "We may have some money . . . You can come out for a visit, see what you think."

She glances at the bus over Angus's shoulder, the grey shapes of her teammates behind the fogged windows.

"If you're interested, Martin here can take you round campus, you can have a tour, meet with a couple of professors. With your parents as well, if they're available."

She still doesn't know what to say, it feels like there's a glob of something caught in her throat. Her ears are ringing.

Angus Graham half smiles, raindrops streaming down his head and face, and there's that certain toughness on his face that she likes. The wrinkles and the strong nose and jaw, but it's mainly in the eyes. *No-bullshit* eyes.

"So, we'll give you a ring to set up a time in the next couple of weeks, if that's agreeable? We're on the road for a bit, but we'll have you out and take it from there. Sound good?"

She sees him noticing her bruised jaw and still doesn't speak, her head storming. The downpour intensifies and the field is now empty except for the four of them.

"Right, then. Let's get you on the bus."

She numbly grabs her bag and they all walk over the squishy grass, leaving the field behind. At the idling bus, she shakes their hands again and notices the firmness of both handshakes, the directness of their expressions, and what still seems like genuine interest as well. Randy stands beside her, quiet, waiting.

"Thank you," she manages, her face tingling.

"Keep working hard. Hope to see you." Angus Graham gives a little nod and turns away, and Martin Crosley joins him.

6

THE TRAFFIC ON FOSTER is Sunday-afternoon light, and as she hikes along with two big plastic bags of clean clothes from the laundromat, she thinks more about the University of Portland and how surreal it all is. That they would want *her*.

It's another drizzly day, and the bags are heavy, but at the spot where she and Kim saw the coyote she stops and pictures the Salmon River up at her grandparents' place. The boulders along the banks and the moss-draped trees. The river sound normally drowning out the distant highway sound. Her special place, where she can relax all the way, at least most of the time. That river air, so fresh and cool in the lungs.

She resumes trudging along the gravel road, wet-haired, looks up and sees Kurt's mom's dented old cream-colored Buick Regal parked in front of the house now.

"Here we go," she says to herself.

From the front porch, she can hear her mom arguing with Rachel. She opens the door and the voices come louder, without pause.

"Are you *listening*?" Melanie says from her chair, her slippered feet planted on the floor. "I don't want him in my house, not after all that last time."

"It wasn't *his*." Rachel's at the kitchen's edge, Elaine off behind her making lunch, what looks like grilled cheese sandwiches, while Adam is standing in the hallway threshold in his red Spider-Man T-shirt and matching shorts, his Chewbacca figurine in hand.

"Like hell it wasn't." Melanie leans forward, the fluorescent orange SEASIDE OREGON across the chest of her white sweatshirt collapsing into warped letters, her frizzed hair down, shower-damp.

"What, like he'd bring a bag of weed into his girlfriend's house and then pull it out—"

"Don't play me, all right? Don't even. Who do you think I am?"

Rachel, in her faded black Jay-Z concert tee, one of her downtown thrift store finds, her frayed brown cords and black lace-up boots to her shins, pale Rachel with her thin build and mussed hair, now with streaks of rust-orange in it, her bangs parted just enough to reveal the still-yellowed bruise beneath her left eye, stands there like a cornered hellcat, glaring.

"I think you're a self-hating power tripper," she says, and it's there that Sara has heard enough.

"Where is he?"

Rachel scowls at her for a few beats, then lowers her eyes. "In my room."

"You mean Adam's room now, since you don't actually sleep here."

Rachel's green eyes flash at her again. "You've already done enough, don't you think?"

"He *hit* you." Sara glances at Melanie, who's rubbing along the bridge of her nose, like she does now and then when a migraine starts, and lowers the laundry bags to the carpet. Adam and Elaine remain still, riveted. "Why'd you bring him here? What are you—"

The power goes out. Sara turns to look out the window and sees lights on across the street. No wind outside. It's just theirs. Again. She's about to ask when the bill was due, but Melanie's eyes start to well.

"I *called* 'em already. They *know* they're gettin' paid . . ." Melanie gathers herself and looks at Adam, who tries to resume his playing, half-heartedly waving Chewie around, and it's then that the smoke alarm goes off. Elaine has been listening and the cheese sandwiches are burning. Adam drops Chewie and presses his hands over his ears, then starts shrieking, the alarm is directly above him, and when Kurt comes loping down the hall he frowns and mouths to Rachel *What the fuck?* His cheek, Sara notices, still tinged a brownish-yellow.

While Elaine gets onto a chair to take out the battery, Sara stares at Kurt.

Rachel likes to say how he's pretty smart actually, and he has a lot of sweetness in him, it's just that he's got a hard family life, give him a break. He just, like Rachel, "wants to live different somehow." But there's something in the guy's eyes, this weird vacancy. Lanky Kurt, with his grey hoodie and ripped black jeans and size goddamn thirteen or something beat-up Vans, staring back at her now.

The alarm finally dies, and she goes over and offers a hand to Elaine, helps her off the chair.

"We'll get out of everyone's hair then," Rachel says, leading Kurt back to the bedroom.

Sara opens the front door to air out the house, returns to Adam and kneels down to calm him. Melanie gazes at the open door, her jaws working. Elaine drops the black sandwiches into the trash, then looks into the fridge while Adam gives Sara a final hug before approaching Melanie and asking if she'll read a book to him.

"Not right now, babe. Mama's tired."

When Rachel comes back out with Kurt behind her, her jammed-full backpack over his bony shoulder, she tells him to meet her outside. Kurt doesn't say anything, just walks out, and Rachel squats in front of Adam and holds him for a minute.

"Can you read to me?" he says.

"I have to go, I'm sorry. But I'll read to you next time, okay? I love you." She kisses his cheek, and as she rises and faces Melanie her expression hardens again. "So, I'll get out of your hair. If I can't even have my boyfriend over."

Melanie eyes her for a few seconds, with just a shade of tenderness. "What's the matter with you, honey? Seriously. What's happened to you?"

"She's brainwashed, is what it is," Sara says.

"What's brainwashed?" Adam says.

"You would have to keep talking with him right here. Nice." Rachel tears up but doesn't cry. "Thanks everyone. Great visit." Without looking down at Adam again, she turns and walks out, shutting the door behind her, and in her wake, a stillness comes and the cool damp air stops drifting into the dim house.

At first no one speaks.

"We got some bologna," Elaine says. "I can make sandwiches with that."

Sara takes a slow breath of the smoky air and is about to join her sister in the kitchen when Melanie rubs her nose again and says to bring her the phone. And the electric bill, it's in her room on the table there. "*Damn* it." She reaches for the TV remote, forgetting about the power, pushes the button a few times and then sets it back on her tray. Adam watches her. Elaine spreads mayo over slices of bread.

When Sara, wordless, comes and holds out the phone and the bill, holding within her all she needs to tell, Melanie hesitates and looks up at her before taking them.

"Thank you, baby. I couldn't do all this without you. For real."

7

OUT IN FRONT OF Marshall, fast-food wrappers, chip bags, school papers. In the bushes near the front doors, along the curbside, overflowing the dented silver trash cans. The surrounding grounds need mowing, too.

Sara stands alone out front finishing off her cigarette, just before the morning bell, and tunes into the freeway. The world speeding past, the daily charge, right on by all the drama down below, the sad-ass poor people and all their endless bullshit. She stamps out the cig and wedges it in the groove on one of the trash can lids, keeps trying not to think of her dad, then walks into the school. Immediately she notices the eerie quiet.

Two days ago, the official announcement: Marshall will close at the end of this school year. Out of all the city's high schools, theirs is the one, as proposed.

The hallways are near-barren, and she knows it'll be like this for the rest of the year. For some kids, it'll be too much of a gut punch, the last straw in some cases, and they'll stop coming. She heads to her locker and thinks again of her sisters, how they'll have to go to Franklin or Madison, probably. Elaine, for her senior year. All that crap from the superintendent about "supporting Marshall students" as they make those transitions: yeah, right. Then there was the *Oregonian* yesterday, the copy she skimmed in the library at lunch, how the editorial board backed the closure but felt also that the district "shouldn't abandon outer Southeast." Talk about lip service. Oh, so you care about outer Southeast now, is that it? Throw down I-205 through the middle of Lents, watch crime blossom, then go ahead and support Marshall's closure on top of everything else. Sweet.

In her English class, the daily prompt is up on the screen: NEIGHBORHOOD. Ms. Engle is sitting at one of the student desks, like she normally does at the start of class, writing off the prompt as well.

Sara sits there in the stillness, throat tight, and looks around for a minute at her working classmates. She thinks of the phone message yesterday from Martin Crosley, how Elaine heard it first and asked her about it. She wanted to be the first to tell mom, she said, and Elaine gathered herself, smiling, and said of course. But their mom had come home in a bad mood, sore and tired, wanting her wine, and so she decided to wait.

Tonight at dinner she'll tell.

She zeroes in on the prompt, lifts her pen and writes, *I live in the wilderness of the economy.*

AFTER PRACTICE, Laney Littlefield drops her off at the corner, and as she walks through the wet dusk toward home she lowers her guard for a moment and dwells on her dad. Nineteen days now. Nineteen, yeah? The familiar avalanche of questions: *What will he do? Will she see him? Will he want to see her and Elaine and Rachel? And what about Adam, what about her mom? What the hell is everyone supposed to feel?*

For dinner they have tater tot casserole with buttered toast and canned pears on the side. From her chair at the table, with Elaine and Adam eating across from her, she occasionally looks over at their mom in the front room, the TV light on her face, the third glass of zinfandel now gone. Maybe it's not the best time. But then when is it ever?

She does the dishes and asks Elaine to take Adam back to his room for some reading, if that's all right. Just for a little while. The house has grown colder, yet the heat stays off. One of those months, heat or eat. Her mom is watching one of her after-dinner celebrity gossip shows, and she goes out and sits on the edge of the coffee table and watches for a minute, too, some crap about some big-titted actress she's never heard of, and at the next commercial she swivels her body slightly and gauges her mom, but the woman stays focused on the screen. Those swollen ankles. The robe and slippers.

"Need to talk a sec," she says, and her mom looks over at her. Her throat feels like it's about to close up, so she coughs once. "This college coach. He came and saw me play the other day. He came to watch one time last summer, too." Another commercial comes on and she sees her mom's tired eyes flit back to the screen. "I guess he talked with Martha."

"Who's Martha?"

Sara hesitates. "My club coach."

"Okay, yeah. Sorry."

"Anyway, this coach from University of Portland . . . He wants me to come play there next fall."

Her mom reaches over and presses the mute button, then focuses on her. "Wow."

"I'm serious. That's what I said. He says they might have some money for me."

Melanie pushes against the armrests and sits up some, the stunned look still on her face. She asks what all this guy said, and Sara tries to calm herself and tell everything.

"So what did he mean when he said he might have some money? What does that mean?" Melanie's face is now flushed and she removes the blanket from her lap. She reaches for her wineglass, sees it's only full of melted ice, and sets it back on her tray. The television flickers.

"I'm not sure. I'm supposed to go out there and meet—"

"You realize how much college is, right? Especially a private one? You know the difference between a public and private university and all that?"

Sara eyes her for a few beats before looking off at the darkened kitchen. She can hear Elaine's door-muffled voice reading to Adam.

"I'm just saying," Melanie goes on. "Look up online how much per year, you'll get what I'm saying. It's not cheap, I'll tell you that. You know about financial aid?"

"No."

Melanie faces the TV, a soundless interview with George Clooney, a movie poster over his shoulder. She opens her robe a little, her large dimpled legs white, shins glossy. "I remember I looked into all that. I wanted to go to college, did you know that?"

Hunched over now, elbows on her knees, Sara gazes at the carpet that needs vacuuming, glances at Melanie and shakes her head.

"What I was gonna do, I had it planned out. First go to Mt. Hood Community College and get my associate's. I was gonna apply for scholarships, do some work-study, maybe take out a loan, whatever I had to do. Then go on to PSU for my bachelor's. You know about all the degrees and everything?"

Sara can hear her starting to get worked up. She doesn't answer.

"Listen, don't get me wrong, this all sounds nice. But you need to find out what 'some money' means, all right? He seem like someone you could take his word?"

"Yeah. He did. They want me to come to the campus and . . . For us both to."

"When?"

"Don't know."

"Do they know I work full time?"

"I doubt it."

"When do they expect—"

"I don't know, okay?"

Melanie stares at her, and Sara looks away. "You don't need to get that way. I'm just trying to—"

Sara stands in front of the TV.

"Hey," Melanie says. "I'm just saying, don't get your hopes all up at this point. Okay? People say shit. People promise shit all the time, right? Just don't want to see you get hurt. You going out there and him telling you they can only cover part of the cost, and then what're you supposed to do? I'm just saying you need to be realistic."

"You never even seen me play! Gramps and Gram have, ask them!"

Melanie rears up in her chair. "And do *they* have to work anymore? Are *they* working almost every day of the week? And you know *why* I work all the time? So you and your sisters and brother have a place to *sleep*? You don't think my feet and back hurt like complete hell after this long, working my butt off for all of you?"

Sara hears the familiar tone, glances up and sees the moist eyes, that expression of hers. She goes over to the hallway threshold, holding words, trying to breathe. She turns around and faces her mom and hears Elaine's low voice off behind her. For a second, as she looks at the woman sitting there in the TV strobe, she wonders what her dad would've said if it were him she had told. If he might've bothered, by this point, on one of his days off maybe, or after work even, to come see her play. Watch her score.

8

THEY FIRE UP THEIR cigarettes and crack a cold beer each, cruise over to Division and go west.

Here's the other planet, especially below 60th or so. The crowded restaurants, cafes, and pubs, the whole buzzing vibe.

"Into the heart of hip," Kim says. "Here we go. Act as cool as you can."

Sara sucks at her cigarette and gazes out her window at the slow-passing scenes. Some Foreigner on the stereo, her pick. The cig makes her think again of her dad, how he was always smoking in the house. Her mom for a while there, too. The place cloudy with smoke, every evening when he was home at least. She looks out at a packed bar, people in skull-hugging hats sitting at sidewalk tables in the chill, and remembers coming down here to lower Division when she was a girl, with her dad, to a hardware store, which was about the biggest attraction on the entire stretch of street.

Kim has on a new lotion or a touch of perfume, Sara can't tell which, some herbal hippie chick scent, but it smells good. Relaxing. Lou Gramm belts out "Urgent" and they keep cruising along, taking in the sights. When Sara reaches back into the cooler for another beer, she glances at Kim's pruners in one of the cup holders and remembers her dad calling her "Roadrunner" when she was little, how she'd run and run all over the house and yard and street, and then, pooped-out finally, climb up onto his blue-jeaned lap and smell his clean after-work smell and watch part of an NBA game with him maybe, his can of Bud in one of his calloused hands, his fresh tank top on, tan lines showing.

"How was work today?" she says, and Kim chuckles.

"Dropped a forty-pound bag of compost carrying it out to this old lady's car. Just all over the place, it was insane. Other than that, good."

"Still like it?"

"Most days. It could pay better, but I like being outside."

"You always did."

"In the blood, I guess." Kim finishes off her beer and asks for another.

"Like my dad," Sara says. "My grandpa, too. He's like that, totally, has to get outside . . . I need to get you up to the mountain for a visit. Ain't been up there in a month, about. Damn."

They're down in the industrial area now, train tracks, warehouses, and Kim loops through the dim streets for another pass up Division. No downtown tonight, as agreed. Maybe next time.

To keep from falling back into herself, back into the memories of her dad, which have been hitting harder and harder with each passing day, Sara takes a long pull on her cig and strains to think of what else to talk about, there's always plenty to talk about, but tonight she can't seem to stop brooding, and this time it's about her mom. How the woman dropped out of Marshall at sixteen years old, got pregnant with her, and everything changed. Everything.

"A couple weeks, my dad gets out," she hears herself say, and Kim looks over at her. She keeps facing forward. Her right foot starts tapping the plastic floor mat.

Kim doesn't pull over, only keeps driving up Division, occasionally glancing at her, listening. Kim had asked, back when they were in middle school, what exactly her dad did, what he broke into and entered, but after getting "I don't want to talk about it" a few times, she kindly backed off.

Sara watches the restaurants come back into view and chews at a hangnail. She downs more beer and looks out at another bar, a place with picnic tables outside, most of them occupied, people talking and drinking, staring into their phones, faces aglow. She presses out her cig in the ashtray and rubs her eyes. Some bad sleeps lately.

As they cross César Chavez Boulevard, Kim says, "You remember his trial?"

For a while longer, Sara's foot taps the mat. "I think one of the craziest things . . ." She chews at her lower lip, battling a sudden rise of feeling, blindsided by all this tonight. "It was the embarrassment, you know? It was so *embarrassing*. For everyone."

Kim only nods, facing the road, and keeps driving toward Lents. At 60th, she asks if it's time for some Journey, it's okay if silence is better, and Sara says sure, bring it on. This time Kim cues "Faithfully," but they don't sing along.

At 82nd, Sara clears her throat, the buzz already fading, and tells Kim about the UP offer.

Kim pulls over in front of a Vietnamese grocery. "Are you *serious*? Oh my God, that's *awesome!*" She stretches over and hugs her full-on, kisses her cheek, and there's that awkward moment that sometimes happens, that current between them. Kim eases back into her seat. "When did you find out? Look at you, all nonchalant."

"Been sitting on it for a few days. Not sure about it yet."

"What do you mean?" Kim's smile falls slightly.

"I don't know, we'll see . . . The shit's expensive, even with a scholarship. Forty-five thousand for just one year, it's crazy. I looked it up."

Kim nods, watching her, while Sara faces the windshield, the traffic passing them by, gently rocking the truck.

———

WHEN SHE GETS HOME from practice the following evening, their mom working overtime, Elaine hands her a Post-it in the kitchen and says that a guy named Angus Graham called, he wants to arrange the visit.

"What visit?" Elaine's eyebrows rise, her jowls pink. "To UP?"

Hair still rain-wet, legs sore, Sara holds the note, rereading it. "I'll cook tonight, what's left in the fridge?"

"Hot dogs. About it."

"So it's hot dogs or hot dogs."

Adam, at the kitchen's edge, post-bath and nude below the waist, his noodle arms raised in victory, looks up at them and shouts, "Hot dogs! Hell yes!"

9

IN THIRTEEN DAYS, HE'S FREE.

It's been like this lately: in his bed at lights out, his cellmate Bernie doing his deep breathing, him with his hands behind his head, listening to all the usual sounds, just thinking.

These past couple of weeks it's been a comfort to him to lay back like this and think for an hour or two or three, try to put things in their place. What all's happened, what'll happen on the outside, what he wants to have happen.

He turns his head and looks at Bernie, who rolls over facing the other way, his normal routine before falling asleep. The guy can do his breathing, then almost immediately crash, it's impressive. He eyes the metal desk and chair bolted to the floor, the toilet, the lights in the corridor. It's still strange for him to think, only thirteen more days and goodbye to this place. Strange and sweet both. One thing, for sure: it'll be beyond strange to sleep in a dark, quiet room again.

Thirteen days. Mother of God.

Keith scratches at his goatee, tucks his hand back under his head, and listens. Someone down the block—Villanueva? Estrada?—babbling in Spanish, something about some señorita. As he listens, stretched out there on his bed, he begins drifting again.

What had saved him was the garden project. That and meeting Lyle and Harold soon after he got in. The gardening, though—each day after breakfast, he would head out to the greenhouses and fields and take care of the native prairie grass seedlings, those perennial bunchgrasses, and then after that, check in on the endangered Oregon spotted frogs. His little buddies. It'd been a fine deal, the whole project they had going for people like him, who could show up every single day and work hard. Breakfast, then work. Lunch, then back to work. He's not afraid of work—that's at least one thing he has going.

After work, the weight room. His legs are still skinny as hell, but compared to when he first got here, his shoulders and chest and arms are ripped now. Not that he was a wuss before, but at least now he's carrying more weight, which in his humble opinion doesn't look too bad.

After the weights and a shower, dinner, then some cards or reading. It was Lyle who got him into reading. Westerns mostly, that's what hooked him. Louis L'Amour, Zane Grey. *True Grit*, too. *True Grit* was an early favorite. Old Rooster Cogburn, La Boeuf, and Mattie Ross, who'd reminded him a little of Sara.

As for Lyle and Harold? It turned out to be a stroke of damn good luck that he loved to play checkers. His first week—it seems, on the one hand, like just one hell of a long time ago, yesterday on the other—that first week in, as the gangs were sizing him up, he came upon Lyle and Harold playing checkers and asked if he could get winners. Lyle looked up at him. A *hard* look. Lyle with his greasy grey ponytail and huge arms. Harold about as large, his bald brown head shining under the fluorescent lights. "Why not?" Lyle said in his deep-down voice, and that was basically it, what helped save him. Because no one ever messes with Lyle or Harold. Ever.

But it was the plants, and being outside, that kept him from losing his mind. Being around all those growing things, always thinking about what they needed. Clean water, clean air, a little sunshine, some care.

He lies there. *Thirteen days, sure enough.*

What he's looking forward to most, besides seeing his girls? Sitting in a bar and having a nice cold Bud. Nothing complicated. Just sit up at the bar and order a cold one or a whiskey and maybe talk to the bartender for a while, or not. Just enjoy sitting there. Maybe catch an NBA game, if one's on. Have a couple of drinks and then get on home, wherever that'll be, and keep on the straight and narrow. Get a job, keep a job, all that. Keep the devil down, stay with the right crowd. Because that's the risk of going back to Lents, of course. The main risk.

His girls, though . . . It nearly killed him sometimes, how much he missed them. He *hated* being gone all these years, those childhoods aren't coming back. For a while, when he first got in, he tried to convince himself that it was almost doing them a favor, him being away, at least there wouldn't be shouting matches all the time; he'd seen it affect them, all three of them, and there were times it about broke his heart. It wasn't supposed to be that hard to be married. Sometimes he couldn't believe how hard things got.

He heard from Sara and Elaine once each, that first year, the two letters he read at least a hundred times—and then nothing after that. Nothing at all from Rachel, not a single letter. Like how he'd received not one letter from his own parents.

He opens his eyes and tunes back into the sounds, Bernie's sleep-breathing, and it's his parents in his head now, where he didn't want to go tonight, not again.

He wrote them twice those first couple of years, telling them how he was sorry. He was straightening himself out, he said, he knew he'd let everyone down. And then he never heard back from them. He wrote again the following Christmas, trying to explain how he guessed certain people just had to take the hard path—and once again never heard back. His entire life, he had disappointed them. The sting of that. That deep cut. His mom, his dad, up there in Welches—he doesn't even know what they look like now. Doesn't even know if they're still alive. Not hearing back was worse than if they'd written and said how what he'd done was unforgivable and they never wanted to see him again. The silence was the thing. Silence and uncertainty: the real killers.

Thirteen days. Hell, almost twelve.

Getting out, it's as if anything can happen all of a sudden, at any time, and he can already feel how that will feel again. He feels it low in his throat. In here, most everything he can predict. But out there?

He scratches at his goatee and shuts his eyes.

There's no doubt about going back to Lents, though. None. It's his neighborhood, and it's where his girls are.

He wants to be near them, he knows that much.

10

KIM TURNS UP Metallica's "Enter Sandman" and keeps the truck humming along up the highway past Brightwood and over the Salmon River. The cab is rocking, they both have their coffee and cigarettes, and even though it's grey and damp outside, even though Sara's hungover, it's still Sunday afternoon and they're almost in Welches.

When the song ends, Kim lowers the volume. "What are your grandparents' names again?"

"Val and Ernie."

"*How old* are they?"

Sara squints, the headache nearly gone. "Gramps is, like, fifty-nine, I think? Gram's a year younger. How long's it been since you been up here anyway?"

"Maybe I was a sophomore?"

"Damn."

Up ahead, the upper half of Hunchback Mountain is cloud-swallowed, most of the other surrounding hills partly hidden as well, while along the highway the firs stand dark and moist, one of the roadside restaurants already has Christmas lights hung. When the stoplight in Welches comes into view, Sara says that's the turn right there, and Kim puts out her cigarette.

"Does my hair smell?" Sara says, and Kim leans over and says no, it's good. Sara puts more drops into her eyes and blinks.

On the narrower road, the greyness thickens and everything slows down. That highway speed, then the mountain road speed. Trees and rhododendrons dripping. Some houses here and there, tucked back in the woods. At Shadow Lane, Sara tells Kim to go right and soon they pull into her grandparents' place, down the short gravel road to the small green house, more of a cabin really, on the riverside quarter acre.

On the tiny front porch, the painted concrete Dutch couple, shin high, are situated as ever so they're kissing, while out on the lawn the mini wooden windmill that Gramps built and the ten or so concrete deer are scattered about. As the street name suggests, almost everything's in shadow from all the tall firs that surround the house and Gramps's garage-turned-workshop. In the driveway, the gold Oldsmobile sedan with the stuffed animals crammed in the back window.

"Forgot how good it smells up here." Kim kills the engine, the river sound flowing into the cab.

"Here they come," Sara says, opening her door.

Her grandparents step out onto the porch and wave, Ernie in his normal uniform of blue jeans with the cuffs rolled up some, his old brown work boots, his jean jacket and the green John Deere cap, while Val has on a pair of beige polyester pants and a light blue sweatshirt that's tucked into the elastic waistband, her behind plump as she turns and closes the screen door.

"Well now," says Val, opening her arms. "There's my girl." At the end of the hug, she says, "You two have been someplace smoky. Did you stop somewhere on the way up?"

"No . . ." Sara blushes, watching her Gram hug Kim, embracing her Gramps now, smelling the wood dust on his jacket.

Inside the overheated house, Val asks about soccer, asks Kim what she's been up to, look how she's grown, look how strong she is.

"Ernie, come over here and feel this girl's muscle."

"Dear—"

"No, now you come here and feel this, it's something else."

Ernie shakes his head and gives Kim a gap-toothed smile, steps over into the kitchen and lightly squeezes her biceps with his thick hand, and now it's Kim who's blushing.

"Well, I'm not gettin' on her bad side, that's for sure," he says.

"I told you so."

Sara watches them. Her Gramps with his deep wrinkles around his eyes and mouth, his yellowed cig-and-coffee teeth, his wiry strength from all the years climbing telephone poles and doing woodwork on the side; her Gram with her wobbly neck wattle, the oversize eyeglasses, permed greying hair. They all move a few steps into the front room, and now she takes in the familiar needlepoint wall hangings, mostly Bible verses, plus all the photos of herself and her sisters and her mom, the two stuffed easy chairs and the couch, the woodstove, the small dining table back by the kitchen. And there's the screened porch out the front room windows, that sweet porch with its river view, the woods out there, and the grey light, all the hours on that porch eating lunch in the summertime when she was a girl, playing cards with her Gramps, or napping on one of the old slip-covered couches.

With four people standing in the front room, it feels cramped to her. When she was little, this place seemed so big, so exotic.

"You two sit down now, my goodness," Val says. She looks over at her husband. "And you, too."

"Yes, Mama." Ernie, giving Sara a glint-eyed half smile, takes off his jacket and cap, eases down into his chair.

Val claps her hands once. "Okay. Now what would everyone like to drink?"

When they're all settled with their cream sodas and tuna sandwiches and Fritos, Val starts in on her questions, asking about Elaine first, and Sara gives the report. She tells about Marshall and how Elaine and Rachel will have to go to Franklin next year, and after Val offers her opinion on that, saying it's just another example of how everything seems to be going to hell in a handbasket, there's a sudden silence.

"And what about Rachel, how's she doing?"

Sara motions that she needs to finish her bite and glances over at Kim, who puts a few chips into her mouth. On the drive up, she'd thought about what she could say about Rachel. How exactly did you tell your grandparents that your sister has moved in with a violent prick? *Actually, she, uh, moved in with a violent prick.*

"She's doing pretty good. Still smart as—"

"How are she and your Mama getting along?"

Sara looks away to her Gramps and feels herself nodding. "Not too bad . . ."

After a few beats, Ernie readjusts himself in his chair. "Well now, Kim, tell us more about that nursery you're at. Where'd you say it was?"

And so the talk turns to plants and gardens, then the latest gossip around Welches, some business about one crotchety neighbor down the road deciding to clear-cut most of his three acres of Doug firs and cedars in order to pay the bills, and after a good while Sara helps carry the plates to the kitchen. Eventually she guides Kim out onto the screened porch and through the door out there, toward the river. They just walk for a time, down the spongy path through the undergrowth, and Sara fills herself with the forest air.

"Can I ask you something?" Kim says. "I noticed there aren't any pictures of your dad."

Sara draws another breath through her nose and doesn't answer.

"They know he's getting out?"

"I'm not sure." She starts down the boulder-strewn bank, some of the rocks shiny grey, others moss-covered, and the sound penetrates her. She finds a rock to sit on, Kim finds one upstream a ways, and for a while they just sit there looking at the river, a mist falling on them.

Across, only forest. Upstream, a wooded bend. Downstream, the property next door with its four Adirondack chairs nestled near the bank, then more forest.

Sara breathes, feeling her body relax. The little soccer aches here and there, the tensions from school and home, from city life, they start to fade some, like they always do when she's at this spot. Her spot, right here. The earthy smells, the light, what her Gramps calls "the primordial feel," how these Mount Hood foothills are about 700,000 years old. She can see how her Gram gets what she calls "the glooms" after days and days of living with this grey dimness, but still, this place is hers. At this exact spot she's spent hours and hours fishing with her Gramps, or skipping rocks, or lately when she comes up just sitting, like now.

For several minutes they remain there on the cold rocks, and as she watches the water she thinks of how her Gramps likes to talk about "river lessons." All that you can learn if you just get still enough and quiet enough and have a good look around. And one of the lessons, one she thinks she has a better sense of today, is how life keeps carrying on. Yet it also feels like she's getting left behind. The feeling comes on strong all of a sudden, in her chest mostly, almost a hollowness there. She tries to block it out, but there's no doing. Life is flowing onward while she's stuck behind.

"You 'bout ready?" she calls out, and Kim soon stirs and gets up.

They find her Gramps in his shop, one of his table saws whining, and she sees that he doesn't have any earplugs in, as usual. They wait there in the wide doorway and she looks around at the organized clutter, the scene that's always amazed her, how he knows where anything is. The bigger tools, sure, and the ones hanging from the pegboard, but nails, screws, all his paints and eyeball stickers and other doodads? They're somewhere in the dusty jumble.

The saw stops. "You two all right?"

"Gramps, we're heading out pretty soon, got a ton of homework."

"I was just making Kim a little something to take home." Ernie holds up the wooden cat doorstop he'd been cutting. One of his specialties, the doorstops. His stubby fingers, with deliberate, almost tender movements, brush away dust from the various grooves. "Here." He sets down the unfinished cat and shuffles off farther into the shop, muttering to himself, finds what he's looking for, and returns with a finished cat painted light orange, complete with eyeball stickers and painted-on nose, whiskers, and mouth. "Take this one."

He hands it over to Kim and she gives him a kiss on his stubbled cheek, and from behind them Val walks up, her steps crunching across the driveway.

"Oh dear. He's not trying to get rid of more of those, is he?"

Ernie grins.

They'll be sure and come to Sara's final game next week, Val says, as they linger by Kim's truck, and Sara still hasn't mentioned anything about the UP offer. She says she'll look for them after the game, thanks again for lunch, and then she's watching her grandparents wave as Kim backs the pickup along the gravel drive.

These two people who've been there for her and her sisters, for her mom also. Always.

When they pull onto the highway it doesn't take long for the forest calm to fade. She opens a beer for each of them, watches cars and trucks blow past, and pictures the river. Ever since she was little, she's always noticed how different the world feels, just from pulling back onto the highway and picking up speed, and Kim seems to realize, too, that some silence is called for as they reenter the rush.

As she drinks at the beer she thinks of Angus Graham and Martin Crosley, how they stopped calling and what that probably means. Besides, her mom was right, maybe. No one in their family, on either side, ever went to college. No one. And there was surely a reason for that. There were some damn smart people in the family, and hardworking, too, in all those generations of Garrisons and Morrises—but not one of them had gone to college, it was just out of their league. And not one ever got all that far above being poor. They could work their entire lives, but no matter. Her Gramps and Gram are probably the closest, what with Gramps's phone company pension, but no one sure as hell would call them rich, even if they do have a river view. There's the world for people who have a way to get themselves established, and there's the world for people who don't. Because here's the thing: there's no *way* someone like her can go to a university where it costs forty-five thousand for one goddamn year. Even half that amount is insane.

She tilts back her beer, then gets another one as Kim drives on.

11

THE NIGHT BEFORE their dad gets out, Elaine hits the light and slips into her bed, and after they lie there for a while she says, "It's good to have you back."

It's the first night in the past week that Sara hasn't slept over at Kim's. The house is still, their mom already in her room, Adam crashed out.

"Rachel wasn't at school today, was she?" Sara says.

"I didn't see her. Have you heard from her at all?"

"She's still at his house, is all I know."

Sara listens to the small fan's purring from atop the dresser, and after a time Elaine says, "What about Mom?"

"What do you mean?"

"I don't think she's heard from her in, like . . . She's been kind of checked out lately."

"Mom or Rachel?"

"Mom."

"When hasn't she been?"

"It's more now. It's weird."

Sara takes a deep breath. "How's Adam?"

"Seems quieter, too. He misses Rachel a lot."

They lie there, Sara on her back, Elaine on her side, facing her, and the little fan whirs.

"Mom knows he gets out tomorrow, right?" Elaine says, softer.

"Hasn't said anything. But she has to."

"Do you want to see him?"

Sara keeps eyeing the ceiling shadows. "No. Why, do you?"

"I don't know. I don't think so."

For a long time after they say good night Sara can't sleep, and she can tell that Elaine can't either.

ON THE WAY TO a house party the next night, she checks again for any texts from Elaine or Rachel, but again there's nothing. All day long she's checked, she's not sure why really, not sure what she's expecting, and whenever she thinks about what to text them, the words never come. Her feet tap the floor mat and she glances over at Kim, who's driving with both hands on the wheel, her forefingers tapping out the beat to "Billie Jean."

"Sure you're cool with this tonight?" Sara says.

Kim turns to her and smiles. "Lee's a dick, but I can handle him, don't worry."

When they reach Lee Shepherd's street, not far from Marshall, cars are parked everywhere and Kim backs up and finds a spot around the corner. She turns off the truck and they can hear the music from here. Eminem.

"Jesus Christ." Sara kills her beer, runs her hands down her sweatpants, and they get out.

With the depression over Marshall's closure, you would think people might be more mellow. But it's the opposite. As they press their way through the crowd, already everyone seems *lit* and it's only nine fifteen. Maybe seventy or eighty people. Some of her teammates are here— Naomi, Erika, Leslie—but she only gives hugs and then keeps moving with Kim farther into the thumping house. She doesn't want to talk soccer. It's the last thing she wants to do, actually. She looks around for Rachel and Kurt but doesn't spot them. Who she does see, though, is Anthony Ferris, Kurt's greasy little homie, pouring a can of Red Bull into the punch bowl that's on a card table by a sliding glass door. Shrimpy Lee Shepherd comes up wearing a brown leather vest, he's wasted, and tries to get huggy with Kim, who half smiles and presses him back gently but firmly, and Anthony Ferris pours another Red Bull into the punch. People all around utterly shit-faced, the house is rocking, the cops will probably show up before too long.

The jungle juice is sweet, strong, and as they down their first cups, she keeps scanning for Rachel or Kurt. Anthony is over in the kitchen now, yelling with a bunch of his skater buds, but there's still no sign of gangly Kurt. In the chaos of bodies, no Rachel. She goes over and ladles another cup, and it's the Red Bull she feels mostly, at first, but the jungle juice has plenty of vodka in there as well.

"Oh my *God!*" Willa Crow, a brawny girl from Kim's class who now works over at 20th Century Lanes, comes up and wraps an arm around Kim. "Ain't seen you in, like . . ." She and Kim start talking loud while Sara downs her second cup and then goes for a third. People are cutting loose here, forgetting their troubles; why not do the same, she thinks. It's only Thursday night, amazing, and she's got a game tomorrow, her very last game in a Marshall uniform, but fuck it anyway. Serious.

With her fourth cup of jungle juice, she leaves Kim with Willa and wanders off through the house, keeping things friendly yet brief with any teammates she comes across, and soon finds herself following a group down the dim hallway and into one of the back bedrooms, where the smell of weed is almost overwhelming. There's a group of naked people on the bed, a bunch of people gathered around watching, and Austin Beam has a video recorder going. Sara's pulse races and her face gets hot, and a few people holler and whoop, but most of the guys watching up near the bed just sip at their drinks, some with tense looks on their faces.

As she turns away, she feels nauseous. Leading with her raised cup, she jostles out of the room and finds the garage door, steps through the garage and out into the packed backyard, where she takes a deep breath of the moist, cold air, her head swimming. It's then, through three huddles of cup-holding partiers half caught by the patio lights, that she sees Rachel over beside Kurt in a group that's passing around a pipe.

The Eminem still raging, her legs slightly numb, she beelines toward her sister, one of Kurt's friends catching sight of her, saying, "Man, watch your ass."

Kurt looks over his shoulder and turns around.

"I ain't even talking to you, so just . . ." Sara takes Rachel by the arm and pulls her away. Her voice sounds slightly garbled to her.

"What up, skank?" Kurt says.

Someone in the group laughs, and Rachel pulls her arm free, but she keeps stepping along with Sara through the shaggy grass over to a row of overgrown rhodies in the yard's far corner. Kurt eyes them and eventually turns back to the pipe circle, while Sara struggles to keep her sister in focus. She thinks she spots Kim over in the bright house near the sliding glass door, but then someone blocks her view. Her sneakers are wet.

"You're fucked up," Rachel says, folding her arms over her black hoodie. Skinny, pale, pretty Rachel in grey hip-hugger jeans with frayed hems and her black lace-up secondhand Doc Martens.

"And you ain't?"

"Not really, no."

Sara searches her face. The thick eyeliner, dark lipstick.

"Have you heard from dad?" she says.

"Why would I?"

"He got out—"

"Today. I know. You don't think I know that?" Rachel stares at her.

"Are you okay? Serious. We been worried. Elaine's been worried as shit."

Rachel looks away then, over at Kurt's group. Sara can hear him laughing with his buddies, but remains focused on her sister's face.

"I'm fine," Rachel says.

"No school?"

"I've been at Kurt's. Or downtown."

"Still ride MAX down there?"

"Almost every day."

So fast they've slipped into the semi-comfortable old back-and-forth, in spite of everything, and Sara feels the urge to reach out and pull her sister into a hug. Kindred spirits, it's basically always felt like to her. Except for the part about Rachel being so damn smart. But she doesn't reach out, only keeps trying to steady the spins and concentrate. Her sister is such a gifted writer, and there's a big heart under the toughness. Rachel even talked once about wanting to publish a book of her poems someday. What the *hell* is she doing now? Throwing away her talents, just like that? For a guy?

"Mom's been worried about you, too," she says, and sees the armor snap back into place over Rachel's face.

"The Great White Whale? She still at it with the iced wine?"

Sara doesn't respond. Just keeps focusing hard on her, her own face intense. They stand there for a minute, and Rachel looks back over at Kurt, as if there's some sort of magnetic pull.

"He kept on asking when dad was getting out, it was sorta strange, the past couple weeks. Like it triggered something in him, I don't know. From his own shit."

"He's still an asshole," Sara says, and sees Rachel get her sad, deep look now. Almost some pity in there, it seems like, and the girl's about to say something so she beats her to it. "I get worried about you."

"I get worried about you, too."

They gaze at each other for a few seconds before Sara makes herself smile. "Well, I guess that's what it's all about then, right?"

"See you later," Rachel says, and heads back across the grass to her man.

———

KIM HELPS SARA into the house. Settles her onto the bed and helps slip off her sweatpants and sweatshirt. Kim's dad is staying over at his girlfriend's again, and the house is quiet. After getting a glass of water from the kitchen, Kim lights some candles and the bedroom glows velvety. The posters on the walls, Jimmy Cliff, Rihanna, the Go-Go's. The old cedar chest that belonged to her grandma, over beneath the curtained windows. The wooden beads in the doorway to the bathroom.

Sara sits back against the pillows in her white tank top and undies, pulls her legs up and holds herself, resting her chin on her knees. The candlelight catches the lines of muscle in her browned legs. Her face is wet.

After taking off her jeans and flannel shirt, Kim has a drink of water, then hands the glass to Sara, who drinks and passes it back. Kim eases onto the bed and curls up next to her.

"You can talk about it, if you want to," Kim says, and a silence follows. She watches Sara, then looks away at the candles.

"Wish I could." Sara sniffs, her head still spinning. The candles are a blur. "I can't believe he's out . . ."

When she begins crying, Kim sits up some and puts an arm around her, and the warm skin touching her own makes Sara cry harder, something inside her just dissolving.

This tenderness. The unbelievable comfort of being held right now. She can let her guard down. She can actually let go, at least for a little while. Kim holds her in the quiet, candlelit, calm-smelling room, and when she turns her head and receives the soft kiss, she feels the melting in her chest and the crowding thoughts start to break up, soon almost seeming gone. As she pulls the T-shirt over Kim's head, nearly tearing it, trembling, she suddenly can't get enough of her friend.

12

HER LAST GAME in a Marshall uniform. It's at home, a rainy afternoon, and Val and Ernie are up in the mostly empty bleachers, a blanket spread over their legs, their thermos of coffee between them. As Sara takes the field, she's still hungover, and the usual bulldog thoughts don't quite come. They're playing Roosevelt, a school in another poor neighborhood across town, a school that'll stay open, though, and seeing how the two teams are cellar dwellers, the game feels a little stupid to her. Still, she wants to go out with a win, can't help that.

As the ref putters around retying his cleats, she shakes out her legs, waiting, scanning the crowd, something she long ago stopped doing before kickoff. She doesn't see anyone who looks like a scout. Not that any scouts ever showed up at Marshall. Just Martha, that was it, from all she knew. Two years ago now. Martha asked her to try out for FC Portland, and if she hadn't taken her seriously and tried out she probably never would've known what a scout even was, would've thought Girl Scout.

The game is crap. Roosevelt goes up 2–0 by halftime and she knows that she's basically been nonexistent. Windy, rainy, potholes all over the field, only a few spectators lingering during the second half. In the sixty-eighth minute, though, she receives a pass from Kylie Valentine thirty yards out and something kicks in. She takes on a defender, flips her right foot over the ball, then pushes the ball with the outside of her left, getting just enough separation to fire a shot that skips once in the goalmouth puddle and streaks into the far corner of the net: 2–1.

But her final three shots miss, one of them ringing the left post, and they lose. That's it. All over. A strange numbness settles in throughout her body. She hugs her teammates, some of them wet-eyed, and when Randy comes over he says into her ear that he wants to talk to her in a few. About UP. He'll see her in the locker room. She hugs more teammates, and part of her wants to cry also, but then something else takes over and the feeling fades. Harden up. The only way.

When her grandparents meet her at field's edge, they say they're real proud.

"That was some goal." Ernie puts his arm around her shoulder. His jean jacket and John Deere cap are soaked. "You 'bout deflated the dang ball."

Val, in her dripping plastic rain bonnet, says, "That team just got lucky today is all. I like how you didn't give up."

Sara wipes mud from her chin and listens, but this time their post-game words don't fully register. Her face remains stoic as she hoists her bag and walks with them over to their car, takes off her cleats, and gets in.

ON THE SHORT RIDE HOME, Val turns in her seat. "Did your mom know this was your last game?"

"I'm not sure."

"Did you tell her?"

Sara looks out her window. "I can't remember." She looks back at Val, the steady grey eyes, and then sees Ernie glance at her in the rearview.

Val turns back around. "Well . . ." And the car goes quiet for a few blocks.

Ernie drives up Foster under the freeway, and right before the turn Sara leans forward.

"Actually, it's kind of weird at home right now, maybe just drop me off in front this time?"

"Everything okay?" Val says.

"Yeah, it's just . . . sort of a weird time is all."

Ernie pulls to a slow-crunching stop out front, and Sara sees lights on. She tells them she'll be back up for a visit soon, thank you for coming to her game, she really appreciates it, and before Val can ask any more questions, says goodbye and gets out.

MELANIE AND ELAINE are in the kitchen. Adam is on the floor in the front room, coloring in one of his Spider-Man coloring books. Sara can tell from Elaine's face that it's one of those evenings already.

"He called," Melanie says, and Sara leans over and sets down her bag.

Melanie shakes her head, adjusts her robe over her chest, picks up her wineglass from the counter and moves to her chair. The TV remains muted for another few beats, the national news, and Melanie seems about to speak but only hits the volume.

In the kitchen, Sara and Elaine stand close.

"He wants to see us," Elaine says.

"What, all of us?"

"What about *me*?" Adam says, looking up at them now, crayon in hand. "He's my daddy, too!"

The TV goes silent again, and Melanie presses along one of her eyebrows. "Sweetie, no. Goddamn it. No, he's not."

"But I want a daddy!"

Elaine goes over and gently touches Adam's head.

"I cannot do this tonight." Melanie wields the remote, sound filling the house once more.

When Adam starts crying, Elaine picks him up. Sara steps over into the front room and gives her sister a look. Elaine, without a word, carries the boy down the hallway and into his room, closing the door behind them.

To the side of her mother's chair, Sara stands in her muddy, smelly uniform. "You really think he needs to see you sittin' there every night, same ol', same ol'?"

Melanie hits mute again, eyeing her. "What crawled up your ass? Don't even talk to me like—"

"Why don't you ever get off your ass around here? Seriously. Just now and then maybe. He doesn't need to see—"

"*Get off my ass?*" Melanie pushes out of her chair, bumping her TV tray, nearly spilling some wine. "I'm on my feet—"

"All day, I know. On your feet all day, we get it."

Melanie stares at her. "You little bitch. Think you're so damn special. Walk around like some badass all the time. Hardly ever around here anyway, and when you are, you gotta act like you're hot shit, don't you? Elaine's gotta do most all your work nowadays, too."

"He shouldn't have to deal with your shit, none of us should." Sara's throat feels like it's clogging.

"Look who's talkin'!"

"Well, then I'll make it easier on you." She picks up her bag and turns for her bedroom. She texts Kim, then empties the duffel and begins chucking clean clothes into it.

Elaine comes in and asks where she's going.

"Kim's."

"Don't leave here. Sara, please."

She keeps packing. "I'm sorry, I can't be here right now."

"Please."

Adam runs into the room, weeping still, and Elaine picks him up again.

"It's always worse when I'm here," Sara says. "Always. This is just till things calm down, okay? If dad calls, tell him we're not even interested, at least I'm not. This is just outta hand, all this."

When she heads back down the hallway, jaws set, Elaine and Adam follow. Melanie is back in her chair, still red-faced.

"So, first Rachel, now you. That how it's gonna be?"

"Hey, at this rate you'll be all alone pretty soon. That's what you obviously want, right?"

Melanie starts to tear up, but then yells, "Get out! Go on!"

Sara pauses at the front door. She looks over at her sister, who's still holding their brother. Tears running down their faces. She swallows and opens the door, hoists her duffel onto her back, and steps into the rain.

Up at the corner, the freeway noise fills her and the traffic on Foster whooshes by. The numbness thick, she searches for Kim's truck in the onslaught of blurred headlights.

13

IN THE COLD early morning at the bus stop down the block on Foster, Melanie waits alone. The hood on her beige coat raised, the ends of her frizzed hair sticking out. She can already feel a light throb in her feet and ankles, and she didn't sleep much last night, got about three hours. Rapid-fire thoughts. Her girls, her son. Keith.

She didn't eat breakfast because her stomach felt off, but she should've nibbled on something. She's a little dizzy now, serves her right. She looks up again and this time sees the bus with its headlights on. The traffic is already thickening, rush hour starting earlier each year. Each passing year.

Here she is, in her usual spot at the usual time, headed back into work. Back to the checkstand. Back to "Find everything all right?" and "Take care now" and all that banter during the entire shift just about, and how she'll keep on like this she's not sure, you can only tread water for so long. Then again, you can get pretty good at it if you have to. True enough.

The bus is a block away, and she steps closer to the curb and glances at some of the passing cars and pickups, once more pushing away the thought that it would be nice to not stand out here in all sorts of weather and catch a bus each day.

Keith is out. He's actually out.

The bus stops and the door opens, and like most days when she holds on to the railing and climbs the steps, the driver doesn't meet her eyes, and so she doesn't say "Good morning."

14

A BAR DOWN ON HOLGATE, about a mile from Keith's new digs. No windows, a long bar and some pool tables, an NBA game up on the TVs, and a cold Bud in front of him. It's just like he'd pictured, for the most part, except it's strange to him not being able to smoke inside of a bar. He keeps reaching for his pack in his flannel shirt, stopping, thinking, *Man, that ain't right.*

It's strange to him, too, how people down the bar and over at the tables keep checking their phones or talking on them. Even here in a redneck bar. That's something that's definitely different, just a hell of a lot more cell phones.

But other than those things, it's still basically the scene he imagined. A good old redneck bar on a good old redneck section of Holgate. Nobody trying to impress. A decent-looking bartender, friendly lady. (*Not bad-looking at all,* he thinks. *A woman about his own age. Real nice body, too.*) His kind of place.

Because what he knows is this: a guy like him would never fit in with more "respectable society," no matter how much he read or dressed different. Too late for that. Just give him this, right here, any day. Give him a decent job, a truck maybe, later on, after he's saved up some, and a couple days off each week. Let him work outside, and in the summertime let him hit the river and fish or tube on the Clackamas or Sandy. Give him some decent books to read and the occasional NBA game, like right here. No peppermint lattes, no pint-size hybrid ride. Maybe get a grill for the patio and come summertime do up some bratwursts or steaks for the girls, have them over.

He hasn't recognized anyone yet who's come in, and no one seems to recognize him. When the bartender comes back over he asks for another one and then asks what all's new in the neighborhood, showing his smile.

"Well . . ." The woman leans forward a little on the bar, and he tries not to stare at her cleavage. "They're closing Marshall, but you probably heard about that."

He swallows his sip. "I didn't."

"It's a shame. It really is."

"I went there."

"That right?" The woman looks into his eyes. "I feel for those kids. It's set to close after school lets out in June."

He takes another drink from the bottle, and another guy down the bar calls to her and she goes. He gazes up at the game for a while but thinks of Sara and Elaine and Rachel. Thinks of Melanie, too, how he met her at Marshall when he was a junior, sixteen years old, she was a year younger. Eighteen years ago. When his hair was down to his shoulders. When he was just starting to hang around a certain crowd, some shoplifting, all those parties. Melanie so fine then, it about killed him.

He finishes off his beer, glancing now and then over at the bartender, and when he gets up she tells him to take care. She's not just decent-looking, he decides. She's pretty.

"See you next time," he says, leaving a good tip on the bar.

RIGHT OUTSIDE, in the drizzle, in the cool November dusk, he lights up a cigarette and takes a deep drag, then begins walking back to his apartment. Through the exhaust from passing vehicles, through his own smoke, he catches whiffs of rain on pavement and wet earth, those smells he loves. The passing cars and trucks: so many models he's never seen. Yet it all looks pretty much the same, the old neighborhood.

He feels the breeze on his bald spot and runs a hand back over the thinning crown. In his jeans, thick shirt, and the new work boots he's trying to break in, he walks along Holgate toward 92nd, hearing the freeway sound grow, pauses to light another smoke, then hangs a right down 92nd and heads along the edge of Lents Park. His landscaping job all lined up, he starts tomorrow. Crew member to begin with. Four days a week, ten hours a day, opportunities for overtime and promotion, so he's been told. As he steps along, he reviews his plan. (Like Lyle talked about, "a guy has to keep his head on his plan.") He'll get some money saved up, first thing. Get that truck. Maybe a little house, way down the line.

He smokes and looks over at the baseball stadium and band shell in Lents Park, at the tall firs and the expanse of grass, and squints to try and spot his apartment building over across the street at the park's south end, but there are too many trees. He remembers hanging out with Melanie in Lents Park back when they were in high school, before Sara came along, how much fun they had. They did have some fun. Hitting Lents Park or Mt. Tabor Park, finding some shady corner to do their thing.

Then he thinks of the phone call a few days ago when Melanie picked up. Hearing her voice after all this time. How light-headed he got. Her reaction to hearing him was understandable. Sure it was. He'd surprised her. Still, he needs to see his girls; it's even worse now, now that he's out, they're so close yet so far. He doesn't know what more to say to Melanie, but he does know that he has to see his girls, and so he needs to watch his mouth.

In the apartment, the place the aid agency hooked him up with as part of their prisoner reentry program, he takes off the damp flannel shirt and drapes it over one of the kitchen stools. Stands there for a moment, looking around. The apartment came furnished and has a view of the park, a separate small bedroom, good shower . . . but it's the *quiet* that gets him, just like he thought it might. Every time he gets back here, so far. The old man next door has his TV going almost all the time, and the sounds come through the wall, accentuating the quiet. It's the kind of quiet that makes him turn on his own TV just to have some closer sounds.

He goes over and pulls a Bud from the fridge, fills a pot of water for boiling, opens two packages of ramen noodles, and then waits, gazing out at the dark park through the sliding glass door. Recalls sneaking out at night to meet Melanie and how his parents had no clue. He thinks of his parents then, and how they never contacted him these past six years, not once, even after what all he'd written to them.

He takes his big salad bowl full of noodles over to the table by the glass door and watches the NBA game that was on in the bar; it's the fourth quarter now. When the game ends, he turns off the TV, and again the quiet attacks.

What he should get is a dog, he thinks. They allow dogs here, he remembers them saying that. And what he needs, also, are some books. He should get one of those library cards that Rachel used to use all the time when she was little. That's the ticket, right there. Good *lord*, Rachel used to want to hit that library all the time. Sara and Elaine, too, but mostly Rachel. Cutie would check out about eight or ten books and then hole up in her room for a few days, just reading, reading, even when he and Melanie were at each other's throats. Especially then, actually.

He stares out at the park and finishes off his beer, noticing the quiet yet again. He'll call again tomorrow, is what he'll do. See if he can get one of his girls on the line this time.

See if he can talk with his daughters.

15

SARA STANDS AT THE stereo cabinet flipping through Kim's dad's CDs—Fleetwood Mac, Miles Davis, Midnight Oil—and decides on some Peter Gabriel this time. In her sweats and a pair of white socks, she goes back for another hit from Kim's bong, then steps over into the kitchen and pours a bowl of hippie-brand honey nut O's.

In the kitchen threshold she eats standing, looking around, listening to "In Your Eyes." It's a house not that much bigger than hers really, but it couldn't feel more different. The wood floors, the books in the built-ins, the fireplace. The bright, framed poster by the front door that says COPENHAGEN JAZZ FESTIVAL. Yet it's still in a so-so part of town, on the edge of Lents, one of those areas that could go either way. Next door, the fresh-painted house where the young couple lives with their Subaru wagon, chicken coop, and two pugs. Across the street, a plastic kiddie pool and rusted lawn chairs in a muddy front yard.

She finishes the cereal and wanders back out to the bong on the coffee table. Kim's off at work, Kim's dad, too. Her dad with his Water Bureau job all these years, steady checks rolling in. Not bad for only two years of community college, Kim once said. Which is Kim's plan, in a year or so, she says. Community college, a better job outside someplace.

As she takes another hit—is this her fifth or sixth this morning?—she can hear Kim in her head, saying how her dad is "way cool" about his weed, the man has "shitloads" and doesn't mind if they smoke some now and then. Besides, he's almost always over at Cheryl's house these days anyway. And so, yes, they've certainly smoked some. She hasn't been to school in nine days. She feels out of shape, misses sweating, that feeling in her lungs from running, it's better than this kind of burn now, all the weed and cigs. Could she *be* any grosser?

She sits at the end of the couch staring at the DVD stand next to her, all the Monty Python DVDs in there, and when she thinks of the one she and Kim watched the other night, the one where John Cleese acts like a chicken, she can't help but let out a laugh. The sound seems weird in the music-backed stillness. It's 10:15 a.m. on a rainy Tuesday.

The soccer thoughts lurk, start to creep closer again, like every morning before she can get high enough, and so this time she makes up a children's book title.

Leave Mama Alone!

She remembers when she was a girl, whenever her parents would yell at each other, she'd run outside to play soccer or go to her room. If she wasn't kicking the ball, she was making up names or titles.

And now more soccer thoughts break through.

Ever since she was little and watched part of the Women's World Cup on TV when her parents were at work, she dreamed of playing on a soccer team. Wearing a uniform. Wearing cleats. Running on a green field, dribbling, passing, scoring a goal. Those women on TV looked strong and tough. Then again, they didn't come from poor families probably. They had money for cleats, all that. They had washers and dryers in their houses when they were growing up. Had food all the time. They had warm houses in the winter and the power didn't get cut, their parents probably weren't always gone, working, and when it came time to sleep or study, the house wasn't loud with TV noise and yelling.

Listen to you.

Sara gets up dizzy, picturing first Adam and then Elaine, their faces when she walked out, and when her own face gets hot she sits back down and takes another hit, a deeper one.

Last night, in bed, Kim: "So, like, what are your plans?"

Herself, stoned: "Not going home. Me and her just don't . . ."

"If you start getting bored or anything, I don't know, I could maybe check if there's something at the nursery. Only if you wanted me to. If you're not going to school . . ."

Working at basically the same thing her dad worked at all those years? It makes sense almost, she thinks. She likes being outside, just like her dad, like Kim. It's true. She could go get a job at the nursery, or with some landscaping company even. What the hell else can she do?

She imagines Kim's arms and hands. The smell of her after she comes in from a day at the nursery, sweat and earth. The power of that. The sexiness, too, sure. But the thing is? She still doesn't know if she's *like* that. Part of her knows, part of her just doesn't. At all. She doesn't know what to think. What if she likes both guys *and* girls, what then? What do people do? And what do you do with this feeling of wanting to *hide* it? Part of her is embarrassed, yet another part loves what they did that first night and a couple of nights since. Last night, though, when Kim, after a long pause, tried to talk about it for the first time, she couldn't seem to say anything back, could only hold Kim's warm hand there in the bed and feel that current and tenderness and that rising moistness. She just doesn't know what to say, there's too much and it's too unclear.

She curls up on the couch, hugging two of the pillows, short of breath. It's happened like this, the past week mostly, at about this time most mornings, if the TV isn't on. It's all too much. *What will she do?* Where will she *live?* How will she make a living? And look what she's doing to Elaine, being here like this. Look what she's doing to *Adam.* This house is so still, this neighborhood, everyone else off doing their thing—

She sits up fast. Wipes her sleeves across her face and reaches for her phone. Elaine is walking to her third-period class.

"Dad called again," Elaine says, slightly out of breath. Kids' voices in the background. "I answered."

"What did you say?"

"I didn't know. He says he still wants to see us."

Sara remains silent, listening to the school sounds, envisioning the hallway. "It can't keep going like this."

"What do you mean?"

"What if . . ." She takes a deep breath. "What if we just meet him?"

Elaine doesn't respond.

"We make plans to meet, see if he's actually serious. You know? What he probably does is go, 'Yeah, hey, see you there, lookin' forward to it,' and then not even show. What do you think? Just throw it back at him."

"I don't know," Elaine says, still walking. "Ms. Engle called. You had some project due? Something about poetry, a booklet or something. The school's been calling Mom, asking where you are. Rachel, too . . . Anyway, I'm here, I gotta go."

Phone in lap, Sara remembers the two poets, the twin brothers, that Ms. Engle talked about a few weeks back. She can't recall their names, but they grew up in Lents. Single mom. They somehow made their way to college and then both went on to publish acclaimed books of poetry, and now, look here, they'd been profiled in the *New Yorker.* "*Look,*" Ms. Engle had said, holding the magazine open at the front of the class. These two brothers. From Lents.

She calls Rachel but gets her voicemail again. Hangs up and decides to text. *Call me. Please.* Rachel never calls or texts back now. Elaine hasn't talked to her or seen her at school except for once, at the beginning of last week. Said she seemed withdrawn, in a hurry.

When the music stops, she pushes herself up off the couch, her legs feeling weak, and puts in one of Kim's Pet Shop Boys CDs. *Maybe it'll help,* she thinks. Maybe she should put the bong away. Shower. She stands there in the middle of the room.

But it's like the couch keeps pulling her toward it, and so she goes over and curls up again, her eyelids so heavy in the sweet haze, better to block tears.

THAT NIGHT, they're watching an episode of *Doc Martin*, one of Kim's favorites, when Sara's phone vibrates. She picks it up and stares. Kim asks who it is.

"No idea."

She doesn't answer the phone, and after a minute listens to the message.

"Yeah, hey, uh, listen. I know you might not want to see me, but I'd sure like to see you and the girls sometime. If there's a way we could meet up, say hi, well, that'd be real good. I'll leave you my number here. Don't got a cell phone yet, but I got a machine here . . . I'm hoping . . . Sara, I'm hoping you'll give me a chance at least. Anyway, I'm at—"

She can barely hear the number over her heartbeat in her ears.

"Fuck this." Before she can change her mind, she gets up and steps into the kitchen, and when he answers on the third ring, she forces a swallow. In the background there's TV noise, and then a jingling chain. He says to hold on a sec, and she can hear him talking to someone.

"Sorry 'bout that. Got a game on."

She tries to speak, but can't yet.

"I'm glad you called." His voice goes muffled and he tells someone to sit down.

"Got company?"

"Aw, that's just ol' Bear. My dog. Got her a few days ago. She gets all riled up for some reason when the phone rings."

Sara swallows. "Me and Elaine'll be at the Lents Commons Coffeehouse on 92nd and Foster"—she can hear him scrambling for something to write on—"tomorrow at four, if you want to meet there."

"I'll be there. You bet. That where that old antique store used to be?"

She doesn't answer.

"Yeah," he says. "I think I saw that place the other day."

"All right then."

When she hangs up and sets down her phone, she feels like she might throw up so she goes over to the sink and tries. But not much comes.

16

UNDER THE THUNDERING OVERPASS, Sara and Elaine walk with their hoods up, past the on-ramps and huge concrete columns, the traffic on Foster racing by, and then out again into the drizzle. Eco-conscious, bike-riding, food scrap–recycling Portland? Sara sucks at her cigarette.

By the bus stop near the cafe, they linger for a while and she smokes yet another, her fingers pink. The air steely. Elaine stands with her hands balled in her coat pockets, watching her now and then, still saying nothing, occasionally biting at her full lower lip. Across the street, there's the New Copper Penny, the nightclub that Sara has always wondered about, what it looks like inside. Most evenings, some scary vehicles parked over there in that back lot. She still feels hungover from last night at Kim's place.

"Ready?" she says, and Elaine nods once. Elaine with purple fatigue lines under her eyes.

Sara gauges her sister again: The girl looks larger, by ten or twelve pounds easy, but there's something else, beyond the weight. It's the eyes. Like walls have raised between her and Elaine. Of course they have.

As they step inside the warm cafe and drop their hoods, she feels short of breath again, and Elaine's face has gone close to red. But he doesn't seem to be there, from what she can tell. Only two guys present, one of them, in his early twenties probably, over at a window table talking to a girl, the other being the slender guy behind the counter with his shaggy mustache, thick-framed eyeglasses, and Kurt Cobain cardigan.

She keeps scanning the place, thinking how it used to be the antique store just piled with stuff, all those old smells. Now it's hip. The two couches, some wooden tables, the small stage with a mic stand and a loud, spooky painting of an old-time sailing ship mounted on the wall behind it.

They sit over at a window table that looks out onto 92nd, Sara hardly touching her coffee, Elaine sipping frequently at her caramel latte. Elaine has on her oversize purple blouse with curly designs on the lapels and her pewter earrings with little flowers; Sara wears her blue sweatpants and red sweatshirt. They've each applied eyeliner, but Elaine's hair is washed and combed out.

"You all right?" Sara says, and Elaine only nods once, then tucks her chin into her jowls. "If he doesn't get here in like ten more minutes, we're outta here."

She checks the clock on the wall and then her phone. She eyes Elaine.

"I'll try to make it up to you," she says. "I don't know how. Everything lately . . . It's just all fucked up. I'm sorry."

Elaine only sips.

"Have you heard from Rach?"

"Saw her at school on Thursday," Elaine says. "She seemed all right. I guess. It was sort of weird. She gets along with Kurt's mom okay, she said. I don't know much else. It's like she's scared to talk for very long, or too tired. Or not interested anymore, I don't know, I can't tell. She looked all right, though. Her bangs are green. Like, bright green."

Foot tapping the floor, Sara glances at the door, then studies her sister again.

Elaine folds her arms over her chest and says, "I got a job at Chuck E. Cheese's."

"Sorry to hear that."

"It's only four days a week, couple hours after school."

"I thought that place used to scare the shit out of you."

"It still does."

Sara sees him pass in front of the window only a few feet from them, smoking a cigarette, it has to be him, and her ears start ringing. Her hands quiver and she presses them together.

"He's here," she says, and Elaine cups her mug in both hands, her eyes closing for a moment as if she's saying a prayer.

Keith hesitates by the door, drawing a few last drags, then steps on his cigarette and comes inside with only a hint of tentativeness. He stands up straight and takes in the scene, and Sara can't take her eyes away from him. He's bigger than she remembered. She'd assumed that since she was twelve when she last saw him, he would seem smaller now. He's lean, sinewy, but also large in the shoulders, under his damp flannel shirt. His hair is thinner, wet, combed back. Blue jeans, new-looking brown work boots. She glances over and sees the guy at the counter take notice of him.

When he approaches the table, they don't get up. She can smell the smoke on him. His hands look strong, the veins there. Grey flecks in his trimmed goatee.

He holds out his hand to her first, and she feels his calloused grip, firm but not too firm. In her glances, the ice-blue eyes rattle her even more, she'd forgotten how blue they are. Though there are more wrinkles around them now, and also the deep vertical wrinkle between his eyebrows. The gap-toothed smile, like her own.

"Can't believe this is a cafe," he says. "Used to come in here when I was a kid with your Gramps and Gram. They used to drag me in here, look all around." He pauses, now observing Elaine, whose face is nearly maroon, her chin tucked into her neck. She still hasn't looked up at him. He lowers himself into the chair between them and settles back.

Sara thinks she can smell alcohol on him now, but isn't sure.

"So, you two. My goodness . . ."

Keith smiles, and Sara looks past him out at the New Copper Penny and thinks he must've been in there tons of times in his life. She eyes him and gives clipped answers to his questions, like how's school going. He says he heard about Marshall, he was real sorry to hear about that. He's not wearing any rings or bracelets, she notices, and there are no tattoos peeking out from under his sleeves. His fingernails are clean.

They sit there in a corner of the cafe, Elaine stone-quiet, and Keith fills the pauses by talking about his apartment next to Lents Park, and how he got a dog, a sheltie-collie mix, she's a cutie. What else . . . He got a job on a landscaping crew, commercial and residential both. Doesn't have a truck yet, "but I got a old ten-speed, one of my neighbors tightened me up, until I can get some wheels."

Sara listens. Watches. Her stomach tight. Now and then he nibbles at the inside of his lower lip, like Elaine does.

"Yeah . . ." Keith scratches the side of his goatee. "They're making me start low on the pole, of course. But it seems like a okay company. No foreman position, but there's the chance for that, so we'll see. Gotta prove myself . . ." He meets Sara's eyes. "With you all, too. I understand that."

"Do you?" The words almost surprise her.

He gazes at her, then gives a half smile, the wrinkles around his eyes blooming.

"I do," he says. "You bet."

A semi downshifts out on I-205, and Keith cocks his head at the sound.

"Good ol' freeway. Your Gramps used to talk about what this was like all in here, back in the day. Farms mostly. Little farming community out here on the edge of the city. Some little businesses. Then the lower- and middle-class houses came in after that, some nice little places." He raises an arm, turns, and makes a sweeping motion back toward the freeway. "When all this came in, he said it was like getting some kind of organ removed. Cut right out."

He looks at them, and neither of them respond. More people come into the cafe, and the espresso machine starts up again. After a while, he leans forward and rests his elbows on the table, folds his hands and then rubs the sides of his forefingers against his lips for a few moments.

"I love you both, you know."

Sara glances at Elaine, who eventually glances at their father.

"And your little sister, tell me about her."

"She's fine," Elaine says, her first words. She clears her throat, a thick sound.

"Still sharp as a bag of finishing nails?"

Elaine nods, then looks away. Another pause hits, and Sara checks the clock. It feels to her like they've been here an hour and it hasn't even been twenty minutes.

"It was kind of hard not hearing from you guys," Keith says, elbows still on the table.

Sara stares at him. "Like we heard from you?"

"Listen, your mom . . ." He stops there and observes her for a few beats, then Elaine. His face changes, there's a sort of haunted light in his eyes, and he gives another half smile. "Listen, I missed you guys a hell of a lot. Just want you to know that. One hell of a lot, you don't even know."

Sara holds his gaze, clicking her front teeth, and then looks away. There's laughter over at the counter, banter with the coffee guy. Keith sits back in his chair and after a while says how he heard a kid in the background when he called the other day.

"It was our little brother," Sara says, her voice low and even, and she can tell that the news pierces him. He only watches her, though. "He's five."

Keith nods slowly; she sees that he doesn't know what to say.

"Is Dad still in the picture?" he says, and Elaine tells him no.

For a time he looks at the rainy scene out the window, still absorbing the information but remaining composed. "You mind if I ask what's his last name, your brother?"

Sara glances at Elaine, and Elaine says, "Garrison."

"Mom kept the same name when you guys . . ." Sara hesitates. "She didn't know what else his last name should be."

Keith nods. Holds the table's edge with both thick hands and just nods.

17

IT DOESN'T SEEM LIKE MUCH of a Thanksgiving to him, being alone and all, being with just a dog. Then again, he's in his own apartment and there's a game on, even though he doesn't follow football much. He takes another sip of his JD and picks at the frozen turkey dinner, now that the apple pie compartment's empty. Bear sits beside the chair, watching him with wistful dark eyes, and occasionally he spoons some of the jellied cranberry sauce out of the can and lets her lick it. He takes another drink, he's had about half of the fifth since lunchtime, and when he glances out the sliding glass door at the park, the grey afternoon light is almost gone.

"What're you lookin' at?" Keith says to the dog, petting her head and neck. "Enough of this, what do you think?"

He gets up. Bear stands, too, tail wagging, and follows him into the kitchen, where he drains the rest of his glass. Before heading out, he gives his toothbrush a quick go, then takes another swig from the bottle.

It's raining and he's drunk, but as he rides his ten-speed along 92nd, holding on to the chain leash, it occurs to him that he's functioning just fine, thank you. Bear running alongside the bike, looking happy to be outside. Not too much traffic. His face and hair get wet fast, the flannel shirt, too, but it feels good to be out and moving after sitting around all day in the apartment. It's good to see other people as well, even if they are just barely illuminated shadows in their passing cars and trucks.

At the coffee shop where he met Sara and Elaine, he stops for a cigarette and to give Bear a rest. He stands astride the bike there in front of the closed cafe and looks across the street at the New Copper Penny. It appears to be open, and he wonders about going in for a drink, see if any other lonely people are hanging out, maybe even get some nookie tonight. Because it's about time. *Man.* What he needs tonight are some *titties.* How long's it been? He doesn't even want to know, actually.

He stands there smoking, glancing around the intersection, sort of thinking, getting wetter, cold now, too, and Bear's panting is hardly audible to him this close to the freeway. It's Thanksgiving, and here he is. Some poor soaked fucker straddling a ten-speed. It's *Thanksgiving*, and Thanksgiving means one thing, it just plain does. Hell with it.

He tosses the cigarette into Foster and with a wobble gets the bike headed east up under the freeway, Bear trotting along. For a minute, as he peddles under the overpass, he thinks again of his parents and what they're doing this evening. He remembers that lime-green Jell-O-and-marshmallow goop his mom made every Thanksgiving when he was growing up, that side dish–dessert combo, and how even through his high school years he couldn't get enough of the super-sweet stuff. They'd about have to pull the damn serving bowl away from him.

But that was then, of course. It's clear enough to him how they want things to be now. Beyond clear. And you know what? They can just keep on with their nice righteous lives, is what they can do. Good luck with that. Because the thing is, a man deserves a second chance. He does. And if you can't give him a second chance, well, then that says a hell of a lot about you, you know?

When he turns onto the gravel road and sees the little white house with its naked porch bulb on and lights in the front windows, he stops and straddles the bike and wipes a hand down his face. He's still drunk, but not quite as much. Jeans wet now, also. He draws a deep breath through his nose and lets out a long, dragon-like plume into the night, and in the pause that follows hears Bear panting.

"This is it, girl." He gets off the bike. "The old street."

He takes another deep breath and blinks hard, trying to sober up, readjusts the leash in his hand, and starts walking the bike toward the house. At the edge of the still-cracked front walkway, he realizes he forgot to bring something.

18

ADAM, POST-BATH, has put on his T. rex underwear over his pants, his yellow T-shirt that says CAMP SHERMAN, OREGON, his green rubber boots with the frog eyes and red tongue, and one of his night diapers over his head. He's hopping around and dancing in the front room to Def Leppard's "Photograph," and Sara has to go tickle him and tell him to keep it down some, Mama has a headache.

"Why does she have a headache?"

"Don't know, man. She just does. Dinner's almost ready."

She checks the space heater over by the front door, it's still pumping, but the room still feels cold to her, even with the warm sight of the table with all the food they're starting to set out. The small ham their mom brought home yesterday, the yearly gift from her boss at Fred Meyer. The bowls of yams, mashed potatoes, Stove Top stuffing, and gravy. She needs to open the can of green beans and the can of cranberry sauce; Rachel's checking on the rolls now. Cans, plates, their glasses of wine all over the countertop.

"Where's that punkin pie?" Elaine says, maneuvering around Rachel. Elaine's overheated, her cheeks sheened with sweat. She lifts the plastic bag the rolls were in and finds the pie, then grabs another handful of black olives from the cereal bowl on the counter and starts popping them into her mouth.

From the front room, Adam dancing off behind her, Sara watches her sisters for a moment.

It's startling sometimes to witness how fast Elaine eats; it's like she's scared the food will get taken away if she doesn't wolf it. As for Rachel, she pulls out the rolls and puts in the pie, Rachel in her black jeans and black T-shirt, Rachel with her bright green bangs. Elaine's the only one among them who looks slightly more festive, clothing-wise, apart from Adam, that is; in her long green blouse and navy tights and dangling turquoise earrings, with her roaring wine-blush, the girl seems almost happy.

Sara glances down at her own blue jeans and MARSHALL MINUTEMEN sweatshirt, then takes the plate of rolls that Rachel hands her.

It's bizarre, sort of, it seems to her. It's almost like how things were last year. Adam underfoot, all loose and excited, her sisters drinking their glasses of zinfandel. The good smells. No Kurt, who's apparently eating dinner at Anthony Ferris's house. Rachel told him she wanted to eat here, and when she, Sara, heard that, it settled things right then and there for her, where she'd go. Kim invited her to her grandparents' place, which was kind and all, but she knew she had to be here tonight. Except for having to watch the noise level, except for that lurking dark energy coming from the hallway and their mom's closed door, it's like they've put all the crap behind them, at least for tonight, and remembered the bond.

"This stuff's kind of awful," Rachel says, wineglass in hand, leaning against the stove. "How does she drink it all the time?"

Elaine shrugs.

"Let's have the schnapps with dinner." Rachel goes over and pours the rest of her wine in the sink, holds up the bottle of peach schnapps that Kurt shoulder-tapped. "What do you think?"

"I'm game," Elaine says, pouring her own wine out.

The doorbell rings, and Adam stops dancing and faces the door.

"What the . . ." Sara goes over and looks outside, blood rushing to her head.

"Who is it?" Rachel says.

"Dad."

"Oh my God."

Adam comes up beside Sara and holds her leg. He sweeps the diaper off his head. "Who is it?"

"Hang on, bud. I just need to talk to him a sec, it's all right."

Sara opens the door and there he stands, wet, glassy-eyed, with a soggy dog panting beside him. A medium-size black dog with a beige and white chest. There's a bike on its side next to the walkway, and he says he hopes it's okay that he stopped by, he just wanted to say hi on Thanksgiving.

"Hi," she says, blank-faced. Part of her suddenly wants to step close to him, hug him, but the impulse only makes her harden up more.

"Where's your mom?" He over-enunciates, and she can smell the booze. It's raining hard off behind him, cold air flowing into the house.

"Doggie." Adam's grip on her loosens.

"You like dogs?" Keith pulls gently on the leash, and the dog steps forward and sits down, tongue bobbing, tan eyebrows raised. "Her name's Bear. She's a good old dog. You wanna pet her?"

Adam looks up at Sara, who shakes her head. She eyes her father again.

"Any chance I could get her a bowl of water? She ran all the way over."

Ankles locked, Sara looks over her shoulder at her sisters. Rachel, slack-faced, is staring right at him, the oven mitt still on her hand, while Elaine has her arms folded and appears less intense, but concerned. When Sara nods once, Elaine gets a bowl of water and brings it over.

"Thanks." Keith bends down and sets the bowl onto the porch, drops the leash, and tells Bear in a calm voice to stay. He rises, smiling, and runs a hand over his hair. "Mind if I come in for a minute?"

Sara feels herself stepping aside, and he passes through and shuts the door on the dog, the slurping sounds cut off.

"Little Def Leppard? Classic." Keith stops in the middle of the room, and Sara watches him take things in. Her mom's chair with the unfolded blanket on it, the same ancient couch, Gram's needlepoint on the wall, all the food on the table. He wipes a hand down his face and zeroes in on Rachel. "Well goodness, look at you . . ."

He steps over closer to her, and Rachel holds her ground, not lowering her eyes once. It looks to Sara like she might cry, but there's more anger there than anything. Keith sees that there won't be any hugs and so he holds out his hand, but Rachel doesn't take it. He smiles and lowers his hand, turns and eases down into a squat.

"And what's your name? I heard about you."

Adam goes back to Sara and hugs her leg, half hiding behind her. He doesn't answer, and she touches the back of his head.

"High five?" Keith holds up a hand.

After glancing up at Sara, Adam steps forward and gives his hand a light slap, then retreats to Sara's leg. Keith pushes against his thighs and stands.

"Brought Bear over to show him. If he wants to go out and pet—"

In the hallway threshold, Melanie, squinting. One side of her hair is flattened to her skull, she's in her robe and slippers, and the sight of her there makes Rachel lower her head. Melanie looks at Keith as if she's trying to figure out who he is, but it's the lights in the room, Sara knows, the migraine pinch.

"What are you doing here?" she says softly.

Keith observes her, a near-dumbfounded expression on his face. "Just wanted to stop by is all—"

"Why are you here?" Melanie steps farther into the room.

"Wanted to say hello."

When she reaches her chair, she puts a hand on it as if to steady herself, and Sara glances again at her sisters. Elaine riveted, Rachel looking down still, her lips pursed.

"You've been drinking," Melanie says, and Keith runs his hand over his hair again, with a closed-mouthed smile.

"It's Thanksgiving."

"Well, isn't that—"

"Mom," Elaine says.

"Don't even *Mom* me." Melanie speaks without moving her squinted eyes from Keith. Her face is glue-pale, and she has a large pimple on one side of her chin. "You think you can just come in here . . ."

Keith raises his hands and backs up a step. "I was just—"

"Come check out the old haunts? See how you left everything?"

He stands, like Rachel, with his head lowered, and Sara takes Adam's hand and steps over and turns off the music.

"Everything look good?"

"Mom," Sara says.

"Don't even." Melanie glares at Keith, holding her robe closed. "He thinks he can show up unannounced, on *Thanksgiving Day*. What, do you want some food? Nice plate of ham, maybe some rolls?"

Keith meets her eyes, his chin raised just slightly, and his voice stays calm. "Only wanted to say hello. That's it."

"Aw, well, what a *sweet* thing to do."

Adam is crying quietly, and Elaine's eyes have filled as well. Rachel's jaws go on flexing. Sara holds her brother's hand and watches her dad move to the door. When he opens it, Bear's tail starts up.

"Oh look, and you brought your dog, too. Would your dog like some ham, maybe some—"

"Would you *stop!*" Rachel shouts. "This is . . . in*sane!*" She pulls at one side of her hair and goes down the hallway, Adam running after her.

At the door, Keith gives Sara a half smile, and his eyes linger on hers for a beat before he turns back to Melanie. "I shouldn't've come. My bad."

"Oh, your *bad*?" Melanie says. "They taught you how to talk in there, didn't they?" When he turns away, she steps over next to Sara. *"So how's the old neighborhood look?"*

Keith keeps his back to her as he picks up his bike off the walkway and leads Bear down to the road, and when Melanie retreats into the house, Sara watches him get on the bike, wobbling with the leash in hand, and how the dog dodges the bike and resumes trotting. They ride away into the night, and off behind her, her mom is crying now, too, sobs rising then dying away behind her bedroom door.

She turns around and shuts the front door behind her. Elaine is standing next to the table full of cooling food, wiping at her cheeks with one hand, reaching for a roll with the other.

19

JACKET HOOD RAISED against the chill, Elaine with her homework-filled backpack walks alone off school grounds and turns left on 92nd. From only a few hours' sleep each night the past few weeks, since before Christmas even, it feels to her like part of her is floating outside of herself. She wonders if this is what jet lag feels like.

As she walks, her face in shadow, she prays.

Lord, please guide us. Please guide my family. Let Rachel be all right. Please let her be all right and find her way. And please guide Sara. And Adam. Please help me to have the patience for him, and the energy. And please let Mom find more strength. She suffers. Please guide her.

Lord, please help me.

Her mom will pick up Adam from Ms. Trinh's today, like every Tuesday now, and after a full day of being on her feet and then the trials of bath time, the woman will be especially cranky tonight. She'll be in her chair, waiting for dinner.

The full-on sensory assault of Chuck E. Cheese never fails to bring on the mild squeezing sensation in her gut. It's not that crowded on weekday afternoons, but even so, after a day of classes and the entire high school scene, the place jars her.

They hired her to wash dishes and clear tables, but soon enough other employees quit and she was wearing the tight purple polo shirt and tighter black pants, the red baseball cap and the waist pack, the uniform that makes her look even larger. But today, as she's about to see if she can squeeze into the outfit again, her manager, Rayette, hurries in, jam-packed into her own uniform, and says, "Gary can't come in today and Janice is late, so you're the mouse. Can you do it?"

"The mouse?"

"You know the moves pretty good. I need to know right now."

"If it fits. I guess so . . ."

"Good girl. It's in the closet there. I need you on the floor in five minutes." Rayette stops at the door, holding it open, turns around and talks over the noise. "Remember, just like when you're not the mouse, when you're the mouse, it's all about keeping the kids happy, okay? *You* gotta have a good time if the kids're gonna have a good time."

"Right."

Alone again in the cramped, cubbyhole-lined changing room, the music and game sounds muffled once more, she sits there for a minute, noticing her pulsing feet and ankles. It's been like this lately, and she's had to buy her own bottle of ibuprofen. The smell of pizza, fries, and cotton candy has drifted into the room, and the usual hunger rumbling comes. She needs her slice of pepperoni and a Coke to get her going, but there's no time today.

The purple jersey with the big yellow *C* on the chest is tight at her belly, but she manages to pull it down over the green shorts, then lift on the huge mouse head with the purple and green cap, get the large grey hands in place, and stand in front of the full-length mirror.

Holy shit.

Out on the floor, though, with the suit on, she notices almost right away how she feels less self-conscious. And the animated life-size animals and happy monsters on stage, the blaring music, all the flashing lights and big-screen TVs, the wobbly car and plane rides, all the star-shaped balloons—from inside the mouse, the onslaught seems a notch less extreme. At one of the long tables, an after-school birthday party for a fourth- or fifth-grade boy is in progress, twelve kids sitting around downing pizza and sodas, and when Mitchell Drake holds up the bullhorn and announces Chuck E. Cheese's grand entrance, she picks up the pace across the room and crashes blindly into a chair, nearly pitching herself over it. But it comes off like part of big Chuck's comedy routine and the kids all burst out laughing.

In front of the stage near the table, she gets in line with Mitchell, Yvonne, and Huong, performing the dance she had to learn three weeks ago: *clap, spin, clap, spin, hula hula hula hula.* But the kids have already lost interest and gone back to eating and talking. The party song keeps going, however, and they're required to keep dancing until it ends, and so she claps and spins, again and again until Rayette whisks over the cake and Huong lights all the candles. Rayette, on her way back to the prize-claim desk, shoots a look at the mouse, and so the mouse moves closer to the table of kids and shifts into mingling mode. She's sweating bad and the suit reeks, but she has ten more minutes of this before she can duck back into the changing room and catch her breath.

At the table's far end, a wizened, peroxide-blond mother is holding a little girl in her lap, bouncing her some. The girl is around three, and from what Elaine can barely see through her sweat-stung eyes, the cute little thing has a wide smile on her face, she loves her some Chuck E. Cheese, and, look, the nice mouse is coming her way! But when Elaine is almost upon mother and child, she catches that the smile is actually a frozen scream, and now the girl unleashes a sphincter-puckering wail.

Her first week here, the other grunts all told her the same thing: either you love it or you hate it.

She waves at the glowering mom, turns and says hi to some of the other kids and parents, a few of whom smile and say something, but she can't really hear them. The lights keep flashing, the kids keep sucking on their sodas, and across the room another group is getting ready for a visit from none other than the main mouse himself, Elaine Louise Garrison.

IN THE WET DARK, FOOTSORE, she walks across the street to the MAX stop, eating from her bag of fries. What she'll make for dinner she has no clue.

Lord, please.

In her entire life, she's been to church a total of six times, most of those with her Gramps and Gram back when they lived in Lents. Those two would never miss a Sunday service, and when they could they'd take a granddaughter or two along, when Melanie said it was all right.

Still, she likes to pray. Always has. When she was little, her Gram told her how the Good Lord always listened, He was always there, and whenever you needed some comfort, all you had to do was try to clear your mind and speak to Him.

Please help me find a way to not be this tired and worried. I'm sorry to ask for so much, Lord.

She rides her two stops, gets out again into the cold January night, hoists her backpack, and eases down the stairs to street level. Under the overpass she hikes up Foster and pulls her hood tight around her face.

20

KIM'S PLACE, a Thursday in mid-January, just past 11 a.m., Sara's about to do something crazy but doesn't quite know it.

She's on the couch in her sweats, stoned yet again, this time sipping from the fresh pint of vodka she just took from Kim's dad's cabinet. There's plenty of booze in that cabinet, but she'll pay him back, she promises herself. Soon. Once she starts at the nursery.

On the TV, *The Bourne Ultimatum*, the one she and Kim watched last night. It's Matt Damon that made her put it in, there's that certain something about him that makes her wonder again. There'd been a couple of boyfriends at Marshall, Toby and Horacio, and she'd enjoyed kissing them and touching them and all, but . . . *Fuck it*. She takes another drink and zeroes back in on the movie, the flashing scenes of New York City, and then smokes more weed, to the point just short of feeling dizzy. After a while, she eyes her books and binder there on the coffee table. She showed up at school a few times in December, mostly to find out what she needed to catch up on, but she still hasn't caught up on much. She told Ms. Engle and Ms. Bennett that a relative's been sick, and she's helping take care of her. Her grandma, she said.

She glances at her phone and thinks of how her dad called three or four times last month and left his messages, how he wanted to have her and Elaine and Rachel over to his place for a wintertime barbecue, maybe a little Christmas party, since the old man next door had a grill he could borrow. There was a view of the park, he said, and he'd pick up some steaks. Even let them drink a beer if they promised not to tell Melanie. But she hadn't ever called back, and Elaine and Rachel hadn't either, from what she knows. She almost did call, one day, when she was here on this couch, but couldn't quite do it. Who says they have to have a relationship? Who says he won't leave again?

She at least saw her sisters on Christmas Day. To watch Adam open his presents. Yet while things had gone all right, no major fights, only a little tension, Rachel disappeared again right afterward, back into her Kurt World. As for Elaine, she seems even more withdrawn lately. When she tried to talk about it with her last week on the phone, Elaine said she was just tired, her job and everything.

But there was more, she couldn't help thinking, and she thinks the same thing now, turning off the movie. Everyone seems quieter, more within themselves, even Adam, and her mom, too. Quieter, like something's building up inside, or maybe something's broken, for good. And maybe it's partly because of her.

The house's silence impales her. She looks around and takes another swig of the vodka, spilling some on her sweatshirt.

On New Year's Eve, at Brianna Chester's party, Kim leaned in close to her in the tight, rowdy crowd and said, "I'm worried about you, man. Been thinking about you a lot."

She gave a nod, avoiding Kim's eyes. Kim was drunk.

"My dad asked what your plans are . . . He said you probably can't stay forever."

She met her eyes then, briefly, but still didn't respond, only raised her cup of beer to her mouth.

Fuck it.

She gets up off the couch and goes over to the computer, vodka in hand. For several seconds she sits there gazing at the screen, which reflects the front windows, the greyness there, bars of rain. Most Portland winters she's fine, she can handle some rain and the short days, she can handle the greyness, but this year is different, it's beyond getting to her, day after day of wet. She touches the mouse and the screen wakes.

She clicks between images of the dorms, the bell tower, the arena's dome, the soccer field, and then for a long time stares at the team photo from this past fall. Some buff girls, squinting into the sun, there in their purple uniforms and polished cleats. They seem so confident and strong. Ready for anything. They know who they are. They know their roles. And there at the end of the standing line: Angus Graham and Martin Crosley, along with two other assistants. One big family.

"Fuck it!"

The walls absorb her voice.

Before she can change her mind, she gets up and showers, throws on a semi-clean sweatshirt, her jeans, and her donated Sambas from her club team last winter, grabs Kim's puffy black coat, an onion bagel from the pantry, and the pint of vodka. She leaves a note on the counter that says *Riding around.*

THE CITY, FROM THE MAX TRAIN, seems calmer to her. Though she doesn't have a ticket and at every stop looks around to see if a fare inspector has boarded, it's mostly relaxing, just sitting there among people, feeling the warm buzz in her head and limbs, checking out the clogged freeway off to her left as the train glides along. People on their missions, playing their parts in the city's rhythm. And here she is, one of the people.

At the Rose Quarter she transfers to the yellow line and rides along Interstate Avenue for a while, gets off at Rosa Parks, and then stops under some trees for another swig of the vodka. It's 1:15 p.m. and she's about as drunk as when she left, about an hour ago, she guesses. She checks the TriMet map again, and soon enough a bus comes along and she tries to get on, but the driver won't let her unless she pays or shows her pass.

"It got stolen," she says, there in the grooved rubber stairwell, the bus idling.

"You'll have to pay then."

She steps back out into the drizzle and starts walking west down Rosa Parks, pausing every few blocks to swig. At Willamette Boulevard she hangs a right, she remembers the campus and neighborhood maps clearly, from all those times on the computer these past few months, and when the campus eventually comes into view after the long sweep along the bluff, she stands across the street, the pint stashed back in Kim's coat.

The rain has stopped, but it's still overcast and cold, and for several minutes she lingers there across from the campus just watching people pull in and out of the main driveway. Some nice cars, some not so nice. An old red Saab parked nearby has bumper stickers that say CHANGE YOU CAN BELIEVE IN and I BRAKE FOR SALTED FILBERTS. She pulls out the pint and drinks.

When finally she crosses and sets foot on the University of Portland grounds, her stomach gets even tighter. Students with backpacks and satchels, some wearing sweats, walk the clean concrete pathways, one tall guy texting as he hustles along. Brick-and-mortar Shipstad, Kenna, and Christie Halls to her left, the old gym up ahead, the dome and the soccer fields off to her right.

I'm actually here.

She keeps moving, doesn't know where she's headed, and keeps on eyeing the students, some who look like rich snobs, like some of the girls on her club team, with their expensive clothes and cool, arrogant expressions on their faces, that certain entitled look that gets under her skin every time. But then there are other faces that don't appear that way at all.

Soon she's beside the bell tower, gazing up at it, it's taller than she thought, and after that she's standing in the middle of the grassy, path-crossed quad, checking out more brick buildings, giant Franz Hall off at the far end with its massive windows, and all the surrounding trees. *Everything's so clean.* More students walk past, some alone, some in groups, and she feels jittery now—what the hell is she doing here? She needs another drink but isn't comfortable pulling out the pint. She looks over her shoulder to the bluff's edge, at some trees and shrubs there, and so she heads over and takes out the pint and swigs, glimpsing the hazy city view, the downtown buildings in the distance, the industrial zone in the foreground, and the brown river. She has another drink, the pint's over half-gone, and stands there for a while with the view.

What the fuck *am I doing?*

She watches the sullen Willamette and imagines the Salmon River, the clear water and the forest. Off to the right, though, across the river, there's Forest Park, that dark expanse of trees right there in the city, and the sight of it relaxes her some. She's here, so to hell with it, might as well finish the campus tour before getting her ass back to Southeast.

Past the library she walks, past a tall old cedar, and then into the parking lot and over toward the rust-colored dome. She can see the practice field through the rows of vehicles, and when she makes her way over to its low fence, there it is, right beside Merlo Field's stadium. It's artificial turf, the practice field, and the goals have new nets on them.

Here's where they train.

The gates to Merlo Field are open, and so she goes in. May as well. See for herself where she could've played if she hadn't been such a complete dumbfuck. Along the grandstand's back wall are blown-up banner photos of famous UP players, including Kasey Keller, Tiffeny Milbrett, Christine Sinclair, Megan Rapinoe, and others. Warriors, all of them. Martha, a former UP player herself, talked about those guys all the time.

When she steps around the corner and the field comes into view, a wave of heat flows up her chest. It's quiet and the stands are empty and the field is the most beautiful field she's ever seen. It's almost painful to look at. The crisp white lines. The flat, newly mown grass. The goals with their nets swaying in the wind. Tall shrubs line each end of the field, the arena dome rising just to the north. She remembers some of the girls on the club team saying how during UP games, from the student section, there were loud songs and drumming, the place would go berserk whenever the Pilots scored.

And here she is—having never seen a college or pro game in person, men or women. Not one. Always too far away, too expensive, even with a club team discount, every excuse you could dream of. Bottom line? It was for people who could afford that shit. For people who belonged in a place like this.

She pulls out the pint and stares at the field for a while longer, getting cold.

Time to go. The wind kicks up and waters her eyes, and as she wipes them she feels like she needs to pee, so she wanders over into the arena, the Chiles Center, and finds a restroom. Sips at the vodka some more, then tightens the cap harder and slips it back down into Kim's coat and this time buttons the pocket. In the concourse on the way out, she pauses at the display case with the national championship trophy and the *Oregonian* photo of Christine Sinclair. There are some cleats in the case as well, but she's too drunk to see them clearly. Across the concourse, though, there's a sign next to a door that says ATHLETICS DE-PARTMENT in words large enough for her to read.

Fuck it.

She swallows and feels herself opening the door, and when the middle-aged, round-faced secretary looks up at her and smiles, she says she's looking for Angus Graham.

"I'm sorry, did you have an appointment?"

"No."

"He's out at the moment. But he should be back within the hour if you'd like to wait."

Sara breathes heavily through her nostrils, glancing around the office. There's a hallway off to the left, some nameplates on the doors, from what she can tell. The woman keeps looking up at her, though not quite as pleasantly, and Sara nods and says thanks, turns and walks out.

On the walk back through the parking lot, she notices that her hands are trembling, and so she slips them into the jacket's pockets and feels, in the right one, some crumpled dollar bills and a pack of gum. Six bucks and a half-gone pack of spearmint Trident, Kim's favorite. Up ahead, there's the Pilot House she spotted earlier, the bookstore and cafe in there; she decides to go on in and grab a snack for the long walk and ride back, now that she's in the money here. Or maybe just some cocoa, she feels so cold all of a sudden. She pops a piece of gum into her mouth, feeling the flavor in her sinuses.

Still, she needs one last look at Merlo—it's like the field has some sort of pull, she has to set eyes on it one last time before she leaves. She weaves back through the rows of cars and stands near where she stood before, at the eighteen-yard line on the western end, and for a long time just stands there with her hands jammed in the coat pockets and looks all around. The high press box. The center circle. The team benches and the goalmouths. A bit less drunk, she makes herself walk away and across the parking lot toward the Pilot House. That cocoa calls her.

She's within herself, picturing the secretary's face, that budding concern in her expression, when she approaches the Pilot House doors and doesn't see Martin Crosley until he's almost right in front of her.

"Sara?" he says, breaking a purposeful stride. He's carrying a manila folder in one hand.

She startles and looks up at him. Martin Crosley with his thick neck and gelled short hair, the black Adidas sweatsuit. "Hi."

"What are you doing here?"

All around them, students are walking in and out of the Pilot House, others are passing through the small brick plaza nearby, everyone doing their thing, in their daily flow. Martin Crosley looks at her, a little worried by what he sees.

"How've you been?" he says. "We tried to reach you."

She looks away again at the passing students. "I had some stuff going on . . ."

Crosley observes her. "We assumed you weren't interested."

Her eyes flash to his, and when she looks away once more, her throat feels dry. "It wasn't that," she manages to say.

There's a longer pause. "Listen, I need to run, but . . ." Crosley glances at the Pilot House, then gazes at her. "Angus is actually inside there, we just had a coaches meeting over coffee. If you'd like, I could take you in. No promises, but . . . he may want to talk with you, actually. If that's why you're here, that is. What do you think?"

Her pulse beats hard in her neck, she's chewing on the gum, and she stands there looking around at all the students, all these college students, all around them. And the thoughts start up again. Look at her sorry ass, a pint of vodka tucked at her side. She looks like shit. The thing is, she belongs where she belongs, and these people belong right here, and what she needs to do right now is just go get on the nice MAX train and get her ass back to the land of gravel roads. It's good she came out here and all, good she saw the place for herself finally, got it out of her system and everything, but now it's time to—

"Sara. I need to know right now, actually. I've got another meeting in, like, two minutes across campus."

Where the word comes from, she's not sure. It just comes. Like someone else inside of her, way down, just cut in line. "Okay," she hears herself say.

Surreal. This door, suddenly opening. And what's even more amazing, what someone like her doesn't even deserve, what makes her heart break even worse, is that Martin Crosley smiles back and doesn't look away.

She walks through the door, eyes filled, following him.

PART TWO

21

AT THE END OF the afternoon session, it's near ninety degrees on the practice field, and Angus Graham stands on the sideline with his arms crossed, his cap shading his eyes.

"Don't let this beat you," he says.

They're on their eighth full-field sprint. Two left. Twenty-three sweat-drenched girls at the end of practice. Sara comes in next to last again and this time bends over and throws up.

"Right, then," Angus says after thirty seconds. "On the line."

Martin Crosley blows the whistle, and as Sara forces herself to run, the thoughts resume their attack: It's too much. She doesn't belong here, this is a fluke. People like her do not do shit like this. She thought she'd gotten herself back into shape over the spring and summer, all the club games, the fairly clean living, but she isn't even *close* to the shape that so many others here are in. They've all trained harder, they've been play-ing longer than her probably, on club teams since they were, like, five. Better training, better coaches, better competition, all kinds of travel for tournaments.

The captain, Lindsay Waxler, is leading again, Siena Vincent and Shannon Wang, two other seniors, cruising right behind her, then the touted freshman Sophie Mack. Compared to the three seniors, Sophie looks short, but she's well-built, she has some biceps on her, a six-pack. Everyone's winded, but only one other person, one of the walk-ons, has vomited so far as well. Olivia, Sara's roommate, chugs along in the middle group. Big girl, strong and tall. Center back.

Sara's legs are cement-heavy and she's dizzy, her lungs torched; but she keeps on running. How will she survive two weeks of camp? she wonders. She's never run this much in her life, never imagined anything near this. When she crosses the end line, she barfs once more.

"Hey, you're reekin' up the field." It's Lindsay Waxler, with only a hint of a smile, her tanned buff shoulders glistening, sports bra soaked. A few other players manage gasping chuckles, Sara doesn't see who.

Sweat scalds her eyes as she rises up again. She wipes her mouth with the back of her salty hand. The sun hitting them all in the face.

"Last one, then," Angus calls. "And, as we do it here, the last to cross has one extra."

The tenth whistle, tenth lurch forward. Sara vomits yet again as she runs, her chin and neck slick, and soon falls back to last. There's a knifing pain in her side now, and her legs are gone, but soon the nauseous walk-on starts to hit the wall, too, slows way down, and at this, Sara clenches her teeth, scraping the dregs, a final push. She catches the walk-on with twelve yards to go, then stumbles across the line and falls onto her front. Her hearing's messed up, everything sounds like it's far away, pulsating, and as she rolls onto her back, her vision is ringed by an orange light. It's through this shimmering light that Angus passes quietly on his way to the locker room, his eyes still shaded, that smoothness in his movements. And it's through this same orange ring that, after a few more moments, Lindsay Waxler moves just as fluidly and powerfully, her golden, lean-muscled body.

"Day one, girlie," Lindsay says, glancing down at her.

THE CAMPUS IS MOSTLY DESERTED, two weeks until classes start, yet as she steps along flush-faced and weak-legged toward her dorm, Mehling Hall, in her white V-neck T-shirt from the trip to Kmart last month, the three-pack that was on sale, and the new soccer shorts and soccer sandals that Martha scored for her last spring, she feels self-conscious again. Like when, a few minutes ago in the training room, she pointed at the Gatorade-filled cooler and said, "How much are one of those?" and some of the others getting treatment laughed. The trainer tossed her a cold bottle. *Day one.*

In her room on the seventh floor with its view of Forest Park across the river, she closes the door and puts on her Rush CD, cues "Limelight," and eases onto her bed, her body still in shock. Olivia isn't there, and she wonders if maybe the girl is still lifting with some of the other players. How they can lift weights after all that: truly incredible.

She gazes over at Olivia's stuff. The Death Cab for Cutie poster. The shirtless Ryan Reynolds poster. The family photos on her desk, one of them taken in front of some beach house, pale dunes and sea grass in the background, her mom and dad with their high-class teeth, a couple of younger, shaggy-haired teenage brothers. Olivia's laptop, her dark green comforter, the glass vase on her desk with the fresh flowers that her mom bought before leaving yesterday, back to Marin, wherever the hell in California that is. Olivia so pretty and tall, like her mom, both of them look like they only eat healthy foods.

But Olivia seems all right to her, at least so far. No whiffs of rich-girl attitude, not yet anyway. It's early, though. Olivia does seem so composed, quietly confident—so totally different compared to how she herself feels right now. And the girl's certainly not shy about undressing in the room in front of a complete stranger. That muscled, tanned body, like Lindsay Waxler's body, actually, but Olivia is even taller, blonder. Killer shoulders, too. A strange thing, trying to fall asleep in the same room with a stranger.

Linus Oinkraisin. Hector Meatsauce.

She turns and surveys her side of the room. Nothing on the walls yet. Bare desk. Her bags on the floor over by the window. The Kmart comforter underneath her, baby blue. No family photos—they never took many, at least that she knows of.

And so now here she is. A twenty-five-minute drive from Lents and it feels like another country, it's true.

She sits up and swivels her legs off the bed. When she stands, her thighs hurt even more. The Rush goes on playing. It's almost dinnertime, but she's not hungry. What she needs is a cigarette, and so she goes over and puts on some eyeliner again, then steps to the window and looks out at Forest Park, the late blue sky above it. On this side of the river there's that trail she spotted yesterday, it looks like it might head down the bank. She opens the wide drawer on her desk and reaches far back to retrieve her lighter and cigs, slips on her soccer sandals and shuffles out to the elevator.

Beside the brown river, she stands on the pebbly beach. The dry docks off to her left, the downtown skyline in the distance. The railroad bridge to her right, downriver. She checks her phone again. Nothing. She thought maybe her dad would text with something like *How was the first day?* But there's nothing. After a time, she lights another cig and walks up the beach, eyeing the skyline, thinking of Rachel. Last Elaine heard, Rachel had been downtown most every day over the summer, hanging out. "She about lives down there, from what I can tell," Elaine said.

Sara stands there for many minutes, smoking, alone. The river smells like warmed aluminum foil. She pulls out her phone once more, and this time texts Rachel.

Hope u r ok. I miss u.

It's been a while since she's tried with Rachel, but she needs to try right now.

She smokes her third, absorbing the scenes, Forest Park looming right across the water, and begins to feel the first twinges of returning appetite. In the lavender dusk she hikes back up another trail, still smoking, and comes out through the undergrowth right near the cafeteria, which sits brightly lit across the mown grass.

As she steps from the woods, she spots Olivia and Sophie Mack walking into the cafeteria, chatting. Two strong, well-bred, freshly showered girls who look over and see a chain-smoking, lank-haired hillbilly emerge from the brambles.

22

IN THE SOUTH PARK BLOCKS downtown, early evening, Rachel's a little high from the last of Kurt's weed. The street kids have mostly taken over the area near Salmon Street, like usual, while on the periphery some older men and women with their shopping carts and dogs hang about. The warm weather has most everyone in a decent mood, it looks like to her, and Kurt goes over to his regular guy to buy more weed with the money his mom still gives him, his weekly payout. If the woman only knew. Then again, she probably wouldn't do anything about it, Kurt being the man of the house and all.

Rachel, her bangs bright blue, eyeliner heavy, finds a free bench and pulls her journal from her daypack. Before opening it, though, she takes in more of the scene. The circle of shirtless hacky sackers. The concert hall's rear marquee through the trees. The respectable citizens staying well clear of the degenerates gathered in the late sunshine. Off to her right, the street librarian is starting to pack up her nifty rolling cart, and there's the old guy she's seen often down here, the guy with the glasses falling down his nose, full grey beard, grey button-up shirt tucked into threadbare brown slacks. He's picking through the books, chatting with the hip-looking, svelte librarian, and, as always, he appears to be discerning, his manner so methodical as he examines that day's selection.

When she opens the journal on her lap, she glances over at Kurt, who's already done his transaction, he's now talking it up with some of the regulars, Kyle, Tree, Vanya with her pit bull mix, Mr. Bill. She turns back to her journal and the surroundings start to fade.

The first draft of a poem, there on the left-hand page, from yesterday. Some possible seed ideas, about sitting at the edge of Pioneer Square in the sun, watching friends hound passersby for change. She likes the phrase "dreadlock disgust." Makes her think of the poem she got published her freshman year, in that Writers in the Schools anthology, how she was in a groove back then, writing-wise, just writing all the time, day and night, stories, poems, essays. And now? Now she's a junior at Franklin. Barely. One visit to that school last spring, with Elaine, to the orientation, and Elaine dry heaved before they went in. How old and dark that school seemed compared to Marshall.

The memory makes her check her phone for the first time in several hours, a lapse that invariably happens whenever she agrees to get high with Kurt, and sure enough there's a message, one from her big bad soccer player sister. *Hope u r ok. I miss u.*

She stares at the words, the last three bringing a faint warmth to her upper chest. Though it could just be the afternoon heat, the remnants of the weed. Whatever the case, she finds herself thinking of Sara off at college now, the lingering surprise of that. The twinge of envy, sure, she'll admit it. She was supposed to be the first in her family to go to college, she was the one who'd said her goal aloud, for all of them to hear.

And then, once again, it's Adam in her mind. Each day, these pangs. Or aches, is maybe a better way to put it. She wonders if Elaine is picking him up from daycare right about now, and what they'll eat for dinner. Who will read to him at bedtime? Most likely Elaine, since the Great White Whale probably won't budge from her precious chair. My God, that feeling of sitting in Adam's bed, pillows bunched behind their backs, just reading to him, him pressed up close to her, his small curled body so fully trusting that she'll finish the book, that she'll then tuck him in and say that she loves him, sleep well, good night. Could she *be* a worse sister? Is that possible?

She types out a quick reply, *u 2*, and tries to clear her head. There has to be something else to say to Sara, but nothing comes and so she hits send. As for any other messages, none. None from Elaine asking when she'll see her, if she's planning on coming to school the first day, and none from her dad, who's been leaving messages all spring and summer, with Elaine and Sara, too. Always a bad scene whenever Kurt catches one of them, how he likes to swipe her phone, listen to her messages, and read her texts, no matter how many times she says it violates her privacy, he needs to trust her, not just say he trusts her. She's tried to reassure him that she has no intention of seeing her dad again, but Kurt always launches into his rant anyway, how "that motherfucker left you guys high and dry, *now* he wants to make it all better?"

When she zeroes in on her surroundings again, the librarian has already pedaled away and the bookish old guy is pushing his well-packed shopping cart off north through the Park Blocks, passing in and out of shade. The hacky sackers are still at it, but Kurt turns and heads toward her now, wiry Kurt loping along in his cutoffs with the chain swaying against his hip.

"You ready?" he says, and she knows to say yeah.

ON THE MAX RIDE back to Lents, Kurt lost in his tunes, she looks out the window at the late rush-hour jam on the freeway. Poisoned air, poisoned water, poisoned land. Why would people do this to themselves and their kids? Cars and trucks sitting there, fumes rising, while the train whizzes by.

When they get home, Sheila has already been home from her day at the auto parts store, smoked her one cigarette at the kitchen table, and left a note that there's frozen pizza, before heading back out for her shift at the New Copper Penny. Kurt checks to make sure it's pepperoni, then takes her hand again and starts down the basement stairs.

Their room has been more cramped, of course, ever since she moved her stuff in, but still, it seems manageable, if they pick up the dirty clothes now and then, something that Kurt struggles with. Her books stacked on the red carpet by the mattress, her posters tacked to the faux-wood-paneled walls, intermingled with his. He's let her put up KRS-One, Radiohead, and Green Day, posters that the Great White Whale always harped on and on about, not wanting them up in Adam's room, too "sour-looking."

"Why does everyone you listen to always have to look so pissed off?" The woman actually said that once.

Kurt pulls the dark red curtains over the three small windows, and the basement goes crimson dim. He sits on the mattress and removes a baggie from his cutoffs, his hand clutched around the contents.

"Try some?" he says.

"I don't want any more."

"It ain't weed."

Rachel steps closer, and Kurt loosens his hand.

"I thought you said you didn't like crank."

"I don't. Just now and then. Ray had it cheap, it's almost a free sample."

"Kurt."

She rubs one of her elbows.

"Fine. Fuckin' smoke it myself."

Soon the room fills with the sick, almost sweet smell, and she lies down on the mattress, on her side; despite her sprinting mind, the fatigue starts to press on her. She knows what's coming and it's like her body is trying to get in a few minutes of rest beforehand. It knows.

Before long he's turning her over, pushing up her T-shirt sleeve, kissing her shoulder. Then it's her neck, her collarbones. He puts on some Nirvana and undresses her, and as things progress, he gets more intense. More like an animal. An angry animal. He goes on for a long time, a lot longer than usual, and at certain points she tries to hold him, slow him down a bit, but he's gone now, in his zone, unstoppable. He's supposed to see his dad this weekend, she knows. The visit they have every three or four months, the guy off in his Gresham townhouse with his new family, and of course Kurt's feeling all edgy about that. Of course he is. She tries again to relax, not control things, let him be a little rough if he wants to, his lithe strong body ramming hers over and over. She just has to hold on, it'll be okay. It's a rough patch, but they'll make it, they only need to hang tough.

Just now and then, he said, about the crank. But from the look on his reddened, sweaty face with the veins at his temples bulged, she's not sure she believes him.

23

THE WORKOUTS usually help a little. The workouts and the talks with Olivia at lights out some nights. But as for her other teammates, she still hasn't talked all that much around them. For one thing, she usually doesn't get the humor, the jokes just aren't that funny to her, especially the ones from Lindsay Waxler or Siena Vincent, and since they're the captains, the tone setters, she can tell that her silence is starting to rub certain people the wrong way. Hard looks, or even comments now and then. A superior attitude. Like two days ago in practice, Lindsay stole the ball from her, bumped her right off the ball, and said under her breath, "Shit's weak." She tried to chase Lindsay down to get the ball back, but Lindsay passed off and then gave a snarky laugh. Angus on the sideline, calm, watching the whole thing.

And now today, three days before the home opener against Florida, Lindsay's at it again, not passing to her. At all. For the past few days, she, Sara Garrison, has been playing with the starters; the week before, she alternated between the subs and starters; the first days of camp it was always with the subs. So she wonders if maybe Lindsay's pissed off about that, Siena and Shannon, too. Whatever it is, they aren't passing to her and it's starting to get on her nerves.

It's another hot afternoon, and the past week or so she's finally been getting her legs under her. Even though she normally comes in close to last in the sprints, she feels stronger, less sore most nights. But she's quiet around her teammates, just doesn't know what to say. And now that classes have started, she sinks into herself even more often. It's like she's swallowing everything, more and more stress, storing it up. Her classes, the loads of homework already, she has no idea how she'll do it, thinks every single day still that maybe she's not meant to be here after all.

So it's the workouts and the talks with Olivia that have helped her hang on. Olivia's unruffled style has been flat-out huge. How the girl stays so composed all the time remains a major mystery, but it's one she's bent on figuring out.

They've been scrimmaging today for ten minutes, the teams mixed, and though she hasn't yet received a pass, the rhythm has started to set in, she's getting lost in the flow, it's definitely awesome to be playing on this practice field on a beautiful warm afternoon in late August. Eighteen years old, in college—on a full ride, unbelievably—healthy and running. It's a damn good thing when it comes down to it. There are a few student spectators beside the field, other students walking alongside the adjacent parking lot, turning to watch the game, too, and for a few moments at least she feels part of things, for the first time really. She feels powerful. Or at least not so weak, almost beaten. She hasn't played on Merlo Field yet, but it's just three days away, that opener, and she'll be damned if she's gonna sit on the bench.

In a burst of energy, she steals the ball from Winnie Baasten, dribbles twelve yards and blasts a left-footed rocket that screams past Taylor Chamberlain into the net. On the jog back, she glances over at Angus, who remains on the sideline in his shades and cap, arms folded. Martin Crosley and the other assistants, Letti Heath and Jason Vanderheusen, all fit, tanned, in a row next to him, shades on. Jason leans forward and looks down the line at Angus, who only faces the field, stoic as ever.

Lindsay, as she runs past when play resumes, says, "Ugly shot," and it doesn't sound like a compliment.

It's then that Sara has had enough.

Three minutes later, when Lindsay collects the ball at midfield, Sara turns and sprints at her, unleashes one of the hardest slide tackles she's ever delivered, and takes Lindsay down. She springs up and stands over her, thinking *Remember that shit*, as Lindsay writhes, wincing. Siena runs over and says, "What the fuck was that?" and Sara breathes for a few seconds, staring down at Lindsay.

"Just playing."

"Really? Playing?" Siena's lower jaw is extended, face dripping, and soon Angus and Letti are close by. Lindsay gets up slowly, then bends over to rub at the side of her ankle.

Angus takes off his shades. "You practice hard, aye, but you do *not* play crap football. Understood?"

Feeling the curtains draw behind her eyes, Sara looks away. Nods once.

"Mother of Christ." Angus puts his shades back on and turns for the sideline, while Letti makes sure Lindsay is all right.

As the scrimmage starts up again, Sara catches Lindsay sharing a look with Siena, and then Shannon Wang.

AFTER PRACTICE, Angus calls her into his office.

On the wall to his left, the photos of his pretty wife and two young children. Photos of him playing for Newcastle and DC United. A photo of a white-haired woman with a younger Angus and two other young men who look much like him.

"Right, then." He takes off his cap and runs a hand a few times over his shiny head, motions for her to sit. He's not that much taller than her, really, but it's still strange to her how he seems a lot taller. "So. What was that all about?"

Sara sits down, the backs of her thighs still sweaty, slippery against the leather, and wonders if he'll tell her she's not a starter now, she had her chance. She doesn't say anything, just keeps her eyes on the wall of photos as Angus watches her. The office smells faintly of suntan lotion.

In a slightly mellower voice he says, "Tell me how you're doing."

She wants to talk, part of her does, but no words come. Will he kick her off the team even, say it's just not working out? He keeps on watching her, for what seems like a couple of minutes, and the longer she sits, the worse her stomach feels. She knew this probably wouldn't work out, she doesn't know how to make it work. Muffled voices come from the lobby, what sounds like the gigantic volleyball coach, Barry Drake, talking with the secretary.

"You belong here," Angus says, and she can't help it, the comment completely blindsides her and her eyes moisten.

"Not only do you belong on this team, you belong on this campus. Do you understand?"

She glances at him. The steady *no bullshit* gaze from across the desk. All those sun wrinkles.

"I'm starting you at left wing on Friday."

She wants to swallow but doesn't. Wants to cry but doesn't. She tries to maintain eye contact.

"It's something you've earned, but it's also something I'd not take for granted if I were you. As you've seen, we've got proper good competition for spots."

Angus leans back farther in his chair, elbows on the armrests now, fingers steepled.

"Tell me about your classes."

She's afraid of what she'll say, that he'll think she's weak. She will *not* cry. None of that.

"I wonder if I'm smart enough." The words come barely audible, and she clears her throat.

There's a long pause, and he only sits there observing her. Waiting.

"Feel like I'm from a different world or something," she says.

"You are." Another pause, shorter. "But that doesn't mean you can't call this home as well. Absolutely no reason you can't. Sara, it's the same world."

She feels his words in her chest, yet they seem not quite believable.

"I grew up poor," he says. "My mam was on the dole for a time, we struggled. I spoke with Martha about your situation, and I understand it . . . Would you let me help you with one thing?" He waits until she gives a tentative nod. "With your grammar. Could I correct you at times, privately? If I notice something that might help? I had someone do the same for me once. I found it, well, not always easy, but quite helpful."

She's blushing hard, and part of her wants to say something sharp. This whole thing's so goddamn insane. But once again something else comes out. "Okay."

"As I told you last winter, if you come here you'll work harder than you've ever worked in your life. On the field and in your studies. This is first about getting a good education. We're still clear on that?"

She nods.

"Right, then." Angus eyes her, starts to push against the armrests, then hesitates. "One other thing . . . It might help, on the team front, if you maybe think twice about leveling one of the captains during training?" With a near-mischievous glint, he lifts an eyebrow and stands. "Or, if it's completely unavoidable, offer a hand afterward? Bloody hell."

24

THE CHANTING FANS, booming drums. Guys in the student section shirtless and bellowing, their chests painted purple. It's a sellout, and as she jogs onto the field for warm-ups on this warm night, the crowd noise rising, she sees the TV cameras ready and feels her forearms goose-pimple. It's almost like the European matches she's seen on TV, except now the fanatics are actually cheering her team. To jog onto the smooth, green, perfectly mowed grass, to feel her clean uniform and cleats fitting just right, to know that her grandparents and Elaine are somewhere up in that crowd—it's almost terrifying. But the more she runs, the more everything outside the field's lines begins to fade. She's a starter on a Division I team, she's never been in better shape in her whole life, and it's game time.

When the whistle blows, she's still nervous, the whole team is jumpy, which Angus said might happen, but what they have to do is be patient, not force things, just concentrate on keeping possession. The pace startles her, it's incredible how fast it is, and the Florida players, most of them, are downright huge. But she keeps up, gets caught in the flow, the surges of energy from the crowd; she makes a few solid passes, finds open spaces, and in the sixteenth minute takes a shot that she doesn't quite get her foot on, one the keeper scoops up easily. She notes that Lindsay, at center mid, almost always looks elsewhere to pass, even in a real game like this, and she briefly wonders what Angus is thinking.

At the half, it's 1–0 Florida, and in the locker room Angus stands in front of the marker board, hands in his black sweatpants pockets, his white short-sleeved polo shirt tucked in and spotless, and calmly says, "We're outshooting them nine to three. We're keeping the ball for the most part. It's about patience now, as we discussed. The goals will come. Maintain possession, keep it simple, take your chances when you have them."

He doesn't pull Lindsay aside afterward, Sara notices.

In the second half, the crowd is every bit as berserk, the field lit up by the towering lights, the sun dipped down behind Forest Park, and in the fifty-first minute Shannon Wang scores on a header off a corner kick. Crowd goes from berserk to apeshit, and on the jog back past the center circle, Sara catches sight out the corner of her eye some shirtless maniac charging along the north sideline with a massive UP flag on the end of a pole. Twenty-five minutes later, Sophie Mack crushes a shot from twenty yards that dings off the post and into the net. Mayhem.

Final whistle: Home 2, Visitor 1. The Florida players look shocked as they walk off the field in the cooling air. Welcome to Portland.

At the railing up behind the bench, Elaine stands waiting like she said she would, and as Sara approaches, she scans for her grandparents.

"Gramps had to use the bathroom." Face pink from raising her voice, Elaine's pressed against the railing as the hordes file out behind her. To Sara, she looks mildly spooked by the overall scene, the drumming, yelling students across the field. Standing there in her oversize Goodwill sweatshirt with *Crater Lake* curved across the chest.

"Mom couldn't make it?" Sara says, deadpan, untucking her soaked jersey.

"Migraine."

They share a quick look.

"How's Adam?"

"All right, I guess."

Sara sees there's more to say on that, but someone bumps into Elaine and says sorry. The drumming starts to fade, the crazed students marching out the far corner gate.

"How's Chuck E. Cheese's?"

"Still want to quit."

"When does school start?"

"Tuesday."

Sara looks away, wondering which bathroom her grandparents went off to, and instead spots Keith shouldering his way through the crowd.

"What in the . . ."

Elaine turns her head just as he reaches the railing beside her.

"Hey, you're *good*," he says.

Sara's calves tense up. Her mouth cracks open, but she can't think of what to say, and Elaine only stares at her.

He's got on a dark shirt over hard-worn jeans, some newer-looking black boots. Hair all combed back. That gap-toothed smile. Against the mass of people shuffling along behind him—plenty of eyeglasses and fleece vests—he looks a little out of place to her. It's clear that Elaine, too, had no clue he was planning to come. Does he know that Gramps and Gram are here?

Keith gives a light laugh. "Can't tell what's going on out there half the time, but that was some game . . . Look at you." He keeps smiling at her, appears genuinely proud, his hands on the railing. He turns to Elaine. "How you been?"

Still red-cheeked, Elaine only nods.

"You drive out here, or you need a ride?"

Elaine glances at Sara, who looks past her for their grandparents. Two spry elderly women pass by and one says, "Nice game," and she says, "Thanks."

"Well, I won't keep you, you better get on back to your team," Keith says. "Or do you need another minute here with your sis?"

"Yeah . . ." She keeps scanning the crowd behind them, she can't help it. "Do you think maybe, for just a sec? Thanks for coming. I didn't expect—"

"Wouldn'ta missed it for anything. No way." Keith gives her another steady, proud gaze, and then faces Elaine. "I'm out over near the end of this first row here." He motions toward the parking lot. "Down there a ways. Old Chevy pickup. White. I'll meet you there, okay?"

He holds up a hand and merges back into the throng, and for several seconds Sara watches him go, looking ahead on his path for her grandparents, still not seeing them anywhere.

"Did you know he was—"

"No."

"You gonna ride back with him?"

"Should I?"

"I don't know. If you want, I guess. Go ahead." She spots her grandparents coming out of the nearest tunnel. "Look, don't tell them, all right? Not tonight, okay?"

"I won't."

"If you're riding back with him, just tell them you're hangin' here with me tonight."

They share another quick look, a sister look, there at the edge of Merlo Field on a spectacular Friday evening, their grinning father walking away from them, their grinning grandparents walking toward.

25

ON THE FREEWAY, the old Chevy chugging along, barely running, Keith asks how she got out to the game.

"Rode the MAX," Elaine says.

She sits there uneasy. Long jangly earrings on, big shoulders rounded forward. She stays focused on the scenes out the windshield.

"So how's work? Those kids driving you crazy yet?"

"Not too bad."

"More the parents, I'll bet." He looks over at her again, smiling, but she only stares straight ahead. "You want some tunes?"

When she gives a single nod, he turns on the rock station, Ratt's "Round and Round" playing. He turns it up some, but not too loud.

"God, I remember this one," he says.

The Chevy rumbles onto I-205, tailpipe gushing smoke, and before long he drops her off in front of the little house. Elaine still has a hard time with eye contact, he notices, but that's all right, it seems to be just how she is now, no use in pressuring her to look at him when he's talking to her.

"See you soon?" he says, and she nods and shuts her door. When she makes it inside, she glances back at him and he taps the horn once as he drives off over the gravel.

On the ride down Foster, he debates about whether to go back to the apartment. Part of him's so damn tired right now, after working all day then watching the game. But hey, how great was it to see Sara out on that field like that? All those fans cheering. For the life of him, he doesn't get some of soccer's rules, heard one lady nearby say "offside" a whole bunch of times, but, man, that was his daughter out there who played the entire game with all those people watching. On a college campus. With TV cameras filming. That tonight was the first time he'd ever been on a college campus, and from what he could tell, the U of P was pretty swank. What he feels goes beyond pride.

He hangs a right onto 92nd, headed toward the apartment, but he's still not sure about going back quite yet. It's only nine forty-five. He's certainly tired, though. Long-ass week. Because what he's been doing is sticking to his routine. That's been the key. Get up at five thirty, make his pot of coffee. Walk Bear over in the park, no matter the weather, then grab a piece of toast or leftovers from the night before, some mac and cheese or something. Ride the ten-speed, or some days now take this piece-a-shit $800 truck, up Powell Boulevard to work. Load the equipment, make sure all the mowers are gassed up and oiled. Pedro, *el jefe* foreman, and Juan, the other scrub crew member—he's usually with those two guys, they make an okay team. Apartment complexes mostly, in Gresham and outer Southeast, sometimes over in outer Northeast. At lunchtime, they usually stop at a McDonald's or Burger King, but lately he's taken to bringing his lunch and eating in or near the truck, usually a salami on white, it helps with saving up for a nicer truck down the line, one that doesn't spew exhaust or make all kinds of alarming sounds under the hood. After lunch, it's work all afternoon, then back to the shop by five or five thirty, clean everything up, ride on home. Walk Bear (who gets let out at noon each day by old Mrs. Spitz three doors down), cook something, then park it in front of the TV with a few beers. At ten o'clock, usually just fucked-up tired, another trip to the park with old Bear, shadows by trees out there in the park sometimes, kids partying a little, no big deal. And then it's time to crash, do it all over again the next day. This is his life now. It is what it is.

When it comes to Friday and Saturday nights, though? A man can't be in his apartment with a dog seven nights a week. It ain't right. It can start to mess with your head if you don't watch it. It's time to get out, mingle with humanity. That bar over on Holgate is his favorite these days, no question about it, that fine bartender, Courtney. She's nice, too. They've been talking more and more, nothing much, just some talk, maybe some flirtation in there, and so what he'll do one of these days pretty soon is maybe just go ahead and ask her out to dinner. She's that fine. And no, it's not all about the titties. But they sure don't hurt, either.

Not that he hasn't had any nookie at all. There was the lady he brought home from the New Copper Penny back in June, he can't remember her name, but my *God* she was loud. Just embarrassed the bejesus out of him actually, what with poor old Mr. Becker next door. The man's hard of hearing, but he isn't *that* hard of hearing.

The thing is, though, it's actually kind of hard to get laid these days. At least for him. At least compared to how it used to be. Seems harder than he remembers, definitely, and he wonders if maybe it's his teeth. They're not doing so good. What he needs to do is go see a dentist, but that shit's out of pocket. There's a molar hurting big-time back up in there. Yet it's not the molar that the ladies see, it's his yellow front teeth. He's tried some of that peroxide toothpaste, but it irritates his gums, and the last thing he needs is red gums to go with yellow teeth. Not a good look.

But the main goal right now? Keep his head down, keep working hard. Try to save up, and pray some good comes from that. Keep saving for that better truck. Try to get himself promoted to foreman, like he used to do, a little better pay. And then who knows, stay on with the company, keep doing a good job, be nice and steady for them, they just might reward that.

But he does like to go out on Friday and Saturday nights. Sure he does. Blow off some steam, have a couple drinks. Doesn't everyone? Work hard, day after day, you need that to keep your head clear.

Maybe the thing that's making him most nervous is Bruce gets out pretty soon and, last he heard, the guy's planning on moving back to Lents, too. Old Bruce. Who's almost done his whole six years. Who's still married, whose wife hasn't divorced him. Bruce Gunderson, his best bud since their crazy days at Marshall, who worked landscaping with him all those years, best man at his wedding. Lord, look at how many of the guys from that old crew went and fucked up their lives, it's truly something to behold. Bruce and him getting caught in that house, Daryl Bell still in for ID theft, Mark Roddick—where the hell is he now? Last he heard, poor fucker was living with his mom, working as a housepainter part time, smoking his weed, getting into some harder stuff. Look at 'em all. The pride of the class of '94. Cream of the crop.

He passes the apartment and heads on up to Powell and hangs a slow left. These streets where he grew up. These old scenes, all around him.

Bruce says he wants to keep in touch, and whenever he thinks of him saying that, he feels the devil on his shoulder. The devil wakes up, starts looking around. Which then of course makes him think of Sara, Elaine, and Rachel, every time now. Because he's a better man these days, he can feel that in his bones. He's making a better life. Being a good example.

It's what he promised himself he would do, and he's doing it. Nice and steady. Paying his rent, taking care of a dog, holding down a job.

Devil, angel, devil, angel. Every single day.

He circles around onto 82nd, the pickup clattering, sputtering, and spots a guy with a ball cap on sideways, wearing a dark tank top and low-sagging, bunched-up jeans, he's probably in his midtwenties, riding a BMX bike across the street, balancing two cellophane-wrapped pizzas on one hand.

"Dinnertime," he mutters.

He turns onto Holgate and soon the bar comes into view. He runs a hand back over his hair.

What he'll do is, he'll go in and just see if she's working. Courtney, who seems to enjoy some talk with him. Who seems to throw him a sign now and then that she wouldn't mind some dinner someplace. It's clear enough. It's been a great night so far, so why not keep it going for a while longer? He's seen two of his daughters again, and that's a fantastic thing. He's seen Rachel only the one time, and he's starting to wonder if she's really okay like they say she is, if something's wrong there maybe, but at least he's seen Sara and Elaine again. His kiddos.

He tells himself once more that what he has to do is just keep on trying, it's as simple as that. Keep it steady. For them, for himself. But there's no reason in the world you can't be on the right path and still blow off a little steam every now and then. The devil and the angel can just learn to be buds as far as he's concerned.

He pulls into the full, dim parking lot, it's mostly pickups tonight, most of them in better shape than his, big surprise. He finds a place out back by the dumpster. Gets out and walks in shadows around front and then into the bar, through that thrill of neon that always makes every-one look better, and in the crowded room he sees her over there behind the bar, pouring a glass from a tap, sweet Courtney doing her thing, maybe wondering when he'd finally show up for another round.

26

RACHEL SHOWED UP the first day at Franklin, and then last Tuesday. Packed classes, cracks in the old ceilings. She spotted Elaine from afar that first day, the girl walking almost right up against the lockers in the congested hallway, her face blushed, books pressed to her chest.

It's better out here, she believes, for herself at least. Especially while the weather is still decent. It's a sunny, mild afternoon in the South Park Blocks, her favorite time of year, where the leaves haven't quite started to turn but the light has changed some, that afternoon light that makes the world seem slightly softer, for a while anyway.

Kurt's over talking with some of the street kids, though there are fewer of them lately, people moving on after the blazing summer. She sits on one of her usual benches and looks over at the kids, she doesn't recognize the ones he's talking to now; the garb almost always looks the same, the battered packs, the dogs on chain leashes. He likes to do that, Kurt. Go meet new people. Unlike her.

Over on another bench nearby, the old guy with the glasses and grey beard, the rumpled professor type with the threadbare sport coat, is reading *Cold Mountain* today, his cart pulled up beside him, his bed-roll on the bottom rack, all his books and clothes and tarps arranged in the basket, everything in its place. He's absorbed, his legs crossed at the knee. His face with that obscure frown when he reads.

She's hungry, they haven't had any lunch, and Kurt has all the money, her wallet's empty like usual. But she remains on the bench, her copy of *The Remains of the Day* in hand. She hasn't opened it yet, it seems to her like the kind of book you don't want to read in a place where there are so many distractions. So she looks up through the trees and sees the half-moon, which reminds her that she's still on a planet. Normally a helpful thought. Then a package truck revs down Salmon Street, popping her concentration. But soon there's a small brown bird nearby that rivets her attention and she wishes she knew what kind it is; it seems important, as her Gramps used to say, to be able to name things. To say nothing of how poetic so many of the names are. *Maidenhair fern. Kingfisher.* The little bird hops around looking for crumbs in the spotty grass, and then a bee appears. She watches the bee for a minute. Which creatures will survive another century of humans?

There it is again. That warm sadness in her chest. She feels it almost every day, can't seem to help it. Just look around. The rich getting a shit-load richer, everyone else pretty much scraping by, such a fundamentally screwed-up definition of "the bottom line." What about Adam's life and Elaine's life? And what about her own—how will she survive in this society? How does a person live an authentic, awake, possibly even *artistic* life and still make a living? She knows no one who's doing this. Some teachers, maybe, but then they're constantly dealing with all the soul-numbing idiocy dished out by automatons who never taught anybody anything.

Again she zeroes in on Kurt, who's still talking with the new people. The scruffy, feral-looking, often sweet-hearted kids. This is partly why street culture remains appealing to her. Certain elements of it anyway. The *fuck you* aspect. The *authenticity.* Traveling close to the ground, the air of grittiness and danger, while the respectable Portlanders go on hurrying about, everyone caught up in their distractions and the mass culture's dominant values. Out here, time moves slower. And there are some smart, like-minded people, too, at least now and then. A share of wingnuts and drug-stoned babblers, sure, but plenty of sharp people as well.

She glances over at the old man, who's standing now, repacking something, possibly getting ready to leave.

While she and Kurt still haven't slept outside, while they've ridden MAX back to his mom's place every night, they've hit all the main day-time hangouts down here. The Square. South Park Blocks. Skidmore Fountain. A few of the shelters for lunch. Plenty of walking, which she normally likes, just taking in the life all around. So much to take in.

Another guy walks up to the group that Kurt's with. Strong build. Looks to be in his late twenties maybe, older than the others. Wearing a green army coat, sleeveless, with black pants cut to calf level, calves bulging, and scuffed-up black boots. His chain-leashed mutt, another pit bull mix. Though the guy certainly appears tough, at least from a distance, Kurt doesn't act concerned at all, his body language remains relaxed, even though he's still coming down from another crank fest. The über-thin, peroxide-blond girl in the group goes over to the new guy and slips her arm around his waist.

It's the guy's buff arms that makes her think of her dad. When she saw him last Thanksgiving. She'd always pictured him smaller, it was odd. From the few photos they had, he did look smaller.

She looks down at the novel in her hands, blocking out the hunger pangs, feeling the walls, the hardness of them. She knows they're always there, and there's not much she can do. She was ten when he went to prison, and right then, a bond snapped for good. For a couple of years before that he hadn't slept at the house but maybe two or three nights a week, always gone, working, out drinking, crashing at friends' places, running around. Acting like a man who felt trapped by his family, his sad little life. He needed his escape, and, well, now she needs hers.

The bearded old guy leans forward and rests his elbows on his shopping cart, then starts pushing it in her direction, out across the brick plaza.

"Great novel," she calls out, partly surprised by her voice, and the man stops the cart, still hunched over, and gazes at her. A frank gaze. As if he's sizing her up. For a couple more beats he stands there.

"He nails the southern Appalachians," he finally says. Gentle, deep voice.

Out the corner of her eye, she sees Kurt striding her way, his baggy black T-shirt fluttering, but she doesn't look away from the old man. It's an intelligent face, his expression slightly wounded, though, wary. He could be around seventy, it's hard to tell. He keeps on staring at her, not in a scary way, just gauging. When Kurt comes up, all edgy, he shoots the guy a look, then says they need to get going, grab some lunch.

The man resumes pushing his cart, and for a moment she watches him go.

"What was that about?" Kurt says.

"Nothing." She slips her novel back into her pack and gets up off the bench, her legs feeling weak. "Just asked what he was reading."

Kurt eyes the old man again for a few beats, then faces her, his jittery expression back. "Check it out, I met those dudes over there, their main man, his name's Tobias. Dude knows his shit. He invited us to meet up later on at the Square, says he wants to talk to me some more."

"About?"

Kurt puts an arm around her, gripping her shoulder, and leads her toward the coffee shop across the street. "I'm fuckin' *starvin'*, man."

As they cross Salmon, Kurt hustling her along, stopping traffic with a firm raised hand, she turns her head and catches sight of the old guy pushing his cart down near Broadway, pedestrians on the sidewalk parting and merging all around him, the city swallowing him up.

27

IN HER FRESHMAN composition class, Sara sits near the basketball players, the three guys jammed into their back-row desks, legs stretched under the chairs in front of them. Up front by the marker board, Jacqueline Mason stands with all their essays resting in a stack on her forearm.

"So, I read these over the weekend," she says. "We have more work to do than I thought."

Mason is in her late thirties, slim, chic in her black slacks and gauzy magenta scarf, her long brown hair with its bold grey strands combed out today. As she passes back the essays she moves with a focused urgency like she's being timed, and Sara remembers how, back on the first day of class, the woman started off by sharing how she's working toward her PhD in comparative literature, this is her fourth year teaching at UP.

When Mason sets her essay in front of her, Sara's eyes land on the red comment up top. *Where's your thesis statement?* Fifty-five points out of a possible one hundred. A heat wave spreads up her neck. One of the basketball players receives his essay and chuckles, and it's then that Mason says, "Funny? Think so?" The class goes quiet. "Do you have any idea what you need to do in order to write in a way that will allow you to earn a college degree, or are most of you just planning on sticking around for a semester or two?"

Jacqueline Mason moves back to the front, half the essays now curled in one hand. That fierce look on her face, familiar to her students.

"Almost all of you are here"—she flattens out her free hand, holds it at waist level—"and by the end of this semester you need to be here." She raises her hand next to her head. "Do you understand this? So we've got work to do. And first, we're *clearly* going to talk again about the structure of the five-paragraph essay, because what I'm in the process of handing back to you shows me that either *I* failed to make that structure completely clear or *you* failed to actively listen . . . This is something, quite frankly, you should already know inside and out."

As Mason resumes passing back the brutalized essays, Sara sits there half-numb and keeps observing the teacher, that edge to her. Thinks of her saying so forcefully back in that first class how they all needed to take charge of their educations and ask questions, that no one else was responsible for that, it's on *them* now. Be *organized*, visit profs during office hours. "You *will* learn how to write a compelling essay. Do you understand?" If only they could stop wasting so much time staring at the internet, or texting, thinking that those things mean genuine human interaction or genuine work, if they'd just get their hands in the dirt, literally and figuratively.

Sara glances down at her essay again, each of the three pages filled with cross-outs and arrows, comments slashed all over the margins. She tries to calm down, even out her breathing, but her efforts fall short there as well.

THE DARK RIVER GLIDES BY. Industrial lights glimmering on the other bank, Forest Park towering, black.

The night is clear and chilly, and she pulls up her sweatshirt hood before lighting her first cigarette. Someone (not Olivia, she's sure) told Angus about her habit, and so last week he called her into his office and said, "You've got to be kidding me." Told her to stop and that if she needed help quitting he'd get her help.

But it's just two per evening, she tells herself, and whenever she thinks about quitting, the idea of living cig-free with all the rising pressure from classes and the team and everything, plus the seriously weird homesickness, it's too much. So here she is again. Nicotine city. There's the rewrite for Mason's class, and also the Hemingway story to read for Sister Toms's class. Francis May-something. It's long, too. She stands there smoking and thinks of Sister Toms with her wiry grey hair and earth-toned blazers and how incredible it is how much that woman knows, it's truly crazy. But it's not just English that's kicking her ass. In biology, Dr. Utrecht up there in front of the auditorium-size class talking about ocean acidification and dead zones. He seems to her like a heavyhearted man, preoccupied, and sometimes she wonders about him as she listens—his life, where he comes from, what all he's seen. Up there with his greasy grey hair tucked behind his ears.

So much homework, plus practice every day, plus the road trip to California this coming weekend, her first time ever on a plane. She lights another one and hears a train going over the bridge downriver, looks over and watches the tiny rectangles of light drift across the darkness.

There's a lot to think about. She's never had this much to think about her entire life, and she wonders once more: Is this what all colleges are *like*? They keep piling it on to see who snaps in half under the load, it's some kind of fucked-up test?

She crushes the cigarette against her favorite boulder, pulls out the crumpled empty baggie from her sweatpants and drops the two butts in, then starts hiking back up the dark, wooded trail, back up to Mehling Hall, where her book-piled desk awaits.

AT LIGHTS OUT, they talk about the California trip, about the two games down there, and at one point Olivia says, "You know, your style kind of reminds me of Rafa Nadal. How you carry yourself."

"Who's Rafa Nadal?"

"The tennis player?" Olivia sits up in her bed, reaches over and switches on her desk lamp. Olivia in her white tank top, her long buff arms lotioned, her blond hair clean and loose. "Oh my God, you don't know who he is." She flips open her laptop and quickly finds a photo, turns the screen and holds it out over the space between them. "Raphael Nadal."

He's shirtless on a beach, water running down his chiseled chest and abdomen, and for a few seconds Sara looks at the photo.

"Hot," she says.

"Uh, yeah."

Olivia takes the laptop back and clicks on another photo, this one of Nadal hitting a tennis ball, his face locked in a snarl. "The swagger I'm talking about. I've seen you look like that. Like you'd rip off their heads if you had to."

"You ain't so nice out there yourself."

Olivia smiles and puts away the laptop and hits the light again. Soon they say good night.

For a long time Sara lies there, eventually picturing Olivia's screen saver, how she finds herself checking it out sometimes. Ryan Reynolds. Hot, too. But then there are also the photos in *People* that Alicia next door lets them look at whenever she's done, and if there's a shot of Jessica Alba or maybe Scarlett Johansson, she usually feels something then, too. Hot men, hot women. Plenty of sexy people in the world, and if she's being honest, it's always been like this, from what she can remember.

And so again she's thinking about Hoban Stellenbach. From Sister Toms's class. Shy, hot Hoban, who she's seen eating alone in the cafeteria a couple of times. That thick, shoulder-length brown hair, usually still drying throughout the class period, the ripped jeans, olive skin like hers. About six foot, lean, with those strong forearms and hands. The multi-colored woven bracelet on his left wrist, shower-wet in the mornings. They got put in the same group last week and each group had to come up with a twentieth-century American poet and do a short presentation for the class. Hoban, at first, was quiet in the group, too, awkward at times, fiddling with his bracelet, he'd never once said anything during the full-class discussions, but after a while he suggested they do e. e. cummings. Which the group ended up going with, even though she had no clue who e. e. cummings was.

Yet after reading a few of the man's poems by herself that same night, those bizarre, sort of catchy poems, she felt even more interested in Hoban Stellenbach. Bursts of questions in her mind, like, *Where does Hoban come from? Who is he? What about his family? Does he feel out of place also, as out of place as he sometimes looks?*

What she does know, though, is that last week whenever they glanced at each other in that small group during those early morning classes with Sister Toms quietly circulating around the room, something would happen that made her wake up more, made her buzz, as much as she often used to around Kim.

She can't let herself think about Kim right now. Can't go there, it's too much. Kim. Lents. That whole other life. All of it.

She lies there in her warm bed, eyes open.

28

DOWNTOWN, IN THE WEATHERED, near-empty furniture warehouse just north of the train station, a three-story building set to be demolished any day now, Rachel half listens to the huddle in the next room.

"—business to run," Tobias says.

She catches snippets like this as she paces the creaking wood floor, smoking another cigarette, looking around at the graffitied walls, the raggedy orange couch, the bed rolls and sleeping bags, the trash swept into a corner, some busted-up wooden dining chairs along the far wall. Out the glass-free windows, below, part of the dim train yard. She passes the open doorway again and glimpses Kurt standing there with them, Tobias in his cutoff pants with his freakish calves, Teena with the peroxide hair and bony limbs and sores all over her forearms. White Fang stout and scruffy, hard-looking, Tobias's right-hand man. And then there's Manfred, a self-proclaimed "heroin boy," mohawked, handsome, tall and lean like Kurt, about their age, but jumpy and prone to giving her these looks, like he's checking her out. Tobias's dog, Finn, at the huddle's edge, scarfs at his bowl of kibble.

"—widen our outreach," Tobias says, and then a while later: "Family, oh man . . . Too many associations with that word, you know what I mean? None of this wacko shit, all these nutjobs with their Viking street names and all that. We're just friends here, man. Don't need to go around calling ourselves a family."

Rachel paces and smokes and thinks of Kurt telling her on their way over here this evening how Tobias comes from a messed-up family, too. Down in Sacramento. She thinks of how Tobias does seem fairly smart, and he's nice enough. But there's something not far under the surface, the familiar anger, and she's caught him leering at her now and then also.

Later on, after Tobias sends White Fang out for sandwiches from one of their favorite food carts, Kurt leads her over to the bank of windows overlooking the train yard, the cool night breeze wafting in, and he tells her in a mellow voice how Tobias wants him to deliver some crank in Southeast. He'll get a cut for every delivery. It's not a big deal, just some extra cash.

A train horn sounds in the distance, and Mohawk Manfred appears in the room. He laughs and goes over to what she now notices is a small pile of stones in one corner.

"Amtrak from Seattle, arriving on time, ladies and gentlemen." Manfred takes up his position in one of the windows, and the horn sounds again, closer.

She looks at Kurt. "God, what an honor, he thinks you'd be a good delivery boy."

"I trust the dude."

"You trust him? Oh, well then."

"Man, come on."

The train noise builds, and Manfred lets out a full-throated whoop. Teena, Tobias, and Finn off somewhere else in the building.

"You don't want to do this," she says to Kurt.

"I do. I will. We need the fucking cash."

The building starts to rumble, the train passing just below, and Manfred begins chucking rocks.

"Welcome to Portland, bitches! Brave new world! Woo!"

He whoops and throws, over and over, and she hears some of the rocks hitting the train, it probably won't be long before the cops show up, good work. She has a hard time looking at Kurt now, and so she watches Manfred do his thing.

She shouldn't be here, she knows. This is absurd, completely. She shouldn't be with him, she feels it in her throat, in her core, she's known it for a while, and soon there'll be more criminal activity, oh joy, these are clearly his leanings and this'll be more than shoplifting. It's an easy out for him, and to say there are echoes of her dad seems just painfully obvious. And yet . . . She glances back up at him; he's been watching Manfred, too, but he lowers his eyes to hers again, with that same mix of stubbornness and rage and pure innocent need for her approval. She's like a mother figure at certain times. Sara said more than once how it seemed like she was under a spell or something, and yeah, it's true probably. So shoot her. The thing is, it's *her* choice. *Her* life. And, okay, it's not that bad of a feeling to be with someone her mother and big sister both massively disapprove of. Classic move, fine, but there it is.

"All right?" he says, reaching out to hold her. "I got this. Trust me."

As she gazes up at him, wanting to tell him what a painfully stupid person he can be, especially lately, part of her sees the scene from just outside of herself, the ransacked warehouse on this chilly autumn night, the retreating train, Manfred's whooping finally trailing off. Two teenagers arm in arm, so much of their lives yet unlived, Kurt's bloodshot eyes steady on hers.

She feels herself giving a small nod.

IN THE COLD GREY MORNING, after a few hours' sleep on one of the musty extra bedrolls, their first night ever sleeping downtown, she wakes to an early train shaking the room. Where Kurt's sleeping bag was, right beside her, is now bare wood floor, and the only other person in the room is Teena, who's over in the nest of blankets and sleeping bags she shared with Tobias, the girl sitting up with a steaming paper cup in her hands.

"They went over to the Burnside Bridge," Teena says. Her voice drowsy, soft. "He said to tell you he'll meet you at the Park Blocks around lunch."

Rachel pushes herself up, head aching, and squints around the room. She remembers how last night, late, someone said that this building will be a condo tower by this time next year, and how she imagined some hip, flush couple waking up in this very spot.

"There's coffee." Teena points at the base of the wall up behind Rachel. "Tobe went out and got some."

The coffee, lightly sugared, helps a bit, but the airy battered room and Teena's waxen, spaced-out morning look keep giving her the shivers, and before long she asks what time it is, then gets up with a story about how she has to go meet a friend, it's later than she thought.

"So, see you later on?" Teena says, wild-haired, languid, still in her nest.

"Definitely. Have a good day."

Midmorning, after wandering into Powell's and smelling the calming scent of all those thousands of books, pausing now and then to browse pages here and there in the various rooms, she makes it over to the mostly empty plaza in the South Park Blocks and finds him on one of the benches, his legs crossed, the shopping cart pulled up next to him. Of course, he's reading. That mild glower of concentration, glasses drooped on his nose, his sport coat on over an equally worn-out V-neck sweater.

When she sits down at the end of his bench, he rests a finger in his novel, *The Crossing*, and looks over at her. Same frank gaze. Wary at first, then more curious, slightly amused. It strikes her that she doesn't feel all that nervous. She digs out *The Road* from her pack, the used copy that Kurt bought her a couple of days ago, and flicks her eyes down at what he's reading.

"Looks like we're both in a light-hearted phase."

The old guy lets out a laugh—a surprisingly full, deep sound—his smile mostly beard-hidden. "Except for mine's going on twenty years."

She looks over at him, and her own smile slowly dissolves. "You've been on the streets that long?"

He nods.

"In Portland?"

"More or less." He observes her for a few beats, again sizing her up. "I took a few years, rode rails all around. But mostly I've been here."

Over on Salmon Street, the traffic streams along, people striding the sidewalks, all that urgent business. Hardly any street kids in sight, only a few on a far bench, listless this early, their packs piled nearby. The rear marquee of the concert hall, over through the trees, shows that Yo-Yo Ma will be in town Friday night.

"What about you?" the old man asks. "I'm Ken, by the way." He holds out a long-fingered, clean hand, and they shake. Soft hand, the nails clipped. "Why aren't you in school?"

She lifts her brow and takes a slow breath through her nostrils. She must look like hell, she thinks, as she scratches at the side of her head. "For one, it's overcrowded beyond belief. I counted forty-one kids in my English class the first day, there weren't enough chairs. Three people had to sit on the heater by the windows. Who needs to feel like you're in a cattle yard when you're trying to read Jimmy Santiago Baca? Not sure I can't learn more out here."

Ken studies her and nods. They sit there for a while, each glancing from time to time at their novels. City noises, distant horn honking, a jackhammer someplace. She feels the pause start to stretch, and soon it gets to be a little much.

"What brought you out here?" she says.

Once more he places a finger in his book. "This morning?"

"I mean, like, your life." She watches him look away. "Sorry, I don't mean to pry. I'm just curious is all."

Another pause hits—he appears to be taking a silent inventory of his cart now. She wonders what else to say, maybe it's best to steer the conversation back to books, but then he turns his head a few degrees back in her direction and stares off through the park. When he speaks, his voice comes slightly softer.

"Well, the short of it is, I used to be an accountant. My wife struggled with schizophrenia for many years. We had two daughters, eight and nine, and one day my wife took them and they never came back. None of them have ever been found. That was 1989, the last time I saw them."

The surrounding sights and sounds obliterated, she only watches him. She wants to reach over and touch his forearm, and she nearly does, but she holds back. She should say *I'm sorry*, she knows, but nothing comes out. Sometimes she hates being a teenager.

Ken opens *The Crossing* again and falls back into it, and still she doesn't know what to say. She turns and gazes at the traffic, and out of the corner of her eye sees him shut the novel.

"My apologies if that was too much disclosure," he says.

"Not at all. I asked. That must be so . . ."

"It is."

They observe the traffic together for several minutes, this pause more comfortable.

"Do you ever feel sort of like . . . you don't quite *fit* with all this?" She gestures at the street, the buildings.

"Made peace with that long ago."

"Like, it just keeps going and going, the *relentlessness* of it all, getting more and more crowded, and you're caught up in it, too. But at the same time you resist, you know?"

Her eyes start to itch.

"I'd suspect," Ken says, "given what we're seeing with all these Occupy gatherings, there are a number of others who feel the same way. If that's any consolation." He looks at her, then back out at the street. "It's not sustainable, the way things are set up in most societies now."

"But how do you, like, make a *life* amidst all this? How do you make a living in a way that . . ." She trails off.

Ken cocks a thumb toward his shopping cart. "You're asking the wrong fella."

She smiles back, but then the conversation falls off again and she looks out at the traffic. At length, Ken gone back to his reading, she wonders where Kurt is right now, what he's doing, when he'll come find her.

Where in the City of Roses they'll end up sleeping tonight.

29

WHEN THE PLANE RISES off the ground, Sara's gut clenches, but soon enough wonder engulfs her. *Look at this shit! I'm on a plane!*

From her window seat, her unopened minipack of Oreos on her lap, she looks out at the specks in downtown on this clear morning, the sunlight shining on the river, and then east toward where Lents must be, though from here it's mostly just greens and grey-browns, all those trees disguising what's really down there. Farther east, Mount Hood looks massive, though still not that snowy, and as she squints at the hazy foothills she thinks of her Gramps and Gram beside the hidden river and wonders what they're doing, Gramps probably out in his shop already, Gram working on another needlepoint. As the plane banks, her stomach squeezing again, she gets a final glimpse of the downtown buildings. Her family, all of them down there somewhere, living their lives, and here she is, speeding through the cold blue above her hometown. Unbelievable.

In the seat beside her, headphones on, Olivia flips through her *People* magazine, munching her almonds and dried blueberries.

AFTER THE SEASON'S FIRST LOSS, 2–1 at Santa Clara, Martin Crosley says that when they get back to the hotel to head straight for the meeting room, Angus wants to talk with them there.

In the large room, they sit wet-haired and solemn at the round banquet tables, and soon Angus comes in with Martin, Letti, and Jason. Still in his game outfit, the usual black sweatsuit, he takes off his cap and walks to the front while his assistants remain at the back. In the middle of the room, Martin's laptop sits open next to a projector.

Everyone quiet, Angus stands there, making eye contact. Muffled sounds from the lobby outside the wide closed doors.

"If you want to play on this team, you will approach the game the right way."

His words hover in the stillness.

"You'll pay attention to the little things. We've already discussed how your boots should be polished before each game, we've discussed jerseys tucked in, and we've discussed how the way that you practice is the way that you play. What I saw out there today, however, completely negated that sort of attention . . . At half, we talked once again about patience. Not pressing. Nil-nil, we'd outshot them, what was it?"

Angus looks to the back of the room, and Letti says, "Fourteen-four."

"Fourteen to bloody four. And so we know the chances are there. It's a matter of not pushing too hard, trusting that the goals will come, the floodgates will open. But what it takes is *patience* and faith in what we're telling you." He pauses. Silence in the room. "And so what do I see? Nearly the lot of you pressing, pressing. Not keeping possession, not marking well, not being stronger mentally than your opponent . . . And there was a last thing I saw, and this concerns me perhaps most of all. In too many moments, it appeared to me that *they* were the more disciplined, hungrier team. *They* appeared fitter."

He takes several moments to look all around the room, and Sara watches how some people lower their eyes when he gets to them. Lindsay stares at her folded hands on her table.

"I see some of you taking this game for granted, and when I see that . . ." Angus runs a hand over his chin. "I can credit football with literally saving my life, most of my family's life for that matter, and so when I see people who've been given a great gift to play this game well, how it should be played, take that gift for *granted*, I become quite angry.

"Right, then. So, this isn't a time for discussion. I want to show you something, and I want you to watch carefully. I don't want you to respond right now, you can talk later about what you saw . . . I'm disappointed, but I also trust you'll think about what I've just said and what you're about to see. You all, every one of you, have a choice to make. You can wilt, or you can raise your commitment."

Angus nods at Martin, who goes over to the laptop and projector. Jason Vanderheusen hits the lights.

"These are a few video clips that Martin assembled last summer, we were saving them. I want to show you the difference between playing like a house cat and playing like a tiger."

Angus turns and looks at the screen and stands aside, and the first clip is of Christine Sinclair, Canada versus China. Sinclair collects a long ball and, with a surge of speed, beats two defenders and buries the ball in the net. Game winner. In the next clip, it's Abby Wambach flattening a defender in a fair tackle, passing off to Megan Rapinoe, then sprinting toward goal and scoring with a ferocious header off the Rapinoe cross, the announcer screaming, *"GOOOOOOOOOOAAAL!"* The clips keep coming, some of them set to music, more Sinclair, more Wambach, more Rapinoe, with some Homare Sawa and Brazil's Marta in there, too, jolt after jolt of fiery, ruthless, beautiful soccer.

At the end, the lights rise and Angus remains off to one side of the screen, his arms folded. Total stillness in the room.

"If you want to play this game the right way, you could do worse than model your approach after these women."

Sara sits there, face tingling.

THAT NIGHT, BEFORE LIGHTS OUT, rooming with Olivia, she stops to notice the clean bathroom, the fresh, cool sheets on her bed. The room's uncluttered style, only the TV and the two landscape paintings, what Sister Toms would call minimalist. It makes life feel a bit better, clearer, having a room this clean and simple. Things can actually be this organized, this uncomplicated.

When Olivia switches off the light, they talk about Angus, and Olivia says that she heard Shannon talking about how he grew up in Newcastle, he and his brothers went hungry sometimes, played soccer in the streets for an escape. One of his older brothers played pro ball, started early in the hometown team's youth system, and Angus would sometimes go check out the practices. Sit there in the rain and watch.

"So I guess one day, he was like twelve, the coach invites him to play in a scrimmage, they need an extra."

He went on to join the Newcastle United system at thirteen, played in the lower leagues for seven years, then in the Premier League for a little while before coming over to play in MLS for DC United.

"How old is he?" Sara says.

"Forty-two. He's married, has two little kids, a boy and a girl. They live about a mile from campus, I guess, this cool old Victorian on the bluff—you can see the river and Forest Park, Shannon said. I guess that's where they normally have the end-of-the-season get-together or whatever. Anyway, he started coaching in Seattle, at a high school up there, then went to UCSB for a few years, then UP six years ago."

Sara lies on her side, watching Olivia's shadowed form.

The words reach her, she's interested, definitely, but she also lets her roommate's voice just wash over her. That relaxing voice. Olivia so composed all the time, with that positive outlook, that quiet, tough optimism. Was the chick born that way? From those family photos of hers, they all look so connected. So damn *healthy.*

Olivia sits up, says she's hot, pulls off her pajama top and lies back down. A murky glimpse of her breasts, the full nipples. Sara feels a shot of warmth and swallows.

"Shannon said someone looked up when he stopped playing pro ball. I guess he was thirty," Olivia says. "There was some kind of heart issue, an irregular heartbeat maybe? I think that was it. Some sort of condition, he was getting dizzy. But I guess he's okay now, on medication. Shannon was saying, don't let the belly pooch fool you, he's still got some major wheels. I guess last year he raced Siena and Lindsay and few of the seniors? He goes, 'All right now, let's have a footrace. I'm looking at the endline over there. Right, so the first one back here across this line gets a chocolate milkshake.' Everyone takes off, Siena and Lindsay are all, like, crazy intense. Angus jogs for a few yards, then turns around and crosses the finish line. 'I said I was *looking* at the endline. It seemed a bit far off.'"

Olivia laughs.

"Nice accent," Sara says, grinning in the dark.

AFTER THE WIN AGAINST SAINT MARY'S, the plane ride back home the next morning. On the approach into Portland, they dip through the thick clouds and the plane bucks and sways. Raindrops on Sara's window.

She looks out as the city appears and thinks of her family. Elaine at Franklin, Adam at his daycare, Rachel in school, too, she hopes. Her dad out working in the rain. She pictures him pruning a rhodie, rain dripping off his cap's bill. Then there's Kim, doing her thing at the nursery, tending all those plants. She still hasn't texted Kim back and that's shitty of her, she needs to do that later today—what kind of friend is she?

The plane keeps rocking, and she hears the wheels descend. Olivia still reading her history textbook, headphones on. Olivia's been studying almost the entire ride. And what about her own homework? Hardly any done on the trip, and definitely not while riding in a plane. The embarrassing thought she still can't quite seem to shake: Maybe her mom was right, people like them don't show up at places like UP for a reason.

There's the world where people know how to get the kind of help they need, they've got connections to help them out, they can handle such a completely ridiculous amount of work—and then there are people like her. She's a Garrison through and through. The plane swoops over east Portland, the still-bizarre sensation of flying, she's not *quite* sure if she likes it, and down there somewhere her mom is probably working her shift at Fred Meyer, standing there scanning groceries, like most days, and maybe that's exactly how the world should be.

People know their place, try to make the best of it.

30

MELANIE DOES STAND THERE.

It's a murky day outside, but inside the store it's dazzling as ever. The long, wide, product-crammed aisles, blank-faced people pushing their carts around, signs everywhere, BUY TWO, GET ONE FREE. She took three ibuprofen on her last break, but her feet and ankles are still wailing. She's wiped out, what else is new, yet strains to focus on the banter. Always, the banter. "Find everything okay?"

A slick-haired old man asks her for a pack of cigarettes and says, "How's it goin' today?"

"It's goin'." What she says maybe a hundred times each day, with the ever-friendly, weary half smile. Or, if the person looks more high class, which is uncommon at the 82nd and Foster Fred Meyer, she might say, "Pretty good, how are you?" It feels inbred to her almost, that kind of kowtowing, but she does it all the same. Automatic. She likes to tell herself it's just her being professional and all—what's allowed her to keep this job going on seven years now—and she's good at what she does, too, good with customers, usually. Plus, when it comes down to it, she's actually a decent person.

Still, with those wealthier-looking customers every now and then— there's that feeling of being inferior somehow. That need to be *nice*. Some days it makes her feel sick. Because that's the one thing, besides the monotony, that gets her most, still, after all these years. So many people think they're better than you. Like you're not smart. Like you're impaired almost. So she's overweight, so she works as a cashier. So what?

She goes on scanning, bagging. But at least now she doesn't have to say, "Paper or plastic?" six hundred times a day, since Freddy's switched to all paper last year. The ankles and feet today, though . . . And now the first twinges of a headache, possibly a migraine. Two more hours until she can go home and rest.

She looks up and sees a man in her line, just the side of his face, he's openly checking out the celeb mags, and for a couple of seconds her heart skips, she thinks it's Keith. The trimmed goatee, the flannel shirt, and thinning hair. But it's not him. She says her usual "Find everything okay?" to the lady in front of her, tells her she can go ahead and enter her PIN, and recalls how she felt when she saw Keith in her living room last Thanksgiving. Coming up on a year ago now.

When the guy moves toward her, he says, "How's it goin'?" in a deep, smoky voice, and she glances at him and says with her half smile, "It's goin'."

ON BREAK, SMOKING OUT BACK near one of the loading docks, her usual spot, she pictures Keith standing in her living room, an image she still can't seem to get rid of. Her pulse is racing, it's been like this more and more lately. A mild dizziness. She stands there imagining Keith and how she about near fainted.

When they first started dating, when they were at Marshall, she was chubby. Nowhere near as chubby as now, but chubby. Reasonably pretty, too. She'd already gone out on a couple of dates her sophomore year, then started up with Keith midway through her junior year. He was a handsome thing, and that gap-toothed smile just about killed her. She'd always thought he was fine but would never go out with someone like her, he always seemed to date these knockout skinny girls like Rosanna Sage or Anne McNulty, he basically had his pick back then.

That summer between her junior and senior years, they were messing around up in Mt. Tabor Park on the wooded eastern slope. It was a warm night, there in their thicket on a blanket, and after a while she took off her shirt. He slipped his hand down her pants, she unzipped his jeans and gave him some attention there. Typical teenage heat. But when he jerked, some got onto her panties, and that's where it all started, right there. "One in a million chance," her doctor said, and all these years later she can still hear that white-haired man saying those words. *One in a million.* Sara. And then she wanted to keep the baby. Told herself it was meant to be. Keith had just graduated, and she tried to go back for her senior year in the fall but was too tired all the time and dropped out by late November. Sara arrived in April.

What she'd planned to do was go get her associate's at Mt. Hood Community College. Then maybe hit PSU after that, if she could swing it.

Nobody in her family had ever been to college, certainly not her mom or her long-gone dad, and there weren't any books at all in the house, ever, but Mr. Jacoby and a couple of other teachers at Marshall got into her head, started to make her believe she could do it, that she was smart enough.

As for Keith, he never had much interest in college. He wanted to get on, like his dad had, with the phone company, or maybe with the Water Bureau or the Parks Bureau as a landscaper. But he never could land those jobs. Never was very good at interviewing, he said. (And never took any steps to improve in that department, either.) So he took a job mowing lawns with a guy, then a year later got on with Drake's 7 Dees Nursery, on their landscape maintenance crew, and it turned out that he was good at pruning, had "a natural flair," according to one of his bosses. An "artistic style." And so he worked full time at that, they got married, and then after Sara came Elaine, then Rachel, the babies flying out.

Not even twenty years old, a mom with three little girls.

When Sara was nine and they still needed extra money bad, after they got evicted from the house out on 101st, the third eviction in nine years, she started studying for her GED, and after a whole year of studying whenever and wherever she could, passed the tests. Started working at Safeway over on Stark Street and slowly began saving up for community college, there were plenty of evening classes she could take.

Not long after that was when Keith decided to break in to that house with Bruce Gunderson.

She checks her watch. Five minutes until the home stretch. The headache still isn't going away, it's beginning to run down her neck. She smokes, watching the rain slap the shrubs across the asphalt driveway.

They'd been fighting since their early twenties, almost every time they were in the same room, but him going off to the pen was the final straw. What gave her the guts.

After the divorce was when she really started to put on the weight. Elaine, too. It all got to be too much, too quick, the change to full time here at Freddy's, the girls starting to act out more, especially Sara and Rachel. And so, not long after the divorce went through, after Wendy Maxwell had been calling and asking for months, Wendy saying they needed to get out for a girls' night and let off some steam, she finally went ahead and took her up on it, they went out for dinner and drinks at the New Copper Penny.

It was there, after she had downed three or four vodka tonics, Wendy off dancing, that the rangy little guy came up to the table and asked for a dance. She never did find out his name. He had on this cream-colored Western shirt with swirly designs on the lapels, she remembers that much. And so they danced, what the hell, and he bought her more drinks. After a while, Wendy wanted to stay and keep dancing, so she went with the little guy back to his apartment and he said in her ear how he liked full-size women. He actually said that. She wasn't sure what to say back except *Well, fuck me then*. So that's exactly what they did.

To feel some skin, some warmth—to feel that someone *wanted* her after all that had happened—it felt so good, even though the sex itself was only so-so, even though he kept on wanting to swing around behind her. And even though she was pretty sure he used a rubber, sure enough anyway, along came Adam. Of course. Get lonely, take up a friend on her offer to go out and kick up her heels, which she hadn't done in God knows how long, years, and then . . . pregnant. No idea of Adam's father's name, but then, hell, she didn't want to know.

One minute left. The black poly-blend company pants feel tighter than ever, they're riding up some. She stands there by the loading dock, adjusts the pants and draws a last long drag.

These snatches of thoughts, like every day.

Here she is in her midthirties, fat as shit, her body giving out, it seems like more and more. The arthritis, high blood pressure, migraines. The feet and legs and back. She feels geriatric. Damn right she wanted more than this. Wasn't supposed to get pregnant at sixteen years old, that's for damn sure. Wasn't supposed to get married so young. Wasn't supposed to get this fat. And then she goes and has yet another kid, after she was absolutely sure she was done having kids. And then this, too: *Her ex wasn't supposed to be an ex-con.*

Can you accuse her of giving up on her life? Maybe so. Of not believing in herself more? Shit, maybe so. Of not following her love of learning to college, of not fighting through more obstacles and doubts, of getting addicted to anger at her ex, the anger over him doing what he did, then leaving her with three children to raise on her own, over the *embarrassment* he brought to her and their daughters, not to mention his own parents? Sure, hell, you can accuse her of giving in to all that. Fine. But what you *can't* say about Melanie Garrison is she's a bad mom. No. Sorry. Because why she's here right now, why she's taken on all these extra shifts? For Elaine. For Rachel. For Adam. Because if Sara can go off to her nice new world and then not call her on the phone and let her know she's doing all right, if the girl can only text and call her sisters, she's too special all of a sudden to fill in her own mother on things now and then, what about the others? What'll they do if they feel like going to college? The cash from all these extra goddamn shifts? It's going, a good bit of it anyway, piddly amount that it is, into that new savings fund for the three of them, so, if they want to, they can use it as a start. Sure, for Elaine and Rachel it's kind of late in the game, but at least there'll be something for them. For Adam, more than a little something.

Speaking of Rachel, though: the school's still been calling about her, wondering where she is. Elaine says she's still at Kurt's. So . . . what? Should she go try to find her, try again to talk some sense into her? The thought of it makes her neck muscles go even tighter. If Rachel, like her big sister, wants to leave her family in the dark, if she can't even find it in herself to visit or call now and then, if she's suddenly somehow so much *better* that she can't even show some common courtesy, then you know what? No. Her mother will not go try to bring her back home. The girl can learn from her own choices. Life's a bitch, get used to it. Figure it out.

She begins moving gingerly toward the loading dock door, but the migraine turns her stomach, it's already to that point. She leans over and tries to throw up onto the bark chips a few feet from the door, it's the best place for doing that, but not much comes, mostly just spit.

She rises and wipes at her mouth. Then heads back inside, tight-jawed, still thinking of her kids.

31

AS ELAINE WALKS DOWN Hawthorne toward the jewelry shop on the next block, she glances at passing earrings. Jade studs, two-toned sterling silver and gold, and then some cool ruby ones with dangling peace signs. It's a rare sunny day this fall, hundreds of people out strolling, and it helps to look at all the earrings, distracts her from the fact that she's the largest person out here.

It helps, too, to think about lunch with Rachel—they'll meet in ten minutes at the falafel place. Because she needs to have one of their long talks, she wants that more than anything. For ten more minutes, though, it's all about jewelry and blocking out the thoughts of Franklin, and blocking out Chuck E. Cheese, where Rayette has her working behind the prize counter now, the sheer craziness of that. Blocking out also, yet again, how she feels like a teenage mom these days, taking care of Adam all the time when she's not at school or working. This is the first Saturday in ages that she's managed to slip away. Finally lied to her mom about having to work.

I'm sorry, Lord.

She ducks into the funky jewelry shop. There are some other women in there, too, so she doesn't feel quite so self-conscious. Checks out some dangling chandelier earrings and pearl studs and thinks of how she and Rachel used to come down to Hawthorne a lot, starting in middle school, to visit the jewelry shops, record stores, the Bagdad for matinees. Sara would usually be at a soccer game, and sometimes they'd even bring baby Adam in his cloth backpack carrier. Where did their (especially her) love of jewelry come from? Probably her Grandma Val, who would let them, when they were little, look through her old wooden jewelry box and try on the fake pearl necklaces, clip-on earrings, and gaudy brooches. Stuff that her Gram had just collected over the years, mostly from thrift shops or garage sales.

She checks her watch. Five minutes. She browses some expensive necklaces with tiny etched hearts on them, the store filled with the other women's calming murmurs and conversations. To just walk along from shop to shop like this, to be out in the city—she feels like she can breathe a little better. Think better. Like this is the first day in a long time that her spirit isn't about to break.

IN THE FALAFEL JOINT, Rachel isn't there yet, and so she goes ahead and orders. Falafel sandwich with everything, extra sauce, large Coke. She finds a window table and sits in the too-small chair, again aware that she's the biggest person in the room. People all around her, some of them so skinny, eating full plates of food.

When her sister arrives fifteen minutes later, she wipes her mouth and sees that Rachel's face looks different: it's more angular, she seems older, even compared to two weeks ago at school. Her bangs are purple now.

"Let me go grab a drink," Rachel says. "Be right back."

"You aren't eating?"

"Late breakfast. You go ahead."

When Rachel returns with her bottle of tea and asks how she's doing, she looks at her for a few beats, there's too much to talk about.

"Have you talked to Sara?" Rachel says.

"She's coming home for a visit later today, if you want to maybe—"

Rachel looks out the window. "I haven't been good about keeping in touch. I'm sorry."

"How's Kurt?"

Rachel meets her eyes again, and this time she sees even more how distracted, worried, slightly agitated she is. "He's fine. Visiting some friends nearby."

"You okay? You seem . . ."

Rachel, mid-sip, arches her brow. "It's just been sort of insane lately."

"How're things at Kurt's?"

"We've only been staying there part time."

"Where else?"

"Just . . . downtown. I'm safe, don't worry. It's just been weird lately."

Elaine gazes at her. Watches her glance around, tap her finger against her bottle. Rachel's eyes are bagged, and there's a pimple on her forehead, a rare sight.

"Dad wants to see you," she says, and Rachel looks out the window again. "He said to tell you he'll stop leaving messages, but he wants to see you."

Rachel gives her a steady, almost blank expression now. A hint of sadness. "I don't think so."

"You don't think so . . ."

Forcing a smile, Rachel lowers her head for a moment, then takes a long drink of tea and gets up. "I'm sorry. It's just been a *really* weird few days. Say hi to Sara? I'm sorry, I really am. I need to go meet Kurt."

She walks out, and Elaine sits there, face hot, a prickling sensation in her fingers, her sandwich half-eaten.

It's like, ever since Marshall closed, everything has changed. Everything. People cut loose into the world, scattered their own ways. Or has she missed something? Sure, Rachel basically moved out early her sophomore year, before the closure announcement, but still. It's the worst, it's official: this feeling of being so close to someone and then just somehow losing the connection, of two ships passing in the night—*and not knowing what to do or say to make things right again.*

She looks down at her sandwich and wants to pick it up, devour it, she's starving all of a sudden, but here she is again sitting alone in a restaurant. She sips at her Coke instead.

Please, Lord. Please.

She has the cornered animal feeling now, in her throat and lower jaw. She needs to talk to someone. Needs to unload some of this. A counselor at Franklin? She wants to see her dad again, is scared to see him again. Wants to talk to her sisters, wants to tell her mom that she can't do so much, she can't keep this up, but it feels like . . . *she can't talk.* To anyone now. The last time she felt free to talk with someone was when Sara was at home, how they would talk at lights out. Just hearing her big sister's voice there in the dark, talking softly like that, it made the world seem a little less scary. Because there was at least one person she could tell how she felt. And to hear Sara's confidence, too, to hear that *bring it on* tone in her voice at times—Sara probably had no idea how much that meant.

So now Sara has her college, her soccer. Rachel has her smarts, her creative writing; in spite of her boyfriend, the girl can do anything she wants in life. Anything. But what does she, Elaine, have? The desire to design jewelry and clothes and no real clue how to start chasing that dream. She can poke into shops on Hawthorne all day long, getting new ideas, but what has she really ever done to take steps toward her dream? Why isn't she working in a shop down here instead of handing out cheap prizes to loud, ungrateful brats? Because of how she looks, is that it? Because she's a gross cow?

She picks up her sandwich in both hands and takes an enormous bite. Sauce all over her lips, dribbling onto her chin, over her fingers.

It helps to chew.

32

ON THE MAX RIDE TO LENTS, half reading *Our Town* for Monday's class with Sister Toms, Sara keeps checking her phone, and finally there's a message. It's not from Hoban, though.

She's not coming. See u soon.

She pictures Elaine thumbing out the text, then looks out at the cars and trucks on the freeway, the clouds above thickening. The day started out bright, Hoban said he would call her this weekend sometime, and now she's speeding toward the gravel road and the house she hasn't seen in over two months and it feels like there's a rock in her stomach. She's still sore from last night's game, her hamstrings mainly, but at least she scored her second goal of the season, a hard volley from fifteen yards, and at least they won. The game thoughts help distract her for a time, images of the crowd going nuts, the students chanting and singing, but soon it's her stop, and when she gets off the train, the freeway noise makes her pull her hood up over her head.

ADAM LOOKS OLDER. In just the four or five weeks since Elaine brought him out to campus for that afternoon game. His height, his face. She holds him as long as he'll let her, then gets onto the brown carpet with him as he shows her his Tinkertoys. In the nearby chair, Melanie sits with her slippered feet up, eyeing the *Bob the Builder* DVD that's on, a glass of ginger ale on her TV tray. Elaine eases down at the dining table.

"Let's build a *spaceship*," Adam says.

"Big or little?" Sara says.

"*Big!*"

The kid gets his building face on—the pursed lips and determined eyes, a look that's often made her smile—and so she starts in also, wondering whether to ask if they can turn off the TV.

"So, tell us about your dorm," Melanie says.

"Good. Roommate's cool."

"I talked to Val and Ernie the other day, they said they've been out there a few times."

Sara nods and tries to focus on the building, on Adam. *Just keep things simple. Keep calm.*

"What're your classes like?"

"Good. Hard."

"What're you taking?"

"Biology. History. English . . ."

Melanie takes a drink, and when Sara glances up, her mother is looking straight at her.

"What?"

Elaine says, "There's more ginger ale, if you want some."

"What's the food like there?" Melanie says.

"Nothing special."

"Nothing special . . ."

Sara grips a Tinkertoy in each hand. She turns and holds her mother's gaze now, while Adam continues building. "What's that supposed to mean?"

"Nothing. You don't seem to have much to say is all."

"Not much to tell, I guess."

"Like to keep your distance, I know. Then when you do come home and someone asks how things are, because they *care,* you get to sit there and act like a princess, is that it?"

"*Okay* now." Sara lowers the Tinkertoys to the carpet and gets up. She keeps her voice even. "Have I ever seen you at one of my games?"

"And do I see you working sixty hours a week on a bad back and—"

"Christ, here we go again." Sara looks over at Elaine. "You ready for the list of aches?"

Melanie rears up in her chair, and then notices Adam, who's raising his hand. "What is it?"

"*Stop arguing,*" he says.

Melanie pushes herself out of the chair, glaring at Sara. "Real nice seeing you. Can't wait for your next visit."

"Me too. Thanks."

Melanie squints. "You really are a little smart ass, you know that? Just kiss all this goodbye, huh? Free and easy. Pretend you never even lived here, isn't that right?"

"*Stop,*" Adam says.

After a last look at Sara, Melanie heads to her room, and soon Adam starts crying, kicks at what they've built so far, and runs down the hall.

For a moment, as she stands there with her knees locked, Sara pictures herself and Elaine when they were around Adam's age, getting up from the floor when their mom and dad started yelling again, leaving their dolls or Legos and going off to their room. Rachel, more often than not, trailing after them.

ON THE WALK DOWN FOSTER to meet Kim, she keeps trying to collect herself. As she passes beneath the freeway, the cafe coming into view, she remembers Elaine and herself meeting their dad last fall and how she thought of calling him yesterday, maybe even stopping by his place today while she was out here and all. But no. Not now, especially. Still, as she opens the door and sees the table by the window where they sat, it feels strange to be so close to where he lives, it's like she can feel his presence.

Kim's already there, in one of her flannel shirts and blue jeans. They hug.

"You all right?"

Sara shrugs, takes off her coat and sits, no drink. Just studies her friend for a few beats.

Kim looks good, the color in her face, her hair a bit shorter than a couple of weeks ago when she came out to the Pepperdine game. Gramps and Gram were at that one, too, and so she and Kim didn't get much of a chance to talk. But then, Jesus, that's not much of an excuse, she decides. It was awkward then, like it is now already, and she can tell from the way Kim keeps taking small sips of her latte that it's not just her imagination.

Kim asks about school, and about seeing her mom, and she answers both questions with "Okay."

The cafe is half-full, some Pearl Jam playing. The eerie painting of the old-time ship still hanging by the stage. For a while they just sit there, occasionally glancing at each other.

"Are you seeing someone?" Kim asks.

"No. You?"

"No."

One thing she'll never stop loving about this girl? How *present* Kim almost always seems. Like wherever she is, whatever she's doing, actually *matters.* Her phone almost always out of sight. Yet this does feel different, there's no way around that. Could part of it be due to what just happened at the house?

"What would you like to do tonight?" Kim says. "Been a while since we cruised downtown." She smiles her blazing smile. *"Don't stop, believin'* . . ." she sings softly.

"Not tonight. Sorry."

Kim's smile fades. "I was hoping to see you more . . ."

Sara feels her right foot tapping the floor.

"It's like you've got your new life and everything," Kim says, "and I'm . . ."

"What?"

"I don't know. Not *waiting,* exactly."

"What are your plans, anyway? Seriously."

Kim gazes at her, eyebrows raised, and Sara looks down at the table, shaking her head.

"God, I'm sorry. That was shitty. This whole day is just completely—"

"Guess I'm not in a rush to escape this place. Like you obviously are."

Sara lifts her head. "What is it with you?"

"What do you mean?"

"Your dad'll pay for community college, you keep saying you want to go, and now you act like I'm the one who, like, *abandoned* all this or something. What the fuck?"

"I didn't mean it like that."

Sara gets up.

"Sara, goddamn it, don't even."

Before Kim can stand, Sara turns and leaves, and when she pushes the door open, the freeway sound rips through her, the traffic air filling her nostrils. It's colder, the grey light dimmer, and as she speed-walks to the MAX stop she pulls up her hood once more.

Just get her away from this place. She can't get on that train fast enough, to hell with all this. For real.

33

WHEN SHE FINALLY makes it back to campus just past eight, the girl across the hall, Heather, invites her to a party over in Villa Maria Hall, the all-guys dorm adjacent to Mehling, where Hoban lives. There was a note from Olivia, she's out with Sophie Mack at a movie, and more than anything right now Sara wants to get drunk, so she washes her face and heads out with Heather.

She doesn't know whose room it is, but the place is rocking. Maybe thirty people crammed in, the White Stripes blaring, people blowing weed smoke out the window, a keg by one of the desks. She drinks through three cups of beer, catching a substantial buzz after not eating any dinner, and then someone passes around a bottle of peppermint schnapps and she downs a quarter of a cup of that. Soon she's over at the windows, smoking from a guy's pipe, four or five hits, she loses track. Seven tops.

After a while she wanders down the hall to Hoban's room and finds the door partway open. But when she peeks inside, no one's there. Two laptops, a TV, ripe for the taking. Joseph's chinchilla, Bö, in his cage by Joseph's bed. The chinchilla watches her. From behind, a door opens, startling her, and one of the long-haired, punk rock guys across the hall comes out of his room and says, "Hoban?"

"Is he around?"

"Went downtown. Joe's around here somewhere, though." The guy hustles down the corridor and opens the party room door, a quick blast of Herbie Hancock's "Rockit," then the muffled yelling and loud conversations again.

Downtown on a date? She stands there, and after a few beats throws back the rest of her beer. The hallway walls undulate a bit. What she needs to do is walk some more, she decides. Get more fresh air, even though she's wiped out.

The night is cold, but her sweatpants and sweatshirt seem to be enough as she makes her way off campus along Portsmouth Boulevard. It's late, there are hardly any cars, and between pulls on her cigarette she catches whiffs of frost and dead leaves. It feels good to her to be high and out walking, that drifting in and out of awareness of surroundings, and she tries not to think of Hoban on a date with some other girl.

For a while she stays on Portsmouth, and just before Lombard, as she's about to hang a right and loop back around to campus, a white Jeep Cherokee does a U-turn, honks, and pulls up alongside her.

Lindsay Waxler. Her white Cherokee. Lindsay's driving, Siena Vincent in the passenger seat, a couple of others in back, Sara can't see who.

Siena rolls down the window and sticks her head out. "Garrison?"

The engine cuts, all four doors open. Lindsay, Siena, Shannon Wang, and another large girl that Sara's never seen. They're all wearing jeans and winter coats, Shannon Wang with a knit beanie on her head.

"Are you kidding me?" Lindsay says, smiling. She looks at Siena, who stands next to her, two feet from Sara. Shannon and the other girl off to the side. "She does smoke. We're trying to make the fucking playoffs and she fucking smokes. How's that working out for you, girlie?"

Sara takes another drag, forcing herself not to drop her eyes, and Lindsay reaches over and takes the cigarette from her mouth, flicks it onto the sidewalk but doesn't step on it.

"Could you possibly be more full of yourself?" Siena says, and Sara smells booze.

Both Lindsay and Siena stare at her, Shannon and the other girl occasionally glancing around the street, clearly uncomfortable, and after a moment Lindsay says, "Get in the car, idiot."

Sara looks down at the still-smoking butt on the sidewalk and notices the cold air on her lips and ears. Her nose running a little. She considers sprinting, but from the expression on Lindsay's face in particular, they'll catch her and force her into the Jeep if she doesn't go on her own, and what's the worst that can happen in daddy's white Cherokee? She steps over and gets in, sits in back between Shannon and the silent beefy other chick. Before climbing back in, Lindsay and Siena briefly confer out of earshot.

Once they're driving—through the Lombard intersection, farther north on Portsmouth—Siena turns around. "So you're from a tough part of town, right? Badass part of town? Where they teach you to be a rude little fuck?"

Sara doesn't answer. She definitely smells booze. She stares straight ahead, face slack. The clock on the dash reads 12:52.

"Proud of being white trash, huh?" Siena says.

Sara's eyes dart over at her, but she still doesn't say anything.

Soon Lindsay turns and now they're driving through a neighborhood that looks strangely familiar. Lots of chain-link fences, small houses. A few vehicles here and there parked on dark front lawns. What even looks like, in the middle of one block, a gravel alleyway. They make a few more turns, she's completely lost, but then they pass a large building that she realizes must be Roosevelt High School. She played soccer there a couple of times, those long school bus rides all the way out here. They pass it and keep on going, eventually rolling by a loose huddle of guys at the mouth of a driveway, two of them turning their shoulders, not so slyly concealing something. Then, at an intersection with a four-lane road, train tracks on the other side, and some industrial buildings also, partly lit up, one of them with white smoke billowing from two tall stacks, Lindsay pulls to a stop. A semi roars by on the busier road.

"Get out," Lindsay says, and both she and Siena unbuckle their seat belts and open their doors.

Sorry, Shannon Wang mouths as she moves to let Sara out.

"So." Lindsay tries to put an arm around Sara, but Sara shrugs it away and Siena laughs. "Feisty little cunt, isn't she? So anyway, girlie, look. Campus is *that way*." Lindsay says this last part like she's talking to a slow child, and Siena laughs again, but then her grin dies off.

"Show us how tough you are now, homegirl." Siena reaches out and slaps Sara's cheek, though a little tentatively, then turns and starts to get back into the Jeep. "Have a fun walk."

Another semi cruises by, and just before the Cherokee drives off, Sara squints up at the street sign that says Columbia Boulevard. One more place in the world she didn't know existed.

FOR A MINUTE she looks around. Wild how fast a part of town can change. She can't be that far from UP, they were only in the Jeep, what, five, ten minutes? Or was it longer? She feels more sober, of course, but her head still whirls, and so she pulls out another cigarette and lights up. Lips a bit numb. It's quiet, there's no traffic all of a sudden, and she stands there at the intersection for another minute taking in the scene. No sidewalks. The small one-story houses. The air over here smells weird, there's a trace of some chemical odor on the chilly breeze, she's not sure what it is. She starts walking again.

After a time, far ahead, she sees the group of guys they passed, their voices carry, and so she turns east, or at least she thinks it's east, and goes down another street that looks familiar. Where one of the houses has a motor home in the driveway. Where a satanic-looking Rottweiler barks its head off at her from behind a chain-link fence. She fires up another cig and picks up the pace a little, turns another corner, south again. She hopes.

Look at this shit. Seriously?

What she'll do is try to finish the season. She can quit after that. It was definitely a nice try, all this. Barely keeping up in every single one of her classes, currently sporting a fat-ass D in Modern World History, essays piling up, each week a new one. The one step up, two steps back feeling, all the time, since she arrived at training camp. The thing is, something's probably not right in her head. There's this demon or some shit, and it always, *always* seems to win in the end, every time, it keeps on shoveling in the coal, keeping the fire nice and high. Hey, maybe she's addicted to being pissed off. Like her mom. Imagine that.

After a while, it has to be one thirty by now—where did she leave her phone anyway? At the party?—she finds herself standing in front of Roosevelt. She pauses there for a minute, then walks up to the front entrance with its tall white columns.

"Grand," she says to herself, as Sister Toms might put it. Better yet: "Stately." Those columns, and all those clean bricks, cast in the yellow lights. Pretty place. And come Monday morning, open for business. Does this neighborhood realize how lucky it is to get to keep its high school open? Do these people around here realize how if their high school got closed it would feel like the rest of the city was basically saying, *Well, when it comes down to it, they don't matter quite enough. Sorry, man.*

She smokes more, turns and makes her way through the neighborhood, soon passing an old VW Rabbit parked in front of a tiny house with a bright fluorescent porch light. The sticker on the Rabbit's back bumper says, I KNOW THERE'S A HELL—I WORK IN RETAIL, and for some reason, she's not sure why, it makes her think of Adam, the feel of holding him today. But then she can't go around thinking about those things, it'll break her. *Fuck it.* Still, it's Elaine in her head now, that look in her eyes, almost haunted it seemed like. That's the word right there, *haunted.* And then there's Rachel, how Elaine said Rachel "looked worried" when she saw her at the falafel place.

Sara goes on walking. At one point she ducks into some shrubs and takes a tremendous piss.

A few final cutting thoughts: There's no place to call home now, it's true. Nowhere she completely fits. And so here she is, drifting. This is the feeling, she can name it. Drifting in the dark, in between worlds. And then of course there's her good old dad, who left another message yesterday, saying he'll try to make it to next weekend's game, he might have a "lady friend" there, too, just to give her a heads-up. Nice.

When she crosses Lombard finally, she knows where she is. Campus another ten or fifteen minutes onward. Calves near cramp stage, feet howling, she's exhausted. Just crushed. Maybe tired enough to fall right asleep when she gets in, not lay there and lay there, thinking.

AS SHE PASSES VILLA HALL, though, she looks over at Hoban and Joseph's window and sees a light on, the curtains partway open. She needs sleep, but she also needs to go over there for a better look. He's reading on his bed, and Joseph doesn't seem to be around, so she steps closer over the grass and raps on the window. Hoban gets up, not appearing all that startled, cracks the window, and tells her to come to the back door.

He's still in his clothes, just jeans and one of his dark blue button-up shirts with the sleeves rolled to the elbows, his knit bracelet in view. At least it wasn't a fancy date, she thinks.

"What're you up to?" he says, holding the door for her.

"Went for a walk."

The hall is quiet, all the doors closed but his, and as they step into his warm room she realizes just how cold her hands and cheeks are.

"How long were you out there?"

"Couldn't sleep." She sits on the edge of his bed and tucks her hands under her legs.

"Can I get you some tea or—"

"I came by earlier."

Hoban looks at her. Wipes a few strands of hair from his eyes. "I went out with some high school friends. We caught a play and grabbed some dinner. What were you up to?"

Now that she's sitting, her head feels woozy again, and when Hoban sits down next to her she leans into him. He puts an arm around her.

"Tired," she says.

"Crash here. Joe's sleeping at Angie's tonight."

Bö, possibly at the mention of his owner's name, stirs in his wood shavings, and she glances at him. "How do you spell Bö anyway?"

"B-O with an umlaut. Joe had some German in high school."

She thinks, *What the fuck is an umlaut?* then turns her head and kisses Hoban Stellenbach. Just like that. It's their first kiss, and she decides not to hold back, to hell with it, and when Hoban gets into it, too, cupping her cold face in his warm hands, there's a high ringing in her ears.

He hits the light and they lie down and make out for a long time, Bö shuffling around, apparently riled up by this late turn of events, and then Hoban curls up beside her and they spoon, and soon she falls asleep. Later, she's vaguely aware of Joseph coming in, but she remains right where she is, warm, the blanket up over her shoulder. Hoban's arm still around her.

34

IT'S AN ODDLY WARM AFTERNOON after several cold days, the rain has stopped, and Ken has already wiped down the bench when Rachel finds him to swap books. She pulls *The Devil's Highway* from her pack, hands it over, lights a cigarette, and sits down.

With his usual glower of concentration, Ken reads silently from the first page, and for a minute Rachel observes him. The beard recently trimmed, the glasses perched on his nose, the frayed sleeves of his grey sport coat. His shopping cart, as always, neatly packed, parked up next to the bench. He finishes the page and closes the book. "I'll take it. And for you . . ." He lifts the book that was tucked against his far side. "This is the first I've read of hers."

She takes hold of *Olive Kitteridge*, and as she checks out the blurbs she notices Ken giving her that look he sometimes gives when she smokes. He clearly has an opinion about smoking, but, God bless him, he keeps it to himself.

"Deal," she says.

For a time they sit there in a comfortable pause, the city flowing all around them, the South Park Blocks full of lunchtime walkers, some street kids. She has maybe a half hour of peace here before Kurt comes and gets her after his downtown circuit, his various deliveries under the Burnside Bridge and over near the Galleria on Morrison. They'll head back out to Southeast this afternoon for more deliveries before calling it a day. She takes another long drag.

"So, what's the plan for you?" she says.

"You're looking at it."

"I mean, like, long term."

"You're looking at it." Ken glances between her and passersby. "What about you? Long term."

"School, I think. Need to go more."

"Sounds like a good idea."

The talk drops away again, Ken nodding and then dipping back into his new book, while she sits there smoking, thinking.

Before, she always knew she could turn it on when she needed to, but now, for the first time, there's this . . . creeping fear. This quicksand feeling, almost. It's Kurt and what all's happening to him; it does feel scary now, okay, for the first time really, like she'd better be very careful, there's that alarm down inside of her that's been sounding off louder and louder. Can she possibly be one of those kids who gives up so easily, who can't even handle graduating from high school, who doesn't seek out help if she needs it? It used to drive her *crazy* at Marshall when kids gave up so easily.

So, does she need help? She goes on smoking, looking around. Kurt says he has no intention of going back to school, has zero interest in it, not since he's making decent money now. He keeps saying how they'll be able to move out of his mom's soon, get their own place.

But it's amazing—she actually *misses* school. And it's not just from Kurt doing crank, what all it's doing to him. It's the situations he's been putting her in lately. Like the place they're supposed to drop by later on this afternoon, the two creepy guys who always have their skanks over and keep asking if Kurt wants to join in. The nasty furniture and mattresses in that apartment.

When Ken reaches over into his cart and pulls out another book, she sees that her cigarette has burned almost all the way down, so she pushes it out against the side of the bench.

"Ever read David Suzuki?" he says, holding the book out to her.

"I haven't."

"Been holding on to this for you. Friend of mine gave it to me last week. There's some of the stuff we were talking about in there. He says how the laws of nature have priority over the forces of economics, the planet can't sustain so much growth. Thought it might be up your alley."

As she takes the book, Kurt's voice calls out from across the plaza: *"You ready?"* He stares over at her, there in his baggy dark clothes with all the pockets, then turns to talk with some of the street kids.

"Sorry," she says, standing. "Looks like I'm outta here."

"Don't make yourself scarce."

She slips the new books down into her pack, but before leaving, she stands there in front of the bench for a moment. This man's presence, it occurs to her, has often reminded her, at least a little bit, of her Gramps.

Ken might be smarter in some ways, more educated certainly, but there's the same gentle bearing, the same courtesy. Sweetness under toughness.

"You take care of yourself," he says, crossing his legs the other way.

She doesn't care if Kurt sees. She leans down and gives him a peck on his bearded old cheek. Then walks away.

THE APARTMENT IN THE Powellhurst neighborhood adjacent to Lents is in a run-down duplex with overgrown rhodies covering the front windows. Inside, the place reeks of crank and, what seems to her, a slight tang of feces. Like the earlier visit, the two guys with their bad teeth and scabby arms inspect the baggie of yellowish powder and the other baggie full of Strawberry Quick, what Kurt calls the pinkish crystals that result from Tobias's cook adding red coloring "for the ladies." Over on the plaid couch, a reedy girl not much older than herself sits cross-legged in a white tank top with no bra on underneath and ripped Levi's. She's glassy-eyed, watching Animal Planet, a show about Burmese pythons running amok in Florida, while across the room in the open kitchen, another girl talks on a phone, pacing barefoot, wearing a guy's button-down shirt that hangs down over her bruised legs.

The larger, ratty-bearded guy, his gums looking like they're about ready to bleed any second, pulls some bills from his shorts pocket. Counts them out and hands them to Kurt while the shorter guy watches.

"You two want to hang, share a round?" The bearded guy glances at her, smiling.

"Naw, we gotta hit it," Kurt says.

"Your loss." The smaller guy has already loaded his glass pipe, and the girl in the kitchen gets off the phone and comes over to him.

"Let me go first," she says, and he hands her the pipe and lighter, watches her in action.

"Chase that white dragon, sweetheart."

She finishes and holds up a middle finger, and then the other girl gets off the couch and comes over to smoke.

"All right then," Kurt says, and as they leave, Rachel sees the bearded guy leering at her again.

When they're around the corner, heading back toward the bus stop, Kurt says, "No way I'm ever sharing you." He walks faster, and she tries to keep up.

"Is that what he—"

"Fuckin' junkies."

Kurt looks around, then stops beside another apartment complex's dumpsters. He checks his coat pockets and rearranges something down in there. He's been doing this lately. After a minute, his face relaxes and he starts walking again.

"So are you paying for what you skim?" she says, and he stops hard. "Or does he just let you have some extra?"

"How you know I'm skimming?"

"I'm not sure you are. Are you?"

Kurt watches her, his lips curled downward. "He said it was all right. A little. Ain't actually none of your business anyway, come to think of it."

"It sort of is, though, don't you think?" When she doesn't look away, his jaws flex and he starts moving again, the bus stop is on the next block. For a while they step along through the traffic noise.

"There's been more in there lately," he says. "A little more with each order, the last week or so . . . I think he's so fucked up most the time he puts too much in. Doesn't even notice. Shit, those fools back there sure don't notice."

They wait at the empty stop. She should shut up now, she knows, this won't help anything, but she can't seem to help herself. The bus comes toward them and she says, "You should watch it. He'll find out."

Kurt's eyes widen and he grabs her by the arm and squeezes hard, but as he's about to say something the bus pulls up and the door opens. The middle-aged driver, a balding, broad-shouldered Black man, stares at Kurt and after a few beats asks if they're getting on.

Kurt stuffs a five into the box and the driver asks if he wants his change, but he only keeps pulling her down the aisle, the other passengers mostly looking away.

35

KEITH JUST TAKES IT ALL IN.

To sit once more in the crowded Merlo Field stands and hear all the cheering, to watch his daughter out there running on the groomed, lit-up field, playing in her last regular-season game, and now to feel Courtney, his clever, voluptuous, high-cheekboned, bartending girlfriend here beside him on this chilly night—it about kills him how fine it feels. He can't stop grinning. And even though, after the final whistle, Sara heads straight to the locker room, not once turning to see him with Courtney by the railing behind the bench, that's all right, the girl's probably just drained, caught up in the win. She can meet Courtney next time.

On the drive back to Lents in the rumbling pickup, Courtney pressed up close to him, his arm around her, they listen to some CCR on the tape deck, "Proud Mary." *Rollin', rollin', rollin' on the river.* And here they are, rolling down the freeway, taking it nice and easy (like he has a choice in this beater), on this November Friday night after a long week at work.

"So what do you think?" he says. "Up for that party, or should we just . . ." He slips his hand down and gently cups her right breast, and she turns and smiles at him, the delicate wrinkles around her eyes blooming.

"Just what?" Courtney kisses his scruffy cheek. "I'm still good with stopping by, if you want. I'd still like to meet some of your old buds. It's your call."

He strokes her breast, feeling the nipple rise under her waffle-knit shirt, and keeps his eyes on the road. Up ahead, there's a cop car, no one wanting to pass it.

"His name's Bruce, you said? Where's he live again?"

"Up off Foster. 112th, down this cul-de-sac." His erection pinned to his thigh by his blue jeans, Keith watches the cop and returns his hand to her shoulder. "Let me think on it. His bashes can get pretty crazy sometimes. Least they used to."

Courtney kisses his cheek again, they go back to listening to the CCR, and he keeps the truck at a cool fifty-five. The smell of her shampooed hair alone keeps the erection going for another minute. That and the thought of them bucking and moaning in his bed.

But then maybe they should stop by Bruce's, he thinks. Just for a bit. He's already told her about prison, been up front about everything from the get-go, and she knows that Bruce just got released. What he *hasn't* mentioned is how Bruce has already been talking shit, been leaving messages every other day or so, and when they went out for beers last Sunday the man brought up their old Marshall pal Mark Roddick, how Mark knew of a few "opportunities." The talk about Mark ended right there, though, Bruce taking him up on a game of pool, and they kept on downing pitchers. But it'll come up again, he knows. It's clear enough where Bruce stands on the matter. Six years sleeping in a cell didn't do much other than make him hungrier for "can't-miss deals." And the thing is, this woman sitting beside him? He's promised not to hurt her, quaint as that may sound. He meant it when he said that. She's been through too much, said she couldn't take it if he hurt her right now, she's seen too much in her life.

At the exit for I-205, the cop car goes the way he's going, and now he's the one right behind it. He slows down a little, wondering if the cop wants to test him tonight. Wondering if cop cars these days have radar guns pointing backward, maybe the driver's partner is aiming one at him this instant. He stays in the right lane, giving the cop some distance, and keeps the truck steady. He only had the two beers before they went out to the U of P, but he can't feel those at all.

Steady on. It's what life's still like these days. It's about all he can do. Just keep things steady, keep the devil in his place.

He is, however, getting just *slightly* frustrated by work. By this point, he thought he'd at least be given a shot at one of the foreman positions. But another guy just got promoted, goddamn Jarrett, twenty-three-year-old scrub. And why not himself? Well, he knows why. Of course he does. But it's best to try to keep blocking it out. Stay on an even keel. He's got a sexy, kindhearted girlfriend, a good lady, he's got a decent place to sleep, a good dog, and even some wheels, even if they are beyond shitty. And look, he's utilizing his freedom pretty well, all things considered. Not taking it for granted.

But he did think things would be different by this point. A year since he's been out. He'd thought that by now, for one, he'd be seeing his girls regularly. He understands how they must feel, but after a certain period of time they have to either find it within themselves to forgive him or not. Open up a little, or not. Elaine's maybe the closest to forgiving him, opening up some, sharing a few weeks back how it's been sort of challenging going to Franklin for her senior year, having to adjust to so many new things. Sara, well, the walls are still thick, but at least she talks to him. Sometimes. As for Rachel? With that girl, lately he's not so sure. Maybe it'll just end up being the case that he'll be one of those parents who're close to some but not all of his kids. Maybe that's how it'll be. Because what he's not going to do anymore is crawl. That's over. No more messages on Rachel's phone, he's left too many already. The tough thing is, Elaine has said how she's worried about her, makes it sound like the boyfriend is maybe the problem, but she won't give much more info, only that Rachel's living with the guy in his mom's basement and "he's not the best of guys."

The cop car changes to the center lane and slows down, and before he knows it he's passed the cop and checks his speed—it's still right under fifty-five. But after only another quarter mile, the cop pulls right behind him. Traffic is light, and the Foster Road exit is still another two miles up ahead. He gives Courtney's shoulder a light squeeze and glances down at her, but she doesn't appear concerned about the cop, her face relaxed, eyes watching the passing night. He checks the rearview and the cop stays three car-lengths back, so he tries to relax his leg muscles and just drive. John Fogarty goes on belting it out.

The thing about his girls, though: What if he never gets all that close to any of them, when it comes down to it, even after giving it some more time? What if that's how it turns out? And then what if he never does get promoted at work and can only afford a small apartment and a beat-up truck the whole rest of his life, barely afford dog food each month? And what if he never does see either of his parents again before they die, and this thing inside of him that's always there, no matter what he does, no matter how much he tries to ignore it, this thing within him that makes him want to show them he's not a total fuck-up, he's making things right, he'll do them proud—what if they never get to see all that before they up and die? Part of him? Sure, part of him wants to see them and rub their faces in his being locked up. Screw 'em. Maybe if they showed a little more goddamn love, you know? But then the other part of him knows that's bullshit, all these sorry fools blaming their parents for everything. That isn't how it'll be with him, not anymore.

Another rearview look: the cop remains back there. What, is he running his goddamn license plate?

Here's the thing, he decides, once again: If his folks don't believe in him, that's their deal. What he's trying to do is just live a decent life. He's not ever going to be a rich guy, might never get much further than where he's at right now, but what he's going to do is keep on trying to make a go of this. He's going to be there for his girls, no matter what.

The Foster exit comes into view, and he hits his blinker early. Checks the rearview and swallows. When he exits and the cop stays on the freeway, he takes a slow, quiet, deep breath and glances over at Courtney: This woman beside him now. This fine, steady, benevolent woman. He turns and starts heading up Foster toward the party, they'll just stop by and say hello, not stay long, then go on back to his place and, with the last bits of energy they each have after working so hard all week, move together under the sheets.

36

RACHEL'S SITTING WITH Ken on their bench, talking about *The Devil's Highway*, when Manfred and Teena walk up.

"Talk a sec?" Manfred, his black mohawk trimmed closer to his skull these days, looks as intense and jumpy as ever, while ropy, washed-out Teena with her tousled off-white hair waits beside him.

"Be right back," Rachel says to Ken, rising off the bench.

At the plaza's edge, across the street from the concert hall, they huddle and she glances over her shoulder at Ken, who's gone back to reading. She can smell now that either or both of them have been drinking.

"Where is he?" Manfred says.

"What's up?"

"He failed the test."

"What are you talking about?"

"His *test*." Manfred glares.

And now Teena chimes in. "T puts in extra, over what his clients order. He wanted to see what Kurt would do, if he could trust him. He likes to give people a chance to come clean, but he's failed three tests."

"Hold on . . ." Rachel looks over at Ken again, then back at Manfred. "He's meeting with Tobias right now, he said, he was going to pick up—"

"Nope. T's looking for him, too. So where is he really?"

Rachel's brow arches. "If he's not with Tobias, then—"

"Dude, *fuck*." Manfred clicks his front teeth, but after a few seconds sees someone come into the plaza, goes over and starts talking. It's a guy Rachel has seen around, but hasn't ever met, and he and Manfred join a group of street kids and soon a burst of laughter comes. It's then that Teena catches her eye. The expression is almost sad. Weary. Teena crosses her arms, her long black sweatshirt sleeves wrapped around her hands, poking out from her dingy black jacket.

"You guys should get out of downtown."

Rachel just gauges her.

"You know almost everyone down here packs now, don't you?"

"What, *guns*?"

Teena gives her this steady, pitiful look, and Rachel glances over at Manfred, who still seems sidetracked, and then at Ken, who's still reading.

"You really don't know where he is?" Teena says.

"I don't, no. He said he'd meet me back at home today."

"Home? Like, his mommy's house? Listen, you'd better just get out of here, okay? You really don't want to fuck around here, you're *so* out of your league now, do you understand? I hope you do. Why, I'm not even sure, since you've been quite the little bitch most of the time."

Rachel's face prickles. Her mouth is dry.

Who knew this pale bony girl could talk like this? She feels herself giving a nod, and as she walks back to the bench she hears Manfred let out one of his crazy whoops, he's still talking it up with the other kids, Teena heading over to them.

When she stands before Ken and he stops reading and looks up at her with those slightly magnified eyes, she has a hard time holding his gaze.

"What is it?" He puts a finger in the book.

"I have to go."

Ken turns and looks around. Uncrosses his legs. "Can you . . ." He hesitates, seeming to grasp that whatever just occurred could mean she won't be coming around for a while, and as she moves to get her pack together, he gets up and reaches down into his cart and pulls out a small black notebook, opens it and removes a slip of grey paper with handwriting on it.

"Been meaning to give this to you." He folds the paper over and places it in her hand.

"I don't know when I'll—"

Ken holds up a hand. She gazes at him. She gives him a peck on the cheek, then tucks the paper into her coat pocket.

ON THE MAX RIDE, her face still tingling at times, she sees that the paper has a few light smudges along the edges, but the black ink is clear, and she wonders how long he carried it around.

It may be that when we no longer know what to do we have come to our real work and that when we no longer know which way to go we have begun our real journey. The mind that is not baffled is not employed. The impeded stream is the one that sings.

—Wendell Berry

The train hurtles alongside the freeway, farther and farther from downtown, and she doesn't care who sees her crying.

———

WEEKS IN THE BASEMENT. Kurt doing more and more crank, only leaving the house to buy more baggies of it. Lots of sex, long sessions where he takes his time, arranging her this way and that way. When it's over, she refuses yet again to smoke with him and tries to lose herself in books. Like she would do when she was a girl, how she wore out her library card, the card with the faded barcode and melted off corners from going through the laundromat dryer. She was so proud of that card, used it until it basically disintegrated and she finally had to get a new one, in middle school, when the reading really kicked into gear. It was all Harry Potter's fault.

THE WEEK BEFORE Thanksgiving, it's a Monday night, late, and Kurt, after being awake for almost three days, is finally sleeping it off.

She sits in the duct-taped beanbag chair at the opposite end of the room, her calculus book in her lap. She has no idea where her classmates are in the book, since it's been almost a month since she showed up at school, but tonight she needs to at least try some math, use that part of her brain. Yet it's true, for her calculus is, for the most part, a painful mystery, there's no way she can work her way through this textbook without plenty of help, and for that she has to get herself into school.

But of course he won't let her go now. The paranoia's out of control. He says Tobias knows that she goes to Franklin and they'll show up there if they haven't already, he's sure of it. So, no, he won't let her leave the house, even when his crank runs out and he goes to score more. It doesn't help that she still refuses to smoke it with him, won't take it in pill form, either, and this only makes him go rougher at times during sex, like he's possessed. Last week, for the first time that she knows of, he raided his mom's old cookie tin in the kitchen, her stash of bills there, and didn't mention anything about paying her back.

She listens to his sleep-breathing and stares at the page in front of her without registering a thing on it. Thinks of Adam and what it was like to smell his hair and hold him and read to him, and she's so *sorry* for all this, she didn't mean for it to be like this. If she leaves, he'll track her down, and then everyone in her family gets to find out what she's done with her life and she gets to feel even more embarrassed about putting herself in this situation.

Rachel? Oh, yeah, she's a prisoner in her meth-addict boyfriend's basement, actually.

Is that right? Well, good luck to her. Let me know if I can help with that.

No. She'll tell no one. She'll figure this out on her own. Find a way, somehow.

She closes the textbook and presses her fingers over her eyes.

THE FOLLOWING EVENING, her phone rings and Kurt flinches.

"Who is it?" he says, propping himself on an elbow on the bed.

She considers lying, but knows he'll check later. "My dad."

He swings his legs over the bed, springs up, and strides over to her where she sits in the beanbag.

"Please don't—"

Kurt snatches the phone. "The fuck you want, man?" He turns and paces back toward the bed. "No, I can't put her on. She don't want to talk to your sorry ass, so why do you even keep calling and texting and shit?" He turns and heads back toward her, his face crimson in the low light. "Did you not hear what I just said? Leave her the *fuck* alone, aw'ight? You want to start some shit, go start some shit with her sisters, 'cause she ain't talkin' to you! No—goddamn it, are you even listening to me? You're a serious motherfuckin' dumbass, do you know that, man? Do you really? *Now leave her the fuck alone!*"

Kurt hurls the phone and it smashes against the concrete wall by the bed. He points at her, breathing hard through his nose, but doesn't say anything more. Just lowers his arm and stuffs his bare feet into his sneakers, grabs his coat and leaves.

37

AT FIRST SHE ZONES OUT. Slouched in her sweats, indoor soccer shoes untied, hair pulled back, she's groggy, like she almost always is in Sister Toms's early class, at least at the beginning. This morning she keeps looking down at Hoban's forearm, that sexy golden skin, the wet knit bracelet. It's cold outside, his dark wool coat draped over the back of his chair, but as usual his sleeves are rolled up, and as the talk about *Uncle Tom's Children* starts, she keeps gazing at his arm, that skin she loves to kiss.

But when Sister Toms, in her oversize glasses and beige blazer, says that today for this first part of class they'll discuss the book as a full group and she's wondering, first off—before they focus in again on Wright's vivid portrayal of racism and oppression—what they think about how poverty is depicted, Sara sits up some.

The serious guy up front, the guy with the dark-framed glasses and buzz cut, says, "Wright showed such a *range* of knowledge in terms of the Black experience."

And then another of the expert babblers, Shelby something, agrees with him: "I was curious about Wright's background, so I did some research and . . ."

Sister Toms stands with a patient expression, just listening, and Sara glances at Hoban, who appears to be listening, too, though with a much more tired look.

From her own reading late last night, it seems to her that poor people are pretty much the same most everywhere, no matter their color. At least overall. A lot of the poverty details in the book rang true. She sits there and looks around the classroom. How many of these people understand what it's like being poor, don't see this discussion as mainly an intellectual exercise? Well, for one, there's Hoban, which at first surprised her. The two divorces, single mom, the tiny rental house over on 59th and Halsey. His work-study job in the English Department office, his two student loans, his academic scholarship: being in college definitely wasn't handed to the guy.

Sara listens, Sister Toms occasionally referencing passages in the book, redirecting, and after a time Hoban speaks up: "Poor parents will often buy their kids nice shoes so they won't get made fun of at school. Same with phones."

And this one comment, she witnesses, injects new life into the discussion. The babblers get all riled up again, the buzz-cut ass-munch going on about how when he worked at a youth center "in a rough part of town" . . .

Language. Like Hoban talked about last week, as they were cuddling one night. It's about language. And she agrees. The ability to name things. Find the right words. There's power there, she still feels that in her gut, whenever she stops to think about some of what's been going on these past few months. Language is *everywhere* here, it's like each day she gets drenched in it, every time she goes to one of her classes. There's power that it seems so many people in the world just don't know about, or maybe in some cases don't want to know about. And there's power, too, in starting to see how certain powerful others want to keep people like them from getting a certain amount of power. Because if they get more *literate*, and if they start to see how small their worlds were before, if they begin to realize how easy it is to get a little too used to suffering, a little too used to drama . . . well, the world can start to look a lot different.

IN HOBAN'S MINT-CONDITION blue Chevy Malibu, the ride he inherited from his grandmother, they drive along eating from a bag of raisins and chocolate chips, some Jelly Roll Morton playing through the speakers.

The city gradually fades, and when they turn off the highway in Welches, she cracks her window to smell the mountain air.

"Have you spent much time up here?" she says.

"Used to hike and sled now and then with my cousins. Mostly we'd go down to the beach, though. Rockaway."

She directs him down the road, Hunchback Mountain looming to the east, and at the mouth of the gravel driveway she says, "I'll show you the river in a while." The same old excitement rises in her, as whenever she first sees the house and the gold Oldsmobile with all the stuffed animals in the back window. Sights she described to Hoban last night as they lay holding each other in his bed, Joseph off carousing again.

Inside, the warm air feels dense, the wood stove is going, and when she jokes about the heat, Ernie says, "I told you so, Mama," with a wink at her and Hoban, at which point Val pushes out of her recliner with a grunt. Her bowl of hard candies and mini peanut butter cups beside the chair, the TV still on, the Travel Channel, a show on Caribbean cruises. Beside the candy bowl, one of her Christian romance novels. Val, in her usual outfit of sweatshirt and polyester pants, shuffles over to them in the kitchen and right off tells Hoban to bend down so she can give him a hug.

"There we go now." She leans back, holding on to his upper arms. "Well, you are a good-lookin' young guy, aren't you. Sara wasn't kidding."

"Gram."

"Oh now."

Ernie stands there, fresh from his shop, in his dusty work jeans and jean jacket. Sara sees that his hearing aids aren't in.

"We were down in Sandy yesterday," Val says. "We stopped by Joe's Donuts and picked up some pastries. So help yourself, Lord knows I've had enough."

Ernie, partly lipreading, goes over to the counter and picks up the box, opens it and holds it out. Sara declines, but Hoban says, "Thanks, don't mind if I do," and lifts out a maple bar.

"Those are my favorite, too." Val gives Sara a look. "You can tell something about a person from what kind of pastry they like, you know." She pulls an exaggerated face, brow raised, lips curled down, and Sara can't help but crack a smile.

After Ernie pours the coffee, Val leads them to the front room and tells them to sit on the couch, she wants to hear all about school and soccer. So, while Hoban eats, Sara fields the questions, her grandparents in their recliners across the room, her Gram's hand soon drifting to her candy bowl.

"I was real sorry you gals had to lose that last game," Val says, "but it sure was a fun one to watch, let me tell you. You played well, that was some goal."

Ernie speaks up then, too loud: "Don't think you deserved that yellow card, though. Why'd the ref give it, do you think?"

"He said the slide tackle was from behind. Said he was thinking about a red, actually."

"Well, it looked fair to me."

Sara glances at Hoban, who's still eating, looking around at the photos and needlepoints, and in the pause she thinks of Angus, pictures him sitting on the bench, how he did that the last two games and even during practices, like maybe he wasn't feeling good, or maybe was disappointed in them or tired of them. She'd thought she heard, but wasn't sure, as she was passing by after practice one day, Martin quietly ask Angus if he was still dizzy. But then at practice the next day, Angus seemed to be back in form, having a post-workout competition with Lindsay and Shannon over who could hit the crossbar, shots from eighteen yards out with each foot. Angus won, as always.

"And so what about your classes?" Val resumes the interrogation.

"Good . . ." Sara nods and doesn't look at Hoban this time. She faces her Gramps instead. "Up for a walk to the river? Shake out the legs?"

Ernie gets up and says he needs to visit "the north forty" first, and when he's gone Val starts peppering Hoban with questions. Where he grew up, where his mom lives, which classes he's taking, how he met Sara. Hoban, calm, friendly, sips at his coffee and answers everything clearly, and it's apparent to Sara that her Gram approves, that pursed-lipped smile.

After a considerable while, Ernie emerges from the bathroom. "Well, let's get your coat on there, lady! Get these two lovebirds to the great outdoors!"

"Oh now, it's too wet out there for me, you guys go on ahead. I'll just wait here."

That sudden flicker of comfortable sadness on her Gram's face, Sara notices. Yet again there seems to be no other reason for it than part of her must enjoy wearing her hair shirt.

And so they hike to the river without her, her Gramps looking small next to Hoban. The grey light low in the woods, the trail moist and springy underfoot, the river sound growing with every few steps. She likes how her Gramps gets quiet on the walk, he's always done that. When she asked him why one time, he said with a half smile that he was in church and you don't talk loud in church, right?

At river's edge they stop on the rocks and she sees how Hoban takes it all in as well, just breathing, checking out the mossy limbs, the old man's beard lichen. The woods rising on the other bank. Her Gramps stands there with his hands in his jean jacket pockets, and she remembers him telling her about the nurse logs and flipping over rocks for her and Elaine and Rachel, pointing out miniature creatures with his thick fingers, holding wriggling worms in those same fingers, teaching her how to hook a worm and then cast it into the water, like how he used to cast into Johnson Creek not that far from Lents when he was a boy, "back when it ran clear." She remembers him talking more than once, while pointing out all the dead leaves alongside the river, about "the pretty side of death." Nature's "hard consolation." The leaves and the nurse logs, sure, but also Mount Hood's age, the constant change all around, the cycles, beneath and on the surface, and all the seen and unseen creatures.

And now Hoban gets to see it, and it makes her proud. Definitely. She glances at her Gramps again and sees that he's still gazing at the river, and, yes, she loves this place like he loves it. This river that'll flow on long after she dies. This ancient ground, everything so alive all around them. This place *hums* with life. It's cold, it's grey and drizzly, and God knows she and Hoban both have tons of schoolwork, but here . . . everything slows down. You can breathe.

"I'm thinking there'll be an early snow," her Gramps says, his voice measured, and she and Hoban look over at him. "Could be some ice storms in town, too." He turns his head and grins at Hoban. "Used to dread those babies, my goodness. Have to get up there and fix the snapped lines."

She keeps listening, but faces the river once more. The phone company days, the good old storm stories she grew up hearing. She listens and breathes, her body relaxed now, all the school tension feels like it's evaporating from her head and limbs into the sky, seeping from her feet down into the loam, and her Gramps's voice blends with the river, here at this spot in the world where she feels most at home.

Before long, her Gramps catches her eye and says he should get on back to the shop, "give you lovebirds some space to smooch."

"Still working on those cats?" she says, battling a blush.

Ernie, already heading back up the trail, looks over his shoulder, smiling. "A man needs his projects."

In the stillness again, they pick out two side-by-side moss-padded rocks and sit, Hoban taking her cue again about quieting down. She loves that he seems to get it, she was wondering how he would be up here, and so she reaches over and takes his hand and gives it a squeeze. As they stare out at the water, she thinks of going to the beach with him next weekend, how he invited her to stay at his aunt's half-built cabin in Rockaway, just the two of them, and she wonders if she'll sleep with him then. They've only kissed so far, and she's enjoyed that, but at times she also thinks of Kim. The feel of her. The taste of her kisses.

Holding Hoban's warming hand, she watches the river and remembers sitting right here with Kim, both of them quiet, observant. Here in this place where death can look pretty, where breath comes so easy, and all around them, above and below, within them, too, life hums.

38

ERNIE'S ALWAYS BEEN LIKE THIS. Has to have a project going. Can't just sit around.

Back in the shop, he surveys the three boxes full of finished cat door-stops, the box of twirling wooden bumblebees, the tools hanging on the pegboard, all the coffee cans full of hinges and brackets, and then settles in again at the table saw, no earplugs in, and soon finishes cutting out another cat head. He screws the parts together, thinking of Sara and Hoban by the river, how he seems like a decent kid, Hoban, and how Sara seems happy.

It's like this much of the time, the careful attention to what he's doing, the craftwork, but also the drifting mind. It helps to work, but the mind never quite stops.

It's time for the final step, and so he takes the cat over to his paint station on one of the heavy wooden tables and starts in, his hand holding the brush almost tenderly. Slow, steady strokes. He paints the toes and whiskers and eyebrows, concentrating, in the moment, yet once more the thoughts come along.

It's his mother this time, as happens here now and then when he paints. Her tole painting. Her hands. Those long-fingered hands that seemed like they would always be in the world, that so suddenly one day were no more. The aneurysm. Dead on the kitchen floor. He was eleven, the one to come in from playing outside and find her there. His world, just like that, gone.

So, yes, it had helped to stay busy, almost his whole life. The long years of being a lineman, the hours of free time spent in his shop, first in Lents, then up here. He'd always been working, always, and with Keith—here he is again, in his head, his son—with Keith, it's true, he'd been walled off a lot of the time. Preoccupied. (Exactly how he's trying *not* to be with his grandkids.) The thing is, he had never, from what he can remember, told the boy he was a good guy. Just didn't know how to say something like that. His own father had never said it to him, the man grief-numbed as he was, alternately sullen and angry. Still, that was no excuse.

Ernie paints. Tries to focus on the cat's eyes. A speck of white in the black, that glimmer.

But then Keith had made his own decisions in life, sure enough. Got his girlfriend pregnant at sixteen, for one. Chose a job where the pay wasn't that good. Chose not to get himself more education. Got into petty crime, then bigger crime, got busted, got divorced. He'd strayed from the virtuous path, strayed from the Good Lord, tried to take short-cuts too often in his life, and then? Well, he reaped the consequences. It worked like that, life. Though some stuff, granted, wasn't a person's fault. For example, an aneurysm.

He finishes painting the cat, sets it in the metal rack to dry and begins cleaning up. But Keith lingers in his mind. Maybe it's having Sara up here, he's not sure, but the Keith thoughts are strong. One of those days.

To say he misses him is about as light as you can put it probably. There isn't a day that passes where he doesn't wonder what all he could've done different, apart from talk more. How he could've guided the boy better. He'd always told himself that his own life and how he lived it, or at least tried to, would be the best teaching tool as a parent, and while that wasn't a wrong way to think, the fact of the matter was, Keith had needed him to say certain things at certain times. To make more of an effort there. The boy needed to feel comfortable enough to *ask questions*, any question he felt like asking, because boys had a hell of a lot of questions, just like girls did, and God knows he'd wanted his own dad to talk more, but instead the man went and retreated behind his walls.

Each day, each night at prayer time, he thinks of his son. Prays the guy will find his way finally. It's the same prayer, always.

He goes on cleaning, sweeping the shop like he does every day, making sure the tools are all ready for tomorrow's work.

It's the truth, hell: As the day of Keith's release approached last year, he got real excited. More than excited. Val was the same, of course. That mix of emotions, boiling inside of him, surges of it. Excitement, anxiety, anger, mercy, you name it . . . It was wrong to have not contacted the guy while he was in prison. Wrong to be so stubborn. Always returning to the safe thought that it was Keith's job to contact them. Downright silly, when it came down to it, yet there it was. Himself and Val about as stubborn as they come, like a couple of old badgers up here in the hills. (Maybe it was why the Good Lord brought them together all those years ago.)

Before hitting the lights, he stands in the doorway, the chill drifting in. He slips his hands down into his jacket pockets. A clean shop: one of the best sights in the world, no doubt about it.

The crazy thing? It still feels like it's in Keith's court. Even now. Even though the guy wrote a couple of times from prison, saying how he was on a better track and all, it still feels like it's in his court to apologize in a better way, for what all happened. For the shame it brought to all of them. Because that's the thing, right there, the shame of it. How it is to have people ask if you have kids and not be able to lie, and when they ask what it is he does, to have to say, *Well, he's sort of taken a hard path*, and then hope the questioning stops there.

So yes. It's still in Keith's court. And here the guy is, a year out, and hasn't once called them. Not one time. The wrongness of that, sharper with each passing day it seems like. And so you're damn right it helps to stay busy.

He pulls the door closed and on the way back over to the house sees that Sara and Hoban are still by the river.

Here he is, a man in his late fifties, but he moves (and probably acts, fair enough) like a much older man. Sore as hell from all those years of climbing poles, it feels like he has the body of an eighty-year-old. He pauses and looks at the little house all lit up inside, the windows bright in the forest dim: how *long* he'd dreamt of this arrangement up here. Their own place in the woods, their own claim in the world, nothing fancy, but enough space where he could have a decent-size shop, where he could take his walks to the river each day and give his thanks. This beauty before him, all around him, reaching his heart, more often than not. Watching that river, my goodness: how the self could just melt away almost entirely sometimes, right into that flow. This sweet place by the river. For so many years he'd worked and worked, and now, by God, it's time to feel happy and blessed.

If only it were that easy.

39

THE DAYS TUMBLE AND BLUR, and whenever Kurt hits her it feels to her like she might detonate. But still, she stays in the basement. Reading whenever he crashes. Lying on the bed, his plaything, whenever he soars. His gums have started to bleed, he's stopped taking regular showers, and from time to time he claims that bugs are crawling over his arms; but nothing stops him every few days from going out again to score more crank.

When he does leave, she tortures herself about what to do. She could make a break for it, just get away, then think what to do next, where to go. As for Sheila, Kurt's mom, she's normally at work, either at the auto supply store or at the New Copper Penny, and when she is home, the woman is clueless as usual, drunk or sound asleep. He says that if she tells his mom he'll kill her, and those words, the way he says them, always keep her in place.

Good Rachel, stay. Stay. That's a good girl.

She tells herself she's weak, weaker than she ever knew, and stupid, too. She should just text Elaine from Kurt's phone and tell her everything, text Sara maybe; but no, she cannot get them into this shit. God knows what Sara would do, what trouble she'd get her own self in. She has to figure this out on her own, she got herself into this. Stubborn gets what stubborn deserves.

Maybe, though? Maybe he'll ease up. He'll get help. She keeps telling him he can get help, he doesn't have to do this, look at what he's doing to both himself and her, look at their lives now, is this *really* what he wants? He often hits her then. Her face, neck, chest. Ribs one time. She curls into a ball on the bed, waiting it out, and usually he tires before long, grabs his jacket, stuffs his gargantuan smelly feet into his shoes, and leaves.

Like a few minutes ago.

She stands topless in front of the mirror in the bathroom, eyeing the bruises along her left collarbone, her chest. She gingerly pulls down her underwear and sits on the toilet, unable to weep this time, still shaking. No sounds from upstairs, his mom at the nightclub by now.

She's late. She's always been on time, but she's late. Going on six days.

After a while she goes and puts on some clothes, digs out her knit hat from her bag on the floor by her piles of books, pulls on her heavy black Goodwill coat, and at the bottom of the stairs pauses and listens. Nothing. Just the fridge hum, faint, beyond the basement door.

Upstairs, the house is dark except for the front room, the floor lamp is on in there, on its low setting. She peeks in. The blue couch, the puffy maroon easy chair. Photos on the wall around the TV, most of them of Kurt as a boy. Kurt in his baseball uniform, crouched, glove ready. Kurt in fifth grade, grinning big, his front teeth a mess. She steps back into the kitchen and looks out into the dark backyard. She waits there for a bit, hearing him say he'll kill her, envisioning his face whenever he says that, Kurt scratching at his forearms.

When she steps out into the cold evening, the air feels like it's slightly lacerating her lungs and she breathes in deeper, nostrils flared. It's been just over two weeks since she's been outside.

She walks fast, chin tucked down into her coat, and in the awful, brightly lit pharmacy grabs a test kit off the shelf, the first one she spots, pays, and pushes the box into a pocket and ducks back out into the night. It occurs to her how incredibly good it feels to move her legs, to feel the sharp air on her face, but then she hears him in her head again and picks up the pace.

Back down in the bathroom, she takes the test and waits there in the basement. He'll come back with a fresh baggie. He'll smoke. He'll want to make up. Another interminable session. Her faking, over and over, trying to get him off.

The stick clearly has a blue line on it.

She takes another test. Blue line.

There's an icy-warm sensation in her abdomen, like her guts are melting. Face slack, she stands in the shadow by the furnace and gazes at the rumpled bed in the pool of lamplight, all her books over there, her bag, their dirty clothes in piles, and after a long time, still just gazing, she hears the door open right above her.

Heavy steps in the kitchen. The faucet turning on, then off. His boots on the stairs now, descending.

PART THREE

40

FOR MOST OF THEM it's their last night, tomorrow they'll catch the flight home, and the mood at their long table in the raucous Stiegl-Keller matches the overall mood of the entire trip so far. This new level of closeness and commitment on the team, this realization that, for the most part, they actually like each other. Which remains striking at times, for Sara especially, now that Lindsay and Siena are graduated and gone.

The beer hall, tucked up against the forested hill capped by the massive grey fortress, this packed hall with its surreal view out the large windows of spires and domes, resounds with songs, most in German, some in English. Dozens of hoisted mugs. Angus is down at the far end of the table with his wife and kids and also Martin and his wife and kids, Letti with her girlfriend, Jason flying solo, all the adults rosy-cheeked and happy, while the kids chatter and chirp, dipping their käsekrainers into globs of mustard.

Sara, short-haired, tanned, lean, drinks more lager and listens in to Olivia and Sophie Mack and Hailey Winters nearby, something about heading out soon to a mellower place for a nightcap.

"You in?" Olivia says, nudging her shoulder, and Sara nods.

Before they leave, though, she takes in the hall again, wanting to capture it in her body. The smells of schnitzel, fries, sausages, and beer. The songs, a chorus of drunken *"Du, du liegst mir im Herzen"* nearby. The feel of her liter-mug in hand, the lager nearly gone. She looks around and sees people smoking out on the patio: my *God* this city makes her want to smoke, there's something about it; though, all right, she also felt like smoking now and then in Munich and Vienna, after the matches were over and they were out touring around, drinking some beers. But there'll be none of that, there's no way she's smoking in front of Olivia, not after she asked her last winter to please get on her ass about smoking, help her quit, help her get through those seemingly endless moments of weakness. Hectic as last year was, barely passing her classes as she did, and with all the shit with Lindsay and Siena, plus all the shit at home, it was a hairy bitch to quit smoking. But Angus demanded it.

So here they are, then. In Europe. It's still insane to her. She's in Salzburg, Austria, eating schnitzel, drinking good beer with her friends, her coaches down there celebrating a successful trip, the three games they played against German and Austrian women's teams, this nine-day tour. Here she is with her better body these days, sixteen pounds dropped since early last fall, with her more chiseled face and abs and legs, her sassy short haircut that Olivia gave her in May after finals were over. Everything still seems dream-like at times.

As for the team, it feels to her like it'll be a decent season. The camaraderie mainly. The vibe. They're young, but they've also got serious speed and toughness and, with the likes of Sophie and Hailey, some serious talent, they went two-and-one against the Euro women. Angus lined all this up, took care of the funding, this is the first time he's done this, and look at the man, he's clearly in high spirits, laughing with his pretty wife, Emily, probably relieved this all turned out okay, shepherding nineteen loony girls all this way, bloody hell. The Grahams will stay on in Europe for a few days, then hit England, visit some family for a while before getting back to the States in time to get ready for training camp.

She watches him for another moment, like she has often over these past nine days. How he interacts with his kids, Charles, age seven, Skye, five, how he usually looks them in the eye when he talks to them, and how he takes the time to stop and teach them about what they're seeing. Like yesterday, on the walking tour of Salzburg's Old Town, over the cobblestones and into churches, a cemetery, an outdoor market. In front of the cathedral, though, it was her whom he approached, as the guide went on yammering.

Angus stood beside her for a minute there at the back of the group, hands clasped behind his back, shades propped on his head, gazing up like everyone else, and then glanced sidelong at her and gave a quick wink. "We belong here, too. Don't forget it." Then he went back over to his wife and kids.

It's true, she knows: he's like her second dad. As she looks away and tilts back the last of her bier, the hall booming with song and joy, it's a silent, solo toast to him.

AFTER STOPPING OFF AT A NEARBY BAR in a cave that's been carved from the fortress-capped Mönchsberg rock, after another liter each of Stiegl and a final shot of plum schnapps, Sara suggests they climb the stone steps right outside the door and go find a view before heading back across the river to the hotel.

Olivia, Sophie, and Hailey, all equally buzzed, gabbing, agree it's not time for bed, the night is warm and they're in Salzburg, and so up the steps they go, onto the wooded Mönchsberg. As they hike, Olivia and Sophie start hurling Shakespearean insults at each other, from the Elizabethan lit class they took last semester.

Sophie: "Thou art a gleeking, rump-fed maltworm."

Olivia: "Thou art a bootless, hedge-born measle."

A needed pause near the top of the steps, Sophie has a fine cackle going tonight.

As they hike on, the banter eventually dies off some, Sara still blindly leading the way, and after a time they curve along the hill's ridge, the city glimmering off to their right in glimpses through the trees. They come to a clearing finally, to some benches that overlook the scene below, and when Sara sits, the others do also.

"Holy crap." She stares out at the illuminated fortress, the cathedral, the churches.

"God, I'm fucked up," Hailey says. "You guys fucked up as I am?"

"I'm pretty fucked up," Sophie says.

And then they all quiet down as if caught up in some kind of spell. Summer night, the air still balmy, the scent of cooling green up here in the woods. This view. It mesmerizes Sara, accentuated as it is by the burst of drunken exercise.

How *surreal*. How many times has she thought of that word lately?

In the stillness, they each fall into themselves, and she thinks of Rachel's due date in three weeks. What she'll do, where she'll live. How she ran from Kurt Draker's house one night and finally made her way home, her face and neck all bruised. How she dropped out of Franklin in April. The thought makes her calves flex as she sits there on the bench beside Olivia, and she can hear Hailey breathing from the mouth down at the other end.

She thinks of Elaine, how large she is now, and then their mom, the woman more on edge than ever, what with Rachel back at home, what with all of Kurt's continuing bullshit. It was crazy, living at home those two and a half weeks earlier this month, that feeling almost the entire time of walking on eggshells, at any second Rachel and their mom could start going at it again.

So clear, clearer than ever: the never-ending *drama* in her family. And so the questions remain. How do you bridge those worlds? How do you engage your family with all its dramas and complaints, all the same old issues? You go out into the world and find yourself changing, in big and small ways, you experience so *much*, new ideas, new emotions, in such a short time, and then *bam*—you go back, even for just the short visits, and it's like at times you meet your old self who never left, who stayed back there, trapped in the old ways, all that suffering, maybe even proud of that shit. It's like the Thomas Jefferson quote Sister Toms wrote on the board that one time: "Travel makes you wiser but less happy." Some truth there, Tom, old boy.

She looks out beyond the Old Town to the smattering of lights at the city's edge, over across the dark river, and wonders who lives out there. Looks back down at the cathedral and hears the tour guide in her head saying how it was bombed during World War II. Her throat's dry, she's forgotten all evening to drink water as well.

She had to escape to Kim's after a while. Part of her felt bad about that, leaving home yet again, not being able to handle even a short visit, especially with what Rachel was going through, but it was either leave or start blowing up herself and adding to the tension, making things worse for poor Adam.

At Kim's, things were all right at first. Some drives downtown, some Journey, a few beers. Yet while they slept in Kim's bed and even kissed a few times, they didn't *quite* ever connect, in all ways. There in bed, especially after they'd had a fun night out cruising, part of her had wanted to go further now and then, badly, just block out everything and feel her, but they never did. It just, for her at least, didn't feel quite right. She told her all about Hoban, and she'd already told Hoban about Kim, in early June, when they went down to Cape Lookout, that three-night camping trip where they had sex in the tent, in the woods, on the beach in the dark.

She pictures Hoban shirtless in the tent. His lithe body and golden skin, his bushy hair. She pictures Kim in her white tank top, slipping into bed, the room candle-lit and nice-smelling. To both of these images, her body responds, and as she looks out at the fairy-tale view, she wants them both here with her, but maybe one at a time, come to think of it. Talk about an awesome place to kiss someone.

Sophie rises, walks over into the woods nearby, and vomits. Hailey and Olivia start heckling her, and Sophie lets out a cackle between hurls. Sara tells her to keep it down over there, Jesus, then takes a last look at the domes and spires, the castle, and the labyrinth of streets.

She's actually here, staring out at this scene, while her family is on the other side of the planet. Sara Garrison, her, getting up off this bench. Home so far, so close.

41

IN HER BEDROOM, sitting up in bed, the application on her nightstand where it's been since Sara left on her trip, Elaine opens her third and final granola bar and listens.

They're at it again, this time about which show to watch next, and Rachel says it doesn't even matter anyway, she's going to bed. But their mom won't let it go. While it's clear that their mom is trying to keep her voice down because Adam's already asleep, it's also clear that the woman wants to get into it tonight.

"Yeah, yeah," Rachel says, coming down the hallway.

"Just run away, like you're so good at."

Elaine hears Rachel turn around.

"Oh my God, what is the *matter* with you? Seriously. You've got some kind of—"

"*Me?*"

And they're off. How Adam sleeps through it, she has no idea. But he does. He's been a lot quieter lately, though. It's getting to him, too, even though he's glad to have Rachel around.

Careful with the empty wrapper, she slips it back into the box, gets up and hides the box in the dresser. Still some other snacks in there among the underwear and socks, an Almond Joy, a bag of chips, small bag of peanuts. But no more tonight. She needs to try to get some sleep, she's working extra time tomorrow, Rayette asked her to take part of Odell's shift, too. Mouse duty.

The house is broiling, this afternoon it got up to ninety-four outside, and their mom still won't let them open any windows. Better to be hot, she says, and get at least some sleep than have the windows unlocked and get none. But the little fan atop the dresser helps some, Sara's old fan, and before getting back into bed she makes sure the breeze is pointed in exactly the right direction.

"This is so exhausting, do you have any idea?" Rachel says out in the hall.

"A pretty clear one," Melanie answers.

In the dark, Elaine pulls off her damp T-shirt and lies down in just her underwear, the sheets pushed all the way down the bed, the warm breeze hitting her legs and midriff and breasts. She listens to them more, for a while, Rachel repeatedly returning to the hallway threshold to sling more words, like she can't help herself, and then finally their voices stop and there's only the low TV noise, Rachel off to bed it seems.

Elaine stares at the ceiling.

What a summer. Her big summer after graduating. Rachel back home, the restraining order on Kurt, Adam uptight. Their mom so protective of Rachel, while at the same time all haunted by the pregnancy and pissed off and even more on edge because of everything with Kurt, to say nothing about her still taking lots of extra shifts at Fred Meyer. It's like she's trying to see just how stressed out she can make herself and everyone else.

But then there's also what she told her about the college money. There's that. It was graduation night, out in front of Franklin right after the ceremony, and in the crowd her mom pulled her aside for a minute and told her how she'd saved up some money from all those extra shifts, for her to use for college if she wanted it. It definitely wasn't much, she said, but if she chose the college route, and she hoped she did, then the money was hers for the taking. Her voice was subdued, almost shy, as she said this. But then Adam escaped from Rachel and ran up, and Melanie shook it off and said it was time for the promised stop at Baskin-Robbins on the way home, and they haven't discussed it since.

She lies there and eventually hears the TV go off. Hears her mom get up out of her chair and shuffle off to bed.

In the sweltering dim, she turns her head and looks at the Mt. Hood Community College application there on the nightstand, illuminated by the alarm clock's red numbers, the pages Sara printed for her, and she wishes that Sara were still here, those two and a half weeks flew by, she'd loved how most nights they stayed up and talked for a while like they used to. About UP, about Marshall, about her year at Franklin. Rachel and Kurt. Adam. Their mom. They talked and talked, and Sara was the same, but different, too. She talked a little differently, for one thing.

Seemed a little more patient maybe. She definitely *looked* different, that was for sure. Her hair, her body.

Elaine eyes the application, it's still not filled out, then faces the ceiling again, sweat running down her temples and cheeks, beading on her upper lip.

Why exactly hasn't she filled it out? Like Sara said, just fill the thing out, send it in, go meet with a financial aid person, and get on with it. *What's stopping you?*

It's been one hell of a spring and summer, though. There's no getting around that. Rachel being home, all the madness with Kurt, like how last February when he finally found out she was pregnant he hit her over and over, commanded her to have an abortion, and it was then that she escaped at last one night when he was out, and soon after got the restraining order, when he started showing up here.

Early on, Rachel knew she was keeping the baby. She's still very pro-choice, she said, but after sitting day after day in that basement thinking about how she'd been on the pill and everything, it "must've been meant to be." Sort of surprising to hear her say that, but there it was. She said how, with all the changes in her body, even early on, she was "in awe of the process." There was this connection, "something primal," with that child inside her, and when she had the ultrasound and saw those pictures, that only cemented the decision.

At first Rachel didn't want anyone to know beyond her, Sara, and their mom. All winter and all spring, she said to not tell Gramps and Gram, or their dad, it was still too embarrassing, she needed time to think. Now, though, with the baby almost here, she says it's okay if people know, and while she called Gramps and Gram yesterday and finally told them the news, Gram apparently supportive and all, she says she can't be the one to tell their dad, it just feels like too much right now and she's not sure what he'll say. Would she, Elaine, maybe tell him for her? Could she do that?

And so that's where that was left.

She'll meet him the day after tomorrow, at the coffeehouse where they usually go, and she'll tell him, yes. Tell him he's going to be a grandpa. She'll try to do that.

She arches her neck and looks out the locked window, the clear night sky up through the black backyard maple, and after a time runs a hand over her slick belly. She looks down at her breasts, her gigantic splayed thighs. Glances again at the application, then over at Sara's bed. The house is so still and she's not done eating, she realizes.

Quietly as she can, her bed whining, she gets up and goes to the dresser.

42

KEITH UNCLIPS THE LEASH and lets Bear wander off to sniff at trees, and in the warm late morning Courtney slips her hand into his as they walk through the grass. Kids and parents are over at the playground and there's a soccer game going near the band shell, guys playing pickup, but otherwise the park is open, plenty of room for Bear to explore, plenty of privacy for him to stop and kiss Courtney's mouth.

"You know what I want?" she says, looking up at him, smiling.

"More nookie?"

"That too." She gives him another kiss and they start walking again. "I want for us to take a trip. I've got some vacation time coming up."

Keith tracks Bear up ahead, the dog taking no interest in a taunting squirrel.

"Sounds good. Where'd you have in mind?"

"I don't know. Someplace with palm trees maybe. It's been a long time since I've seen a palm tree."

He holds her hand and they keep strolling. In the pause he thinks of how he's never laid eyes on a palm tree, ever.

"What do you think?" she says. "Could you get the time off, maybe this fall or winter?"

"Depends how long."

"A week maybe?"

His lips curl downward and he finds himself nodding, still watching the dog. He notices how his pulse seems faster, he can feel it in his throat slightly. "I could probably swing that. I'd have to see."

She squeezes his hand and starts talking about Mexico and the Caribbean, and while he listens at first, soon he's half listening, thinking about Friday night, how he had beers with Bruce and how Bruce talked about a guy over in his neighborhood who must've come into some money somehow because he just bought "this beauty of a boat," a tricked-out Sea-Doo Speedster. Bruce: "Sumbitch's got twin supercharged engines, four hundred and thirty horsepower." The neighbor drives a new Navigator, too, and here's what he, Keith Alan Garrison, knows: Bruce wants to hit that house, or at least the garage, for that boat. Bruce has a pal out in Estacada where they can take it and hide it, "Terry'll paint the thing, he'll do a nice job on the serial numbers, then we resell the bitch for around $30K, maybe more, and what we do is just split it three ways, cool $10K each. Beyond easy."

The crazy thing? He found himself listening. Like just now. A trip to Grand Cayman, on a landscaper's salary? Hey, no problemo.

Bear begins to slow down, drifting over closer to them again, and Courtney's still talking about travel possibilities, she's excited now. He holds her hand. Under a humongous fir, she stops and smiles up at him again and says, "What do you think?" Her full lips parted, a thin band of sunlight across one of her smooth cheekbones.

"One thing I think is you're about as pretty as they come."

This makes her get onto her tiptoes and kiss him long and deep, and as he loses himself in the kiss he can feel once more how she wants to be with him, and how he wants to be with her, there's this real affection they have, this care with each other, like they know how fast things can change if the wrong words get said, if certain lines get crossed, and they've lived long enough and through enough to understand this in their bones.

"Well, we should make it happen," he says, and she lets out a giddy laugh.

Bear leashed up, they start heading back to the apartment, and as Courtney talks more about possible destinations, comparing, thinking aloud about research plans, whether or not to talk to a travel agent maybe, and as they pass the playground where he used to play when he was a boy, where his parents used to take him, this wholesome, regular, honest neighborhood scene, he tells himself that he'll stick to what he told Bruce on Friday night, *No thanks*. Because this life, right here, it has to work. He'll keep on working, saving up, stay on the right side of life. And for inspiration, beyond the daily thoughts of his girls? All he has to do is look at this lady here beside him.

AT THE CAFE IN THE AFTERNOON, he gets there first like he usually does, except for that first time when Sara came also, and after getting his cup of black coffee he sits down at one of the window tables and waits.

The place is about half-full, the day still warm and sunny, and like she normally does, Elaine comes in ten minutes late, gives him a shy wave, and then goes up and orders her latte.

As she stands up there at the counter, he watches her now and then, noticing how she's taken to wearing more billowy clothing these days, like today, that button-down black shirt out over flared grey sweatpants. Her face is rosy, like usual after her walk down here, but as she carries her mug toward him he sees that she looks especially nervous, a lot like that first time, coming up on two years ago now, when she barely said a word. Dark semicircles under her eyes, too.

"How do?" he says.

Elaine settles into her chair, takes a drink, and has a hard time meeting his gaze.

"Everything all right? You look like—"

"Rachel's pregnant."

He stares at her. No words come.

"She's due in two and a half weeks, actually. She didn't want people to know."

Elaine reaches again for her latte and looks out the window, and for a few seconds longer he only stares at her.

"She all right?" he says, and sees something pass behind her eyes when she turns her head and glances at him. Some real fear there. "What is it?"

Her face flushes even more, and she takes another sip. "Her boyfriend, ex-boyfriend, hasn't been much help."

"What's the guy's name again?"

"Kurt."

"Is he in the picture still or—"

"He won't leave her alone. She doesn't want anything to do with him." Elaine stops herself. She's more flustered now, cheeks blazing. "She just wanted me to tell you about the baby is all. She wanted you to know. It's a boy."

Legs tensed under the table, he watches her. Their surroundings gone.

"What do you mean he won't leave her alone?"

"I shouldn't have brought that up. He just—"

"Has he hurt her at all?"

After a few moments, Elaine's eyes begin to fill, but he only keeps watching her. Toes curled in his boots.

"He hit her when he found out. He didn't want her to keep it."

She gathers herself and takes another sip. He tries to take a deep breath through his nose.

"What's his last name?"

"Why?"

"Just, what is it. I'm curious is all."

"Draker. Kurt Draker. They dated for a long time." She suddenly seems startled that she uttered his full name, and for several beats afterward focuses on her latte. She tilts it up, nearly killing it off. Some foam lingering on her upper lip.

He motions at his own lip, and Elaine, with a dazed, drained expression, wipes her mouth with the back of her hand.

AFTER HUGGING HER OUT FRONT, thanking her for telling him, telling her to hang in there, it'll be all right, try to get some rest, he sets out along 92nd again, glad he decided to travel on foot this afternoon. He needs to walk some more, clear his head. He stops to light a cigarette, the familiar neighborhood sights lost on him, and once again senses something risen up inside of him that he hasn't felt for a good while now. The facts.

He walks and smokes, heart still beating in his throat, and those two words keep floating through him. *The facts.* And what are the facts?

Redneck walking along a street, the sun hitting his back, his bald spot. Vehicles keep gliding by, there's the freeway hum, the world going on as it always does, and a boy has hit one of his daughters. His pregnant daughter. The boy is still harassing her, scaring her. A boy with a restraining order against him is scaring his family.

Fact: guy walking in Lents on a summer afternoon, heading home. A guy smoking, thinking.

43

RACHEL'S SORE. Her back this morning, mostly. And tired, like almost always now.

It's hard to get out of bed, even though she already did, earlier, to help get Adam ready for daycare. The house is quiet and warm, it's much cooler outside, it would help to open a window, but she doesn't dare.

It's as if she's a shut-in these days. Up until a month ago, she went out occasionally, but even then, she often thought she saw Kurt. Once at the coffeehouse with Elaine, in April, right after she stopped going to school altogether—it looked just like him, loping past the windows, the baggy dark clothes. Then, two weeks later, when she badly needed to escape the house, escape her mother, she went for a walk and saw Anthony Ferris's dad's grey Ford Tempo parked at the end of the block, near the apartments, both Anthony and Kurt inside, from what she could tell. As she turned back for the house, the Tempo started up, then drove off in the other direction.

It's 10:40 a.m. and she needs to eat, the baby's stirring. She gets up bleary, huge, and slow, her brown bangs flopping into her eyes, and looks through the blinds out at the empty street, as is her habit these days. No one. No Tempo.

The first time he came to the house, a Thursday afternoon in May, Kurt knocked and knocked until finally she peeked out the front window, Elaine off behind her, phone in hand. He looked wasted, there on the porch, and when he saw her, he came over to the window and said that they needed to talk. His face was pallid, almost ghoulish, and his gums were dark, and that night, when Elaine let it slip that he showed up, that's when their mom called the police and they got the restraining order soon after.

Hands pressed to her yowling lower back, she waddles in her robe to the kitchen, pours another bowl of the generic raisin bran, and takes the last of the OJ. Sits down spraddle-legged at the kitchen table.

The house is silent. She chews and looks out at the living room. The front door. Her mom's chair and TV tray. The old brown carpet. She should've turned on the stereo, but she's not getting up right now, so it's just her and her thoughts here for a couple minutes.

Sara's back in town from her trip but staying out at UP, doing some part-time work with the groundskeeping crew out there, a gig that her coach apparently arranged. Can't blame her. Two weeks in this nuthouse and you're ready for absolutely whatever, just about.

And then there's Ken, her image of him sitting on his bench there in the South Park Blocks, reading—the scene always seems to calm her down some. Ken with his old sport coat, his books, the neatly packed cart, sitting there with his legs crossed on their bench. Maybe it's the thought of books that helps soothe her also, and what she'll do right after breakfast of course is go on back to the bedroom, get into bed, and read. This is the routine.

She hears herself chewing, swallowing in the dense quiet.

Her dad knows now, it's official. He's already texted her a couple of times, saying how he'll support her no matter what, and each of those two texts made her bawl.

At length she rises, sets her bowl and glass in the sink. Goes over to the front window and peers through the blinds and tells herself yet again: it's batshit ridiculous, this habit. It's like she's some heinously wacked-out paranoid, look at her, seventeen years old, massively pregnant, here at eleven in the morning in her robe. Then again, after the note last week, it's understandable, spying like this.

The slip of paper was sticking out from under the doormat, and Adam was the first to spot it. He handed it to Elaine, who came back into the house and showed it to her. Lined notebook paper, a torn half page, folded over. Blue ink.

Time to talk, Rachel. YOU KNOW IT IS.

That was all it said. No signature.

Was he high when he wrote it? High when he delivered it? Was he on foot? And what time was it when he was standing right over there on their front porch, ten feet away from where she was sleeping in a room with her little brother?

Part of her still wants to show the note to her mom, ask if they should let the police know. But there's no way, it would throw the woman over the top, and the baby's due so soon, any day. Her baby boy, getting ready to come into this world.

She stands there a while longer, then lets go of the dusty blinds.

44

LIKE MORE OFTEN LATELY, Sara wakes in a good mood. Today she's up before Olivia even, and their view of Forest Park on this early September morning looks especially clear to her. Other residents of Mehling Hall stir, the day is sunny, and her American Lit class with Sister Toms starts in just under an hour.

In the shower, running her bar of soap over her abdomen, she wonders if Hoban is up already, imagines his room over in Villa, the room he's sharing with Joseph and Bö again. They're in a good spot, the two of them, sleeping together but taking it slowly, hanging out but not suffocating each other, and that's another thing that has her in rhythm these days. She's in the best shape of her life, things with Hoban are smooth, the team won its first game last week, and even life on the family front is a bit more stable now, at least from what she can tell.

Like most mornings, she luxuriates in the hot water. (No need to cut it short. No water or heat bill to worry about.) She stands there, face tilted up under the stream, and thinks of how Gramps and Gram offered to take Rachel in and how Rachel took little Ben up there last week. From their phone call yesterday, she gathers that it's a lot calmer in Welches, even though Gram's driving Rachel mildly crazy with all the fussing. "But at least it's not as bad as Mom's fussing," Rachel said. Rachel building her strength back up, taking Ben for walks in the woods even.

In American Lit, she sits beside Hoban and listens to Sister Toms introduce *The Sun Also Rises*. The Paris expat scene, the festival in Pamplona. She's glad she signed up for another class from Sister Toms, but from time to time she glances down at Hoban's tanned, veined hand on the desk just inches away. She wants to slip her hand into his but doesn't, and it seems that he's aware of this desire. It's like he's teasing her, he knows how she feels about his hands, he just keeps his hand there, taunting, distracting from some genuinely interesting words coming from the front of the room. The beautiful bastard.

After class, as usual, they hold hands on the short pathway over to Franz Hall, where she'll head off to her Media and Society class, and he'll go to his astronomy class, these their last few minutes together on Tuesdays and Thursdays until the evening homework session in one of their rooms.

"That was cool what Toms told at the end there," she says. "That quote. What was it again?"

"We are all apprentices in a craft where no one ever becomes a master."

"That's right."

"From a guy who won a Nobel Prize in Literature."

"I know, right?"

Here on a college campus, she thinks, talking about Hemingway with her hot, smart partner, walking to their next classes. Sometimes, like right now, it still hits her. Strange, though, how since late last spring probably, it seems to happen less.

"See you tonight?" Hoban says.

They share a quick kiss just inside the building, and she likes how they don't say, "I love you," too much, don't cheapen it with overuse. While they began saying that over the summer, at the beach on their camping trip was the first time, there in the tent, and while they haven't laid down any rules about saying those words, they have this mellow, sort of graceful understanding.

ON THE STROLL FROM MEHLING over to practice after her short nap, her mood remains bright like the weather. Have the normal light workout today, talk about tomorrow night's game, then grab a tasty dinner, do some reading, hit the sack at a decent time. Big home game tomorrow against North Carolina, and they don't get much bigger than that. "If you want to be the best, then have the guts to play against the best," as Angus put it.

As for all the reading she has? As for her grades this year? He had this to say, also, at their one-on-one preseason conference two weeks ago: "Just keep your head right." Looked her straight in the eyes. Plenty of worse advice in this world.

The team seems loose to her, confident, maybe the perfect temperature helps, seventy-five degrees, light breeze. But Angus doesn't appear to be quite so laid back today, he keeps stopping the scrimmage and reminding them to "pay attention to the little things." At one point, after

Sophie throws the ball in, Erin Cox trapping it high on her chest, Angus halts the action again, comes back out onto the field, and pauses to look around at each of them. "Throw-ins should preferably be directed toward your teammate's feet, or at least thigh, yeah? Let's go now. All of you. More quality."

He eyes them all once more, the late afternoon sun blazing the side of his face, outlining a rare protruding vein there, and after adjusting his cap to further shield his eyes he walks over to the bench and sits down, something he still hardly ever does.

When play resumes, Sara glances over at him, he's sitting there with his palms pressed against the bench's edge on either side of him, shoulders hunched, and when she looks over there a minute later, Martin is approaching him, saying something she can't hear. On the following trip downfield, she hears Letti Heath say, "Oh my God," and sees Angus slumped over on the bench, Martin with his hand on his shoulder.

Everyone starts drifting over there, but Martin says to hang on, give some space, and tells Letti to call 911. A few players have their hands over their mouths, they're all standing there sweating, watching, soon staring in shock as Angus falls unconscious, there on his side on the bench, and Martin reaches to take his pulse. The next thing Sara knows, there's a siren, and then a small fire truck pulls into the parking lot and three paramedics jog out onto the field, wheeling a gurney. Hailey Winters and Olivia are holding each other now, some of the others holding on to each other, too, holding one another up it looks like, as the assistant coaches block part of the view and the paramedics work on Angus. He remains unconscious, and after a while they lift him onto the gurney and wheel him to the ambulance that arrived after the fire truck. A small crowd of students has gathered at field's edge, and as the siren starts up again, cutting through the clear afternoon, Sara stays put there on the field, rooted, watching the ambulance take her coach away.

———

SHE'S IN HOBAN'S ROOM. He's holding her as they're curled on his bed. Joseph at the library, Bö sipping from his water bottle. Down the hall, Zeppelin's "Going to California" drifts from someone's open door. She can't read, couldn't eat dinner, could barely shower. Her phone on the bed beside her.

Hoban understands he should only hold her now. He listens when occasionally she speaks. She's told him a couple of times already what happened, a moment-by-moment account, and he asked a few questions the first time, somber, gently asked questions. She can't get the image out of her mind of Angus slumped over on the bench, or of him being wheeled off the field, or of Olivia on her bed a while earlier, how she came out of the shower and found her like that, big strong Olivia balled up, crying, clutching her pillow to her chest. But Olivia didn't want to talk about it, only wanted to wait by the phone to hear from Martin or Letti or Jason, and since she, Sara, *did* want to talk, *needed* to talk, had to try to put words to what she'd witnessed, she leaned down and kissed the side of Olivia's head and said to call her if she heard anything first, she'd be over at Hoban's for a while.

They lie there, his arms around her, his hand stroking her arm now and then. Bö shuffles around in his wood shavings and Zeppelin still plays. At 9:12 p.m., finally, her phone rings. Olivia.

When she answers, there's only the low hiss, and she feels her face tightening.

"Sara . . ."

Olivia starts crying, louder than she's ever heard her cry, and she keeps holding the phone to her ear. Then Olivia speaks again.

"There was another heart attack at the hospital, a bigger one. His heart just stopped."

She hears herself say something into the phone, she's not sure what, possibly about being back at the room later, and they hang up. She lowers herself. Rests her head on Hoban's pillow.

At first she weeps almost silently, for a long time, but when Hoban places a hand on her lower back, the sobs come. And keep on coming.

45

EVEN NOW, IN MID-SEPTEMBER, everything is so green. The undergrowth, the mosses. Only a few of the vine maples have just started to turn. On the old wooden bridge a hundred yards upriver from her grandparents' place, Rachel stops to catch her breath for a minute and surveys the scene, the shafts of late afternoon sun through the branches, the low water, all the boulders.

Here in the green, in the real world.

This is the first time she's gone out without Ben, and at first, right when she set off on the trail, she almost couldn't do it. But as she turns and continues over the bridge, breathing the sweet forest air, she thinks again of him in her Gram's arms, sleeping, and a rhythm starts to set in. Her steps on the worn wood, then on the trail beyond. Her legs are weak, but it does feel good to walk on her own like this, take this hour to herself. The lack of sleep toys with her, as ever these days, and when the trail heads up the slope she breathes hard. But the movement, this movement, feels so great.

For another ten minutes she hikes up the hill, stopping frequently, hands on her hips. She forgot to bring a water bottle. Up ahead, the forest abruptly ends, the clear-cut begins, and when she steps out into it the sun hammers her. This is the cut that her Gramps talked about, it's barely a year old. Though there's some undergrowth here and there, and what looks to her like blackberry bushes off in the distance, the land still appears as if it's been bombed, stumps and debris everywhere, a nine-square-acre blast zone.

As she stands there squinting, absorbing the spectacle, she also wonders if maybe there's phone reception and finds herself reaching into her pants pocket. The world drowning in chatter. Guilty. One hand cupped over the phone so she can see it better, she finds another text.

Fucking BITCH. Where the FUCK r u?

He called again, too, but didn't leave a message. Two calls a day, at least two texts a day for the past three weeks, it's even worse now that Ben is here. She slides the phone back in her pocket and stands there sweating in the clear-cut, looking around in the stillness.

Should she let the police know finally? Tell Gramps and Gram? But there's no way he knows where she went, right? And there's no way Elaine would ever tell, if he tried to confront her, which he couldn't be stupid enough to do. Right?

So hot here after the forest cool. No sunscreen, no water, faint wind. All the shadows along the cut's stark borders.

The urge is sudden, almost overwhelming: she has to get back to the house. Hold her son.

46

THEY'RE IN A TAVERN way out on Foster, the dive where Bruce likes to go, out near his place. It's windowless, dim, a few pool tables and video poker machines, and they sit at the bar again, Bruce with his large belly and his slouch, his shaved head to deal with his accelerating baldness, his arrowhead tattoo on the side of his neck that peeks up out of his tucked-in XXL T-shirt. They sit there and take sips of their first cold Bud each, not talking much, mostly just banter with the guy behind the bar, football talk.

There's a new quietness in Keith these past couple of months, something Bruce has long-since pointed out, something Courtney has brought up, too, on a number of occasions lately, how he needs to calm down and let it go, it's okay, Rachel's in good hands. She needs him to lighten up again, she says. What happened to his sense of humor, is it in there somewhere?

When the bartender goes away, Bruce reaches back and pulls a folded-up piece of paper from a back pocket of his jeans, sets the paper onto the bar, and slides it Keith's way. "Two places. One's down on Glenwood, other's over off 89th and Tolman."

Keith unfolds the paper and reads the names there. Chester Draker on Glenwood. Sheila Ann Draker on Tolman. *So here it is, then.*

"You didn't have to do this, I could've found these if—"

"I know. Just take 'em. If you need 'em. And I'm here if you need any help, trust me on that."

Keith refolds the paper and slips it in the warm space between his wallet and jeans. Takes another drink of his beer.

For a while they sit there drinking, looking up at the TV, the Lions–Saints game, second quarter.

"You know which one it is?" Bruce eventually says, still focused on the screen.

"He lives with his mom, Elaine said. That's all I know."

"She know what you're thinking?"

"Elaine? Naw, hell. She said I should let it go. Smart girl." Keith holds up a finger for another beer. "May still do that, I'm not sure yet. But thanks, I owe you one."

Bruce glances over at him and lets out a low chuckle.

"*Except* for that shit," Keith says with a half smile, then tilts back his bottle, catching the last drops. "Go get your own damn boat."

The bartender brings over the cold-beaded fresh ones, and for a time they all watch the game. Sweet distraction. But beneath the chitchat, still, Keith thinks about someone hitting his daughter. He can't seem to get the image out of his head, thinks about it all the time when he's out pruning rhodies, say, or shearing an arborvitae. It's stuck there.

ACROSS THE STREET from a white ranch-style house on Glenwood, the place with its manicured yard and little porch swing, he waits in the pickup and pictures her up in Welches. When Elaine mentioned that a few weeks ago, about Rachel going up there, his guts about twisted up on him. His grandson in his parents' arms. Talk about a hard image to shake.

After forty minutes an elderly man shuffles past the gap in the curtains and so he starts the truck and pulls away. Then at the house over on Tolman, he waits for close to an hour. Shabby, small grey house in need of a paint job. Ratty yard, dandelions everywhere, overgrown shrubs. The place depresses him. He sits there in the truck, smoking, watching some kids down the block shooting hoops.

Just past six fifteen, a cream-colored, late eighties Buick Regal pulls into the driveway and a skinny, short, haggard woman gets right out. She's wearing a red company shirt with a logo on the breast pocket, black slacks, black tennis shoes, and she's clearly in a hurry as she finds the house key on her big jangling key ring.

He waits there in the truck, finishing his smoke. Her head appears in a window, once, but there are no signs of anyone else. Before too long the woman hustles back outside, now dressed in tight blue jeans and a low-cut purple blouse, her hair's pulled back, and she gets in the Buick and backs out fast, not once looking across the street, the lady's in her zone, watch out.

He starts the truck and lets it idle for a minute. Squashes out his smoke and looks once more at the house, sees no one inside.

The curtains in the basement windows unmoved.

47

CLOSE TO TWO THOUSAND PEOPLE show up in the Chiles Center, the arena dimmed, and up at the lectern Lindsay Waxler stands speechless, straining to compose herself, finally unable to. Martin comes to her aid, helping her down off the stage. Many people are quietly weeping, looking at the projected image up behind the podium: Angus in his cap, black shirt, and shorts, teaching something during practice, players gathered around, including Sara.

She sits between Olivia and Sophie Mack and listens to another of his former players, someone well before her time, a fit woman in a dark business suit, talk about how Angus saw you as a person, cared about you beyond just as a player on his team. "He cared about your education, and about you living a strong, full life, and I think that's partly what made him different."

It's been six days since he died. Six days since she's been to practice. Though they canceled the UNC game, practices resumed two days ago, but she hasn't been able to go. How everyone else has, including Olivia, she has no idea. *How can they play soccer now?* She could hardly get herself presentable to come here today.

Back in the room, the curtains still pulled over the view, Olivia says she needs to hit the library, she's way behind in biology. Can she get her anything on the way back? A snack maybe?

"No thanks," Sara says, pillow muffled.

Olivia, on her way out, leans down and touches the side of her head, and when the door closes, Sara reaches and pulls her comforter up over her.

Later, when Hoban calls, waking her, he asks if she's okay, can he bring her some dinner, she has to eat; but once more she says no thanks. She just wants to be here in her room. Be alone.

THE FOLLOWING DAY, she skips practice again. As she skipped Sister Toms's class again. Her limbs still feel heavy, as if she's been drugged, but she pulls on her grey sweats and purple UP sweatshirt, then leaves a phone message for Hoban saying she has to get away from campus for a while, she doesn't know how long. She gathers some underwear and socks, pants and T-shirts into her duffel and leaves a message for Kim that she needs a place to stay tonight, if it's not too much trouble.

Slightly dizzy, she hesitates there in the quiet room, looking around. Olivia's desk. Her desk. Their beds, Olivia's with the covers pulled up as usual, hers like some sort of wolverine's nest. She has absolutely zero energy for walking, but she needs to leave this place, all of a sudden she can't stay here, anywhere near UP.

SHE RIDES THE MAX TRAIN alongside the freeway. Beautiful fall day, the afternoon traffic slow, the train whizzing by. She watches the scene dazed, with the same feeling like she's been sedated, like she's lagging a few moments behind the relentless pace of moments. She swallows a lot. Thinks of Martin and Letti and Jason, what they'll do. Already a couple of calls and texts from each of them the past few days. How are those guys carrying on right now? How does a person *do* that, so soon?

At Powell, two stops before Foster, she decides to get off. On the platform she shoulders her bag and finds herself hesitating once again. *This spaciness, Jesus Christ.* She should probably grab something to eat. Go over to McDonald's. But the thought of food still makes her epiglottis twitch, there's no way.

Over on 92nd, instead of heading south, she walks down the Marshall driveway. This is probably the last place she should be, but to hell with it, she wants to see it. As she approaches, she eyes the tall grass, a few cars in the lots, a few parked in the loading area over near the front doors. She stashes her duffel behind the shrubs near the doors and, before she can change her mind, goes inside.

From what Kim told her, the building is now used for "professional development," but from what she can tell there's not much of that happening today. The place is totally quiet. No one in either direction down the long main hallway. And so she walks, soon passing the spot where she hit Kurt, wishing she could have another crack at that, break his eye socket. She passes her locker, Ms. Engle's old room, darkened, and then loops around to the front again and goes out the doors into the spacious inner courtyard where she ate so many lunches. The courtyard empty, too. In almost ten minutes, she's seen not a soul. She stands there in the middle of the courtyard and looks around at all the windows, sees nobody in any of them. Empty. Perfectly nice, solid building, in good repair from what she can tell, large campus, plenty of classrooms, just sitting here. No one. Only ghosts.

ON THE SLOW WALK down 92nd, she considers hopping a bus, but there's something about the weight of the duffel, the fatigue and discomfort, that seems strangely right to her. She keeps on walking, eventually passing the park and then her dad's apartment. It's almost five thirty, he'll probably be home soon, and for a minute she considers going over and waiting on his steps. But her body keeps moving, it's like she's on autopilot.

There's plenty of traffic on 92nd, and off to her left the freeway blares. But it strikes her: there's some beauty around here as well, even in the middle of ugliness. The well-tended yards here and there, parents playing with their kids back on the playground, all those towering trees.

As she keeps going down this familiar street, though, she sticks to the familiar thoughts.

To just walk, step after step, to feel this thirsty and weak, about ready to cry again—to wander like this, all light-headed and numb, stubborn as fuck, freeway noise in her ears—hey, it's who she is, right? It's what she needs. Because this is always, *always* where she'll be from, right here. Redneck with a duffel bag, on foot, proud as goddamn hell.

48

KEITH HAS BEEN LEAVING MESSAGES or texting every other day for ten days when finally Sara picks up. He stops pacing the apartment and mutes the TV.

"I heard about your coach. Talked to Elaine . . . I was real sorry to hear about that."

There's only the low hiss on the other end, but she stays on the line. He doesn't know what to say next. Clears his throat.

"How's school been?"

When she speaks, he can't hear her clearly and asks her to repeat that.

"I'm in Lents. At a friend's."

He turns and looks out at the park, and as he stands there at the sliding glass door something surges in him, he can hardly stand it.

"So, listen. Come on over here tomorrow night and we'll grill up some steaks, drink a beer or two, how does that sound? Actually, I don't care how it sounds, let's do it anyway, all right? Sorry if you have other plans."

After the gush of words, the pause stretches and he winces.

"Okay," she says, softly, and he lets out a quiet breath.

"Pick you up around seven?"

"I'll come there."

He watches his reflection in the glass give a single nod. Sees Bear looking up at him. "All right then. See you here. Some beef and brew."

"Bye."

SHE SMELLS OF CIGARETTE SMOKE and her face is pale, looks like she hasn't slept well. Grey sweatpants, purple sweatshirt, flat-bottomed soccer shoes. She carries a Safeway pint of potato salad over to the kitchen counter before squatting down to pet Bear. Playground sounds from across the street, through the patio screen.

"Beer?" he says.

"Yep."

His hair still wet, combed back over his ears, he opens another bottle and hands it to her, considers making some kind of toast and decides against it. He heads back out onto the patio, to the grill, and both Sara and Bear follow. It's an overcast evening, mild, and as he tends to the steaks he steals glances at her. She looks thinner. That short haircut's grown out a little. She's also becoming a woman, it's clear. Her face, her eyes. She takes another drink, then rests her elbows on the railing and gazes out at the park, while Bear stares at the grill.

"Talked to Elaine lately?" he says, flipping a steak, and Sara only takes a sip and keeps observing the playground, the kids over there running around, some parents watching. "I talked to her, let's see, think it was Sunday. She said she talked to Rachel, young Ben's doin' all right."

Sara just nods. His head storms for something else to say on the matter and he's not sure how he'll be able to eat his dinner.

But after she finishes her first Bud, she asks if she could maybe have another, and soon she seems less nervous. Not that talkative, just less nervous. At the kitchen table they eat their steaks and baked potatoes and the potato salad, Bear sitting off a few feet, eyeing them, and after a few bites her appetite kicks in and she puts more butter and sour cream on her potato. Some CCR playing low on the stereo, they talk about his work, how more and more they have him doing specialty pruning jobs on his own, "some rich clients who get picky about their bushes." And then she asks about Courtney and he tells her how they're thinking about a short trip to Jamaica in February, maybe.

"Never pictured you hanging out in Jamaica," she says.

"You and me both. But, hell, why not, mon?"

When she makes a face and then smiles—the first time since she was a little girl that he's seen her actually smile—he notices how it looks a lot like his own smile, that gap-toothed Garrison charmer, and this makes him let out a laugh. They're each on their third beer, he cooked the steaks right, there's a nice-lookin' apple pie over on the counter, and so far the evening hasn't been a disaster. Far from it.

Over the pie and ice cream, though, when he asks like he did yesterday about how school's going, he wonders if he's ruined it all. For what seems like a good minute Sara only takes slow, small bites and looks off through the screen door at the shadowed park. But he makes himself not fill up the silence with any words. He takes another bite of the not-that-bad store-bought pie, occasionally glancing at her.

"Don't know if I can go back." Her voice is barely audible. She sets down her fork and rests her elbows on the table, hands folded in front of her mouth.

He wipes his mouth with his paper towel and just watches her.

"He was the reason I even . . ." She hesitates.

"He meant a lot to you."

Still looking out at the park, Sara gives her head a quick shake, then focuses on her pie again. Before taking another bite, though, she sets down her fork. "Let's talk about something else."

In the pause, he catches her eye. "So, you maybe aren't goin' back then, you're saying. You sure about that?"

Sara pushes her chair back and stands, takes her plate and fork into the kitchen and says she has to get going.

"Hang on." And suddenly here it is again, this fire rising up in him. Whether it's beer-fueled or what, he's not sure, but here it is. When he gets up, Bear slinks over toward the TV and watches from there. Sara, by the sink, turns and faces him, her hands pressed against the counter on either side of her. "So, let me get this, just so I understand . . . You're saying this man recruited you to come play soccer, he gave you a full scholarship to go to college and get yourself an education and play on a good soccer team, and then he passed away. And so now you think the best way to honor him and all he did for you is to just say, well, let's call it a day?"

He steps to the kitchen's edge, paper towel crumpled in one hand. Sara folds her arms over her chest but doesn't look away. Fire in her own eyes now.

"Spare me the pep talk, I'm not—"

"Oh hell, listen to you. You're damn right I'm gonna give you a pep talk, but I'll try to keep it short for you." He catches himself and lowers his head, breathing through his nose. "Look. I'm sorry. I'm real sorry for what happened, that's hard. Real hard . . . But you know what?" He makes sure she's glaring at him again. "It's fucked up how easy people quit. You know?"

"I'm not—"

"Yeah you are. You're sittin' there telling me you might not—"

She pushes herself away from the counter and starts past him. He nearly grabs her arm, but stops himself, and over by the front door she turns and faces him again, hand on the knob.

"Thanks for dinner," she says.

"Hold on. Now goddamn it." He goes over to the stereo and kills the music, and old Mr. Becker's TV sounds come clearer through the wall. "You think he'd want you to quit school? Quit the team? You telling me your coach would *want* that for you? You just say, hell with it all and not keep making a life for yourself? *That's* what he'd want?"

In the brittle pause, she looks down at Bear, who's lying down as if trying to make herself invisible.

"You can't quit now. No fuckin' way, girl. I'll hound you like a god-damn yard dog if you do. Count on it."

She makes no sound as she stands there gripping the doorknob, pressing her lips together, tears flowing, and when he steps over to her, tentatively at first, and pulls her into a hug, she doesn't resist. Just slips her arms around him and rests her forehead against his chest.

BACK AT THE TABLE, after she's collected herself and they've mostly finished their pieces of pie, he tips back the rest of his beer and says he wants to ask her about something else. His words sound strange to him, nearly garbled.

He wipes his mouth on his paper towel ball. Puts down the ball beside his plate and runs a hand over his face. It's hard for him to look at her now.

"Something that's been on my mind," he says.

Silent, puffy-eyed, Sara observes him. Bear comes up to the table and he pets the dog's head for a while.

"There's some people I need to see. My grandson, for one. About time." Sara nods slowly, waiting, and he goes on petting the dog.

"What I need to . . . What I need is for you to help me out, by being there. Just keep me company. Tomorrow."

49

THE CLUNKER CHEVY rumbles through the small town of Sandy, one of Keith's old mixtapes playing "Rock You Like a Hurricane" by the Scorpions. Sara reaches for another piece of beef jerky from the half-gone pack on the seat between them and watches Joe's Donuts glide by, then farther up the highway, Shorty's Corner Gas Station and Cafe. This trip she's made at least fifty times in her life.

They haven't spoken much on the ride so far, it's clear to her that he's struggling some, often wiping a hand down his fresh-shaven face, occasionally tapping on the wheel with his forefingers. Now and then she catches whiffs of his aftershave or deodorant, she's not sure which.

"You good?" he says, shifting the truck as it slows on a hill. "Lookin' pretty thoughtful over there."

"Sure. You?"

He keeps his eyes on the road and nods, his lips curled down, and again they slip back into themselves and she views the forested hills and half-clouded Mount Hood. Some of the vine maples on either side of the highway have started to change colors, but most everything else is green. Douglas firs, cedars, hemlocks. Alders and cottonwoods. Mötley Crüe's "Wild Side" comes through the speakers, and as she chews another bite of the jerky she sees out the corner of her eye how her dad has resumed his drumming on the wheel. Fifteen more minutes to Welches.

But her other thoughts continue to cut in. Elaine back in Portland, watching Adam, who apparently has a bad cold. Their mom working an extra shift today. And then it's Angus again, the photo of him they showed at the funeral, Angus coaching, teaching, that sunlight on his face. Mainly, though, she thinks of what they're driving toward and how this is all still a bit surreal, her coming up here with him, without anyone else knowing.

Near Brightwood, only a few miles below Welches, her dad reaches for another piece of jerky and bites off a chunk, then lets it soften in his mouth for a few seconds before he starts chewing. Hard chewing. She looks back out at the highway and the hills, half listening to the song and the groaning truck.

Here she is, with her dad, on a Sunday afternoon. Riding toward the mountain.

50

THE CLOUDS HANG just above the treetops, and in the soft light the house looks especially small to her for some reason, the firs looming on either side and over in back, down toward the river. When her dad turns off the engine, the whine of her Gramps's saw comes through, and she looks to the warm-lit garage with its cracked doorway. Lights are on in the house, too, but there's no smoke from the chimney, not quite cold enough yet. Her stomach feels tighter and she glances over at her dad, who remains there with his hands resting on his thighs, staring at the house. They sit like that for a minute, and when she sees a curtain move in the window by the front porch, she opens her door and dangles a leg out. The scent of green tinged with a hint of wood dust drifts into the cab.

She looks over at him again. "All right?"

After a quick deep breath Keith gets out, and as they step toward the house, gravel crunching, he runs a hand back over his hair and inhales through his nose once more. The saw lets out another wail. On the porch, after she knocks, Sara sees his right hand shaking slightly. He slips his hands in his jeans pockets just as Rachel opens the door.

"Oh my." Rachel clearly stunned, her voice higher pitched than normal. She gauges them for a few beats before stepping aside.

"Hello to you, too." Sara gives her a light shoulder punch as she passes.

"How do?" Keith says, and in the pause that follows Sara hears her Gram's recliner squeak.

Rachel turns and leads the way into the front room, Keith trailing last.

Val, in her chair holding Ben, the back of her hair sticking up, a faded orange dish towel over one shoulder, lets out a deep moan when she sees him, a sound that stops their approach. She cups one hand over her mouth, still holding the baby to her chest, and Rachel goes and takes

Ben, whispering something soothing into his tiny pink ear. Val, like a child, holds her hands up over her face, as if she wants to hide.

After getting a steady first look at his grandson, stroking his dark hair once with the backs of his trembling fingers, Keith goes over to his mother. He squats down and then reaches up, touching her arm near the elbow. At his touch, Val peeks through her hands.

"Hello there," he says.

She looks at him briefly, her lips pressed and slightly contorting, then tries to push up out of her chair and asks if anyone wants coffee or tea. But she can't gather herself and surrenders, settling back into her chair. She takes his hand, covers her eyes with her other hand.

Off to the side, here in this room lined with dozens of photos and framed needlepoints, Sara stands still beside Rachel and Ben. Through the sounds of weeping and Keith's low-spoken words, the persistent sawing from outside cuts in and out like high notes from a song.

51

IN THE KITCHEN, after he's had a chance to hold Ben, after his mother puts on coffee, Keith watches her turn and give him another long look, her wrinkle-edged eyes still wet.

"Go out to him first," she says in a hushed voice.

The girls are with Ben over in the front room, talking. Keith observes his mother setting out mugs. How she's aged.

Out on the porch, he draws some lungfuls of the clean air, the forest and river smell, he can't seem to get enough. It's like he's been starving, is how he thinks of it, and at the first scent of good food something in the body gets triggered. You didn't realize how much toxic crap you were breathing in, in the city, until you came to a place like this. He'd almost forgotten.

But when he hears the saw again and looks over at the garage, it's harder to breathe. He goes down the steps and hears the gravel beneath his boots and it's still dream-like, this whole scene, what just happened inside, what he's walking toward now. When the sawing stops, he hears the river for the first time and then notices that his hands are shaking again. He stuffs them in his pockets and continues, but right outside the garage doorway hesitates. The saw starts up.

He's safely out of view, he thinks. Sees his dad in there in a dusty flannel shirt with the sleeves rolled up, dusty jeans. The man's still got some forearms on him. The thick hands, too. Green cap on his head, safety goggles on. The saw stops and his dad surveys his work, and it's then that he feels himself stepping closer, pulling the door open wider.

When his dad lowers his goggles and stares at him, he freezes. It's like he's a kid and got caught spying. His dad stares longer, then comes out from behind the table saw and walks toward him.

Despite the forearms and hands, the man's smaller than he remembered. Older looking, too. The shoulders not quite as broad, the deep-lined face. When they're a couple of feet apart, he's aware of looking down a few inches into his dad's blue eyes. The air rich with pine dust. The longer his dad looks straight at him, the shallower his breaths come. But he holds the gaze.

"You been inside?" his dad says.

Hearing that voice: It's like the sound is a key for some long-locked rooms inside of himself. He feels the sound in his rib cage. The voice is louder, though, as if the man's hard of hearing these days.

"Yep. Was just in there."

His dad clears his throat. "How'd that go?"

"All right. I think."

"She okay?"

"Think so . . ." There's the thickness in his own throat that makes his voice sound weird to him.

His dad keeps staring at him, then nods. Slowly raises a calloused hand, and they shake. Firm grip, brief. As he tucks his hand back into his pocket, before the trembling starts again, he observes the man's face once more, the smile lines and the crow's feet, some stray grey nose hairs. The dusty John Deere cap.

"Quite a shop—"

"You planning to—"

"No, go ahead," he says.

His dad watches him. "You planning to visit for a while or . . ."

"Came up with Sara. Gotta get her back later this afternoon. But we got all afternoon."

The river sound fills another pause, and after a time his dad shakes his head once, still looking at him. The pause keeps on stretching.

"Your hair's not as long," the man says.

"Because it's falling out."

His dad lifts his cap some, shows his close-cropped grey hair, the high widow's peak. "Get used to it."

They each restrain a smile, but then his dad's face changes, goes serious again, and the man looks down at the floor as though he's searching for something.

"She's making coffee."

His dad looks back up at him. "Guess we should go on in then."

"Sounds about right."

His dad goes over and switches off the lights and pulls the door closed, and he waits until the old man's beside him out on the gravel before turning to walk back to the house. Only a few paces onward, though, he feels a grip on his upper arm and they stop and face each other.

Wind in the boughs above. The river. The house nearby, the people in there.

"Goddamn, kid."

The hug is as firm as the handshake, and about as fast, and as his dad pulls away with a final hard backslap, he sees him wanting to hide his eyes just like his mom did.

52

THEY SIT IN THE FRONT ROOM drinking coffee. Occasionally the girls snack from the passed-around bowl of animal crackers. Rachel gives Ben his bottle, and for a good while they talk mainly about what the baby has been up to, how he likes going along for walks in the woods.

Across the room from Keith, his parents are on the quiet side, understandable enough to him, but they're clearly happy to have Rachel and Ben around. He drinks his coffee and listens for the most part, glancing over at them from time to time, absorbing more details. His mom's neck wattle. His dad's gold wedding band, how it looks like it's about grown into the skin on his finger. The way his mom keeps looking at him, almost like she's checking to make sure he's still there. The way his dad looks at Rachel and Ben.

When Sara suggests a visit to the river, he hears himself say that he could use some more of that air, and then Rachel says she and Ben are in, too. He should stay right here in the house, he knows, talk to his parents more, try to anyway, there's a lot to talk about, after all. But he's up, Sara and Rachel are up, and maybe it's best not to push it too much today with his folks, they should save that talk for some other time probably. Besides, the girls and the baby are around and what if his parents ended up getting mad, how would this day turn out then? One thing at a time. Take it in doses.

By the river, Sara says with a friendly half smile that she's going to take a few minutes to herself, then goes over and sits a ways off on a moss-covered boulder. It's still cloudy, but not too cold, and in the pause after Sara heads off, he and Rachel stand taking in the river and the woods, Ben bundled into a small pack on Rachel's chest.

He breathes, scrambling at first for what to say, but soon decides to just breathe. To be away from the house, to stand here in the woods like this—it makes his gut relax. Dense forest rising up the opposite bank, the rapids upstream, Sara over there on her rock.

"They ask about you sometimes, you know," Rachel says, and he looks at her. Her cheeks with healthy color. Her brown hair clean, pulled back. Not much makeup. "She's probably in there crying some more. You know that, right?"

Ben starts to fuss, so Rachel begins unclipping the pack, struggles with one of the clips, and asks if he can give her a hand.

"Go ahead and lift him out," she says.

When he adjusts the blanket around the child, Rachel doesn't make a move to take him back, and so he holds his grandson and eventually the boy calms down. Rachel watches them briefly, and he notices how she doesn't seem overly concerned. Wasn't that long ago he was holding young Rachel like this. Not long at all. One thing he definitely remembers: how much body heat a little one gives off, my goodness. All that bright-burning life inside of them. He bounces slightly up and down, the earth soft beneath his boots, and Ben makes a happy cooing sound, like a little owl.

For a while they linger there on the bank, gazing at the scene. He turns around and eyes the house, doesn't see anyone in the windows, and wonders what they're doing now. No saw sounds. As he faces the river again, he catches Rachel's tense expression as she's looking at the water.

"What's up?"

"Nothing . . ."

He resumes his light bouncing and remains focused on her. Ben drifting off, Sara still downstream, sitting.

"Ask you something?" he says.

Rachel hesitates, then nods once, not meeting his eyes.

"Any issues with your ex-boyfriend?"

She shoots him a caught-off-guard look, then goes back to watching the river.

"He been bothering you at all?"

For a good many seconds she only remains still, fixated on the flow, her jaw occasionally working. She bites her lower lip, and when she speaks finally, she speaks toward the water. "He keeps leaving these messages. He wants . . ."

There's the sudden high ringing in his ears, but he keeps trying to take slow breaths. Keeps gently jouncing his sleeping grandson, so warm against his chest. "Ask you something else? He ever hit you?"

Rachel stands there for a while, blinking. There's almost a disoriented look on her face now. Cautious, too. But then something opens up in her, there's a moist-eyed rush of words: "He's high most of the time, I'm not sure what he'll do, if he'll try to . . . He keeps on leaving these messages, he didn't want me to have the baby." She stops herself and glances over at Sara, who's out of earshot. The river's din. "Sorry. It's better up here. For now. We're okay."

She turns and looks at him then, at last, and when she does, he sees just how scared she really is.

53

HERE IN HER SPOT, her dad and sister and handsome nephew nearby, she tries to notice things. A pileated woodpecker in one of the larches on the opposite bank. A finch on a boulder mid-river, for a few seconds. The cool moss under her hands. At length, she pictures Hoban sitting over there on a rock to her left. Kim, too. Pictures her Gram hiding behind her hands a while ago.

Then, yet again, it's Angus in her mind.

It may well be corny, but screw it anyway, for some reason it helps: just sitting here looking around, holding still, thinking about the cycles of life. She's witnessed this view in all seasons, and human life is short no matter how long a person lives.

But even so, how do other people deal with this kind of pain? She'll never be able to absorb it all, it feels like. No matter what the woods and the river so steadily teach.

MORE SMALL TALK back in the house, the friendliness still tinged with the shyness and nerves and all that hasn't been said. Her Gramps, when she and her dad are getting set to leave, becomes more talkative all of a sudden, saying how he needs to cut down several trees on the property, he gets worried more and more with some of these windstorms they've been having.

From the porch overlooking the driveway, her Gramps continues, pointing out a good-size Douglas fir between the house and garage. "That old gal right there, she's one of 'em. That crown gets swayin' . . ."

She sees her dad look up at the tree and then down at his father again. Her Gramps clearly waiting for him to offer a hand with the cutting, talk about a wide-open invitation if ever there was one. But her dad only gives him this even, almost wistful look, there's this sort of quiet sorrow in it, and it makes her face tingle. Since the river hike, he's seemed more within himself. More tense. But also more tender. Maybe it's just that it's been one hell of a day, he must be wiped out.

"Well," her dad says, all of them out on the porch now. His voice is crackly, subdued. "This lady's got class in the morning, should get her on back to town."

He steps over and holds out his hands for Ben, and when Rachel gives the kid to him, he holds him for a minute against his chest, then kisses the top of his head. His eyes get red, a little wet.

"You be good for your mama, all right?" He kisses Ben's cheek and hands him back gently.

Gramps clears his throat. "Don't be a stranger."

Though he's looking her way when he says this, she knows he means it for both of them. "I won't," she says, like always, then hugs him and turns for the truck.

When she stops at the truck and faces the house again, her dad is hugging Gram. It's a short one, but her fingers press into his shirt. With Gramps, it's only a handshake, but with solid eye contact, and then her dad turns and heads her way, the gravel crunch. They get in the truck and he starts it up, the river sound gone, but before shifting into reverse he lingers for a few beats, gazing at them there on the porch. Rachel has one of Ben's arms raised, waving it back and forth, while Gramps and Gram only stand there stoic, almost numbed-looking, still stunned, watching their son.

The truck backs up and the view widens. The house and the gold Oldsmobile. The trees. Four people, family, watching them leave.

On the road out to the highway, there are no words. There's no music. Her dad just faces forward, his back teeth clenched, tears silently running, and drives.

54

WHEN THEY PULL UP outside Sara's dorm in the lavender dusk, Forest Park already black across the river, Keith tells her to go ahead and take the rest of the jerky and shuts off the truck. Many lights are on in the dorms, and for a time they sit there in the parking lot, the engine clicking.

They've been quiet almost the entire drive, but Sara's been understanding about that, she has a lot on her mind herself, he knows. She waits, occasionally glancing over at him, and after another minute reaches back behind the seat for her bag and sets it in her lap.

"Glad we went up," she says.

"Listen . . ." He wipes a hand down his face and turns his head. He can hardly look at her, this beautiful daughter of his, the oldest of his beautiful daughters. This young woman in college. His mouth starts to move, but no sound comes before it does come. "You remember our talk last night, you hear? I mean it."

There's an edge in his tone, but she doesn't look away. Doesn't say anything, either.

"You just stay on your path, all right? Don't let no one push you off it. Promise me that, all right?"

She seems a little startled, bewildered maybe, it must be strange being back out here and everything, and here he is acting all intense on her. But she only gives a nod and says in a quiet voice, "Okay." She opens the door and gets out into the evening, holds on to the door and looks back into the cab.

"Go study," he says.

He thinks maybe there's more he should say. Hell, there's more he should *be*. More he should've always been, for everyone. Better dad, better son. A better man. Smarter, that's for damn sure. But for the good goddamn life of him, no more words come, and he is who he is, there's no getting around that.

He turns the key and the old truck roars. Sara shoulders her bag, closes the door, and holds up a hand.

FROM THE SAME PLACE he parked last time, now in shadow, he sees lights on the main floor and in the basement windows. He sits there for a while, and when his phone rings and he sees it's Courtney he almost answers. But his voice might sound tight and he can't be getting into a long conversation with her right now. He waits, then listens to her message.

"Hey. Just wondering how you're doing. Been thinking about you today, wondering how it went . . . I miss you. Call me, okay? Or just come over if you want, I'm making up some of that taco casserole you like. We could talk some."

He tucks the phone back in his pocket, her sexy voice still coursing through him. Envisions her internet printouts on Jamaica, the brochures she sent away for, all arranged at one end of her kitchen table, "Trip-Planning Central" she calls it. He imagines them on one of those palm-lined beaches drinking some beers, smelling that salty breeze. Courtney in a bikini.

The woman passes in front of a window and the pictures in his head stop. His heart beats in his neck. The street is empty, no vehicles pass, and when he gets out he hears the distant freeway sound. Sunday night, still some traffic. He crosses the street, eyeing the windows, and sees no other movements. The thoughts of Courtney, and then of his daughters, start to come again, the closer he gets to the house the more insistent they get, trying to distract him, divert him. But there's something deeper inside of him still that keeps him stepping forward. He walks alongside the house, then around to the front, and wonders if once he's on the porch he'll hesitate before ringing the doorbell, but he doesn't. He watches his finger push the bell and hears it muffled. The bell's inside, of course, but his hearing is muffled, too, he can hear the low thud of his pulse now. There's too much in his head, and too much to take in, and so he blocks out everything else except for the sight of the curtains moving in the front window right near the door and the woman's mousy face peeking out.

The curtain drops and then she's on the other side of the door, he can hear her there.

"I need to talk to Kurt," he says. "I'm Rachel's dad. Need to talk to him for a minute."

She says something, but he doesn't catch it, and her footsteps move away from the door. He looks over his shoulder. There's no one on the street. No one in the windows of nearby houses, from what he can tell. He's light-headed.

He holds his breath for a few seconds and hears them talking inside, and as he breathes again the boy's face appears in the window. He's taller than he imagined. He also looks hopped up, from what he can see. The eyes. The sores around his lips. The mom's voice rises in the background, but he still can't make out what she's saying.

"Need to talk a minute," he says.

Kurt only glares at him, holding back the curtain.

"If you won't invite me in, at least be a man and come out here and talk."

The kid just keeps glaring. Greasy hair falling in his eyes. Pouty, bony face, trying to look hard.

"I saw her today," he says, and sees the expression change slightly, Kurt seems almost rattled for a moment, but then goes hard again. "She wanted me to tell you something."

He watches the kid. Wants to swallow but doesn't. The street still quiet.

"Get the *fuck* outta here," Kurt says. "Don't care what that bitch said. Get the fuck away or I call the fuckin' cops. You probably wouldn't want that, would you?"

He stands there on the porch, breathing faster through his nostrils.

"You think I'm *playin'*?" The kid looks bolder now. "Get your fuckin' deadbeat ass outta here!"

When he punches out one of the four small squares of glass in the door, there's a flash of his parents standing on their porch with Rachel and Ben. As he reaches through and flips the deadbolt, a flash of Sara getting out of the truck with her duffel bag. He steps in fast and the spindly kid takes a wild swing but misses, so he tags him in the face, knocking him down, while the leathery short mom with her bagged eyes is over in the front room, her eyes wide.

Everything comes in snatches.

Kurt getting up, getting hit again, this time in the windpipe. Kurt dropping hard, and then he's kneeling on the kid's chest, bending in close to the blood-streaming face. The terms of his probation flicking through his head before he speaks.

His voice is measured, even when he hears the mom on the phone off behind him.

"No one fucks with my family."

He stares at the bulged eyes.

"Is this getting through? *No. One.* And if I ain't around, I got friends who know all about your sorry ass, too."

He slides his knee off the bony chest, straddling the wheezing kid, and leans down even closer to his face.

"You ever come near my daughter or my grandson, I will hunt you. *Do you understand?*"

It's then that something hard hits him on the back of the head, but he doesn't fall over. The mom's holding a thick broom in both hands, and as he looks back at her Kurt rages, writhing, tries to push him back but can't. The woman swings again, and he blocks it with his arm, then punches the boy in the nose, blood pouring. Pounds his cheek, his temple, the nose again, his ribs. A flurry. He gets up fast, the mom going wild, still coming at him, swinging, swinging, and when he glances down once more at the crumpled, moaning kid he hears sirens, at least he thinks he does, but it could be his ears after that broom hit, he's not sure—until he gets hit in the face with the broomstick and staggers back out on the front porch, where the sirens get louder and then the colored lights start to flash.

The crazed woman is still screaming, and he hears voices off behind him, but he only stands there, hands raised a little, breathing hard, breathing the air of this neighborhood where he grew up. And all he can think at this point is how every now and then, when it comes to certain things in this life, it's true, the angel and the devil both have to win at the same time.

PART FOUR

55

THE SATURDAY BEFORE THANKSGIVING. Cold, bright afternoon.

Rachel's borrowed the Oldsmobile with the stuffed animals, she's driving into Portland on I-84 in light traffic when a MAX train glides by.

Ben back in Welches, it's just her, driving along with the radio off, eyeing the downtown buildings up ahead, the buildings she hasn't seen in so long, and as she takes the Morrison Bridge over the river it feels to her like her heart has floated up into her throat.

With her normal hair color still, the same old brown, and with one of her Gramps's jean jackets on, she knows she looks different, yet when she finds a parking spot near the art museum adjacent to the South Park Blocks and gets out, she pulls down her blue knit beanie nearly to her eyebrows. Plugging quarters, she keeps looking across the street and tries to calm herself. From what she can tell, Ken isn't there on any of the benches, and the huddle of street kids over near Salmon Street doesn't appear to include Tobias, Teena, Manfred, or White Fang. Or Kurt. Then again, she's needed glasses for a while now, and of course any one of them could've changed their appearance, too.

She crosses the street, her hands balled in the jacket pockets, head lowered a bit, and gets a better look at some of the bench-sitters. A near-elderly woman with her crammed shopping cart, a mucus-eyed cat beside her on the bench. A guy with matted hair curled up sleeping under a soiled grey blanket. On another bench, down near Salmon, two street kids, a goth couple she vaguely recognizes, sit eating from a fast food bag. She approaches them, glancing again at the larger huddle close by, and asks if they've seen an old man who used to like to sit right over there and read almost every day. Shopping cart, sport coat, beard, and glasses?

The guy looks at her, his silver-ringed lips still moving, and then swallows. "Always reading, yeah. Haven't seen him for a couple months." He turns to his girlfriend. "Remember that dude?" The pasty, stoned-looking girl only keeps chewing, eyeing her, and the guy takes another bite of his soft taco and with his mouth full says, "Sorry."

For a time she walks the Park Blocks, through the PSU campus and then back toward Salmon. No sign of Ken. Not even any other old men with carts. Just a few more street kids, and what seem like PSU students, plus some middle-aged people out strolling with their dogs. Near the statue of Abe Lincoln, a dad plays with a toddler, letting him push the stroller, and she can't contain a smile as she passes.

How *different* life feels as a parent. That searing threshold. What kind of mother is she, though? What kind of mom will she be? Same daily questions.

Back at the Olds, she lifts her backpack out of the trunk and then goes up to the cafe she spotted near PSU. Still no Ken sighting, but she gets a window table and, after ordering a drink, sits there gazing out at the Park Blocks. The cafe is crowded, mostly people in their twenties, college kids, several chatting, many doing what looks like homework, typing on their laptops, earbuds in. Which is what she needs to do, and soon.

But when she pulls out her books and notebooks finally—the heaps of homework from each of her classes at Sandy High, from her full load of English, Spanish, biology, US government, and calculus—she hesitates over the sheer amount of it all and resumes looking out the window at the city scenes, all the people walking by, the buildings through the trees.

Her other daily question, even more insistent now that she's a mother: *Where will she fit in all this?* Can't live with her grandparents forever. But for now, yes. Ben has a home. Sandy High is all right, she's the new kid again, but things are steady, for now at least. Ben's okay. There in the woods, near the river and the mountain, with her Gramps and Gram.

This scene out the window, though . . . All the passing vehicles, the fumes rising, day and night, particles in the lungs, even in Ben's, even up in Welches. Human beings bent as ever on conquering nature, no matter how many signs nature gives. "We are what we breathe," as Ms. Harrison, her biology teacher, put it last week in class. And this, too, from the woman, early in the semester: "We come from the stars, literally, and yet most of us have no idea. It's us, then it's everything else."

Her coffee gets called, and when she returns to her table she opens her US government notebook, the half-done outline for the persuasive essay on lobbying in Congress. She takes a sip, but before starting in on the homework has another look out the window. Still no glimpse of Ken, the man whose name inspired her son's name. And no Kurt, either. Phantoms from another life, it almost seems like, already. Okay, not quite true.

At length she zeroes back in on the outline and makes herself concentrate. Because she *will* finish high school, like her sisters. And after what her dad did, she owes the man that much.

She takes a drink and slides the cup and saucer aside. Uncaps her pen. It's a cold November afternoon, this downtown cafe is warm, and here she is. Girl at a table with a bunch of books, one of the students in here settling in, getting down to some work.

56

IN SISTER TOMS'S CLASS, she sits beside Hoban, her feet tapping the carpet. It's almost her turn. The girl up front is talking about Willa Cather's *O Pioneers!*, but Sara catches about every eighth word. What they had to do was choose from a list of novels, read the book, then come up with a presentation for the entire class, and while the first two tasks were easy enough for her, it's this last one that about has her ready to vomit.

Hoban doesn't reach over for her hand or try to catch her eye. He knows it's just her now, about to stand up in front of these twenty-three people this morning. She thinks of Angus, but that only helps a little, and so she thinks of her dad, which bolsters her feeling that she might not actually puke. Before she knows it, she's coming up with names again, something she hasn't done for some time.

Jennifer Rumpdevil. Gail Schtinkenmachen. Ted Hump.

This helps, but when the other girl finishes and Sister Toms looks her way, she feels like she might faint.

Up in front of everyone, she hesitates. Coughs once. Looks down at her notecards for a few seconds and then sets them on Sister Toms's stool. Hoban doesn't avert his eyes, just gives a slight nod.

"I chose *True Grit*." She hears herself, in her head, proceeding with her rehearsed line about how the novel captures something quintessentially American, but then hears her voice go elsewhere. "I saw the latest film version, with Jeff Bridges, a few months ago. Liked it a lot."

People smile, including Sister Toms. A hint of condescension in some of those smiles? Screw it anyway, doesn't matter. No way she'll tell the real reason she chose the novel, though, how it was because Elaine mentioned last year that their dad liked to read now and apparently one of his all-time favorites is *True Grit*.

"Anyway, I liked the book, too. Wasn't too long."

More smiles. She catches herself looking at the floor and makes herself raise her head again. Makes herself make some eye contact. Half outside of herself, in a state of wonder almost, she goes on telling about how she especially liked the main character, Mattie Ross, how Portis captured her feisty, precocious voice but didn't go overboard. Mattie's got grit, sure, and she's also real on the page, and Portis captured the idea of the rugged, persistent, crafty-at-times American pushing on in the face of obstacles, facing the elements, facing the land . . .

When she finishes, she can hardly recall what the hell she said. It feels like she has a fever, her face is burning. But she's done. People clap even. Sister Toms gives her a kind smile, then calls on the next student.

She sits down again, and now Hoban takes her hand. As she gives a squeeze back she wants to call Kim, they talked last night and she shared how she was so wigged out over this damn presentation, and Kim wants to know how it all turned out. The girl's at work now, though, of course. She settles back into the chair more and pictures her, like she often does, loading a big bag of mulch into someone's car, her flexed shoulders and arms, her beat-up cowhide gloves. Such a seriously sexy girl. Best to call tonight.

The presentations go on, words on Steinbeck, Toni Morrison, Faulkner filling the room, words about words and the American psyche, words about people and the land, and as she calms down further, her feet flat on the floor now, more of the words start to sink in.

———

IT'S THAT LATE AFTERNOON autumn light that about shatters you. She's on the practice field running, scrimmaging. Playing with the other starters, Olivia and Sophie among them, getting ready for Saturday, their quarterfinal match in the NCAA Tournament, here at home versus Notre Dame. Sold out Merlo Field.

On the sideline, Martin stands in his puffy black coat and black sweatpants, his arms crossed, black cap pulled low, while Letti and Jason stand nearby in the same outfits. The three of them, these past three months, acting steady, in this season dedicated to Angus Graham.

In the fading amber light, she runs, and eventually it comes. The flow. That rhythm. She starts to lose herself. Like so often this season, there's the feeling of Angus urging her on. There's this sense of him, especially here on the practice field, like he's still over there on the sideline not missing anything, Martin next to him.

Her dad's words, too—they drift often into her mind, and her promise to him—they seem to come at some of the hardest moments, like late during a game when, spent, she glances over at the sideline expecting to see Angus there and feels the last bits of energy drain from her legs, or during study time when she doesn't understand what the hell she's reading, or now and then during the walk from the locker room, cleats clacking on that smooth cement, when she passes the athletic offices on her way outside.

Here she is. Sprinting. Fit. Shoelaces tied in a double knot, her practice jersey tucked in. As Martin continues to demand, they practice full-on, all of them, they're on a mission, these scrimmages can get brutal, and just as it's getting hard to see, that sweet light about gone, she collects a pass near a corner of the eighteen-yard box.

Maybe it's the same old electric thrill of gathering the ball to herself, almost like the ball is a part of her own body, returned after a short trip. Maybe it's the sudden surge of speed that catches Dana Harmon-Blake wrong-footed, or maybe the burst of cougar-like focus that makes her lower jaw extend, this mouth-watering prospect of a clean, clear strike.

It's all of those, or it's just Sara Garrison on the ball, the goal nearby.

She flicks the ball once more with the outside of her right foot, Dana still scrambling after her, and as she feels the lethal warm coiling in her body, her left foot planting hard in the turf, time seems to slow and sound muffles. The goal seems so large, so close. So pitifully beaten.

57

THE BUSIEST DAY OF THE YEAR. Long lines at each of the fifteen check-stands, some tense shoppers. Melanie's ankles and lower back are shriek-ing, she's near the end of her shift, but she makes a point of looking at each customer, saying hello.

"How you holding up?" asks a pint-size, white-whiskered man, his fro-zen turkey, three cans of jellied cranberry sauce, and two boxes of Stove Top stuffing there on the conveyor belt, headed her way.

"Not bad," she says. "Did you find everything all right?"

She half listens to him talk about his Thanksgiving plans and thinks about how she has tomorrow off, her first full Thanksgiving off in . . . she can't remember how long. She hands over the receipt, smiling, and the man hoists his bags, while the next customer, an elderly Asian lady, is already in front of her.

"How are you?" she says. "Find everything all right?"

For the next hour she stands there scanning, trying to block out the pains, chatting, bagging. Her line, like all the others, never goes down.

WHAT SHE WANTS IS THIS: her glass of wine, her pajamas and slippers and robe, three ibuprofens, some of that leftover ham and Elaine's scal-loped potatoes, her evening news and then the celebrity gossip shows. That's it. That's all.

She looks down the busy street and sees the bus coming this time. Headlights worsening her headache.

Then again, she might not make it much past dinner tonight, she's that tired. Extra shifts all week. Maybe just dinner, one celeb show, then straight to bed. That sounds about right.

She grimaces as she climbs the bus steps, holds on to the poles and sometimes the seatbacks as she makes her way up the aisle. There's a seat toward the back and she takes it, but notices before she does the group of young guys in the very back. One of the kids looks a little like

Kurt, lanky, dressed in baggy black, his hood pulled up. Skate punk with his three friends. She listens to them, it's hard not to.

"Dude, fuck, chill."

"Not even."

"Suck my dick, yo."

None of the other passengers look back at the kids, and from what she can tell, the driver doesn't bother checking his rearview.

"Ring the fuckin' bell, dickwad."

"Man, I ain't your bitch."

The bell dings, and when the bus starts to pull over on the next block the kids get up, one of them gets pushed from behind and bumps her shoulder as he passes. The kid doesn't say sorry, and the others only laugh, jostling toward the back door. When the door closes behind them, she can hear them whooping and swearing. No one else on the bus shows any sign of relief, and the bus rolls on up Foster.

She rides, looking out at the night, at the reflections. At her own reflection. The New Copper Penny eventually passes by, like always.

Say what you will about Keith and what he did—and there's plenty to say, for sure. But Kurt Draker hasn't come around since, and Rachel hasn't heard a peep. No one has.

The bus passes under the freeway, through the thrumming cavern of Lents, and soon enough she'll ask the lady next to her to ring the bell. She'll push herself up and get off the bus, shuffle wincing that half block up Foster and then turn onto the gravel road. She'll eye the little house there with the porch light on, with Elaine and Adam inside and dinner heating up, Adam watching one of his DVDs or building something or other with his Tinkertoys or plastic blocks. It isn't much, the house, God knows, but it's home and she's paid her bills this month and the place will be warm on this chilly night, her wine nice and cold.

She gathers her purse and turns to the woman beside her. The day's almost done.

58

IN A LARGE GREENHOUSE, row after row of five-inch-tall starters, native prairie grasses. It's clear and crisp outside, Thanksgiving Day, late morning.

Keith steps slowly down each row with the nozzle on shower, the hose trailing him along the clean concrete floor. As he goes, he speaks in a soft voice, though the others are all the way at the other end of the greenhouse.

"Rain time. Drink up."

He takes care not to give too much water, keeps on moving. It feels good to him to be walking, even at this speed. Good to be working out here with some green things. Because, for one, what he can't do right now is think of his girls, or his parents, what all they're doing, the food they're probably getting ready to share. He can't think of his grandson, not today. Courtney, either.

What he'll do, he knows, is go back in after a while for the big lunch, then probably go read, maybe in the rec room if he can find a good chair, maybe on his bed. No checkers today, no backgammon. Just the book he's into. Get him lost in those scenes, in those people. Get him those sentences that carry him off.

As he walks along, he pulls the hose with him, keeps the nozzle high enough so the spray doesn't bend the grass blades too much. *Because what these babies here need is a little TLC. That and some time. Sweet time.* Whenever he imagines them getting out and getting planted in the earth, growing out in the open in all kinds of weather, taking root, it makes this work seem even more important. Like it matters. Like it means something.

He has a purpose.

59

THE SATURDAY AFTER THANKSGIVING, rain on its way, Hawthorne is bustling, the sidewalks are packed. People hitting the sales in all the boutiques, the record store, the toy store. As she steps along through the afternoon crowd, Elaine reminds herself to keep her head up, not tuck her chin, move with good posture, and make some eye contact. The little things, as Sara put it two days ago, after dinner when they all went for the stroll to the river.

She has on her vintage silver drop earrings with the turquoise stones and also her purple satin ribbon necklace with the ceramic painted red lotus on a soft square, both of which she got from Goodwill last month, and then her violet scarf, black pants, and black coat. Not bad, she thinks. It's that good, this outfit, yes. She's got some taste. She carries the blue glossy folder at her side and pictures Sara there by the river in that mellow grey light, giving her that pep talk of sorts, their Gramps and Gram, Rachel and Ben, and even their mom just upriver a ways, looking out at the forest after all that turkey and pumpkin pie.

Every now and then, though, she catches herself feeling self-conscious. Once again, she's the largest person on this sidewalk. Catches herself tucking her chin into her wattle and raises her head. So many thin, pretty people in this crowd, with expensive shoes, even the people who purposely dress down, at least some of them.

After a time, the store comes into view and she takes a few deeper breaths as she walks. The closer she gets, the more she thinks of Sara. *Why not you? Who says? Seriously, who says?*

Outside the store she hesitates, opens the blue folder and acts like she's reading something in there. Her face and neck so hot now. Is she hyperventilating? Armpits moist. Passersby occasionally brush her shoulder.

Look at her: beached here on this sidewalk, choking big-time. Like she knew might happen. It's sad, really. What is she doing? *Lord, please.* What the hell is she doing? She glances at the store through the river of people. Look at this place. How long has she loved this shop? How many nights has she lain in her bed thinking about working here, or someplace just like it? How many times did she and Rachel come down here to browse?

She stands near the curb, surveying the street, trying to breathe. The day spa, the upscale Vietnamese restaurant. The brewpub and the condos. People everywhere, out spending money, eating and drinking, people out in the world, part of things, here in this neighborhood where no freeway cuts it in half, where fences are made of wood, the side streets are paved. All this here, in this part of town—and then there's her. Good old Elaine. In her Goodwill outfit. Outside one of the coolest jewelry stores in the entire city.

Once more she opens the folder and looks down at the lone piece of paper tucked in there. The heavy, cream-colored bond paper. Expensive, that paper. She raises her head and eyes the ice cream shop half a block away, it doesn't appear too crowded right now, she could go grab a sundae and then sit there inside for a while, watch all the people pass by the windows. Or she could just go get back on the bus and get out of here, people like her can visit but not stay.

When she turns, flushed, and goes into the store, she watches herself step to the register and ask the hiply dressed, thin, greying woman if she could please speak with the manager.

The woman holds her gaze for a couple of beats, kind-eyed. "How can I help you?"

Why not you? Who says?

Before she can tuck her chin, before she can turn around and leave, she pulls her résumé from the blue folder and hands it over with a red-cheeked smile, refusing to look away.

ACKNOWLEDGMENTS

THE AUTHOR WISHES TO THANK Helen VanBelle, John Tuggle, Nate Pomeroy, Jon Bell, Marc Poris, Tom McKerlick, Joan Saalfeld, Bob Fulford, Clive Charles, Tom Jenks, Stevan Allred, Literary Arts, Meredith Stabel, James McCoy, Margaret Yapp, Allison Means, Meghan Anderson, Amy Benfer, Karen Copp, Angie Dickey, Susan Hill Newton, Danielle Johnsen, Oksana Duncan, Kasey Poserina, Nicole Wayland, Ron and Cindi Pomeroy, and especially Brooke Tuggle.